T0265866

# The Imposter

# Johanna van Zanten

# The Imposter

Addison & Highsmith

# Addison & Highsmith Publishers

Las Vegas ◊ Chicago ◊ Palm Beach

Published in the United States of America by
Histria Books
7181 N. Hualapai Way, Ste. 130-86
Las Vegas, NV 89166 USA
HistriaBooks.com

Addison & Highsmith is an imprint of Histria Books. Titles published under the imprints of Histria Books are distributed worldwide.

Library of Congress Control Number: 2023948265

ISBN 978-1-59211-376-7 (hardcover)
ISBN 978-1-59211-397-2 (eBook)

# Chapter 1

The sound of singing, children calling out, screams of delight, a barking dog, music from a radio. A light appeared behind Johanna's closed eyes. A soft paw touched her cheek. Enveloped in the warmth of a down bedcover, she resisted opening her eyes. She listened, but the voices had disappeared. She didn't want to return to the living, the present. She knew nobody would suddenly pull the cover off her, sing *Gutenmorgen,* and then throw open the window on the second story to hang the bulky feather-and-down duvet over the windowsill to air out the night sweat and make it snow, like *Frau Holle* in the fairy tale.

A pervasive pain in her hips and knees woke her. She wasn't young and didn't have her whole life ahead of her anymore. She was nearly a century old and in bed on this cold, watery morning in a *foreign* country by the sea. Johanna took a deep breath and forced her eyelids to lift, disheartened she was still alive. The curtains were too thin to completely block the daylight, allowing a bleak sun to shine through on this chilly winter's morning. She quickly closed her eyes and let her thoughts return to her favorite time of life, her childhood.

Preferring to live inside the ethereal dreams of the past, she let her memories come on as they wished, more robust than ever before, and with each day, the yearning to be back there became all-encompassing. Nothing else in life could please her. Familiar with death from an early age, she knew the difference between life and death, aware that three years before she was born, a brother — a precious boy — had preceded her, stillborn. Another dead sister was born when she was eight. She remembered it well. The little, limp body like a rubber doll on *Vati's* arm reminded her of a butchered chicken, its skin slippery. "Can I touch her?" she asked when Vati showed the children their baby sister.

"Better not," he said, but she touched the little leg hanging down over the edge of his open hand.

***

Johanna was born the second daughter of Friedrich and Friederike and grew up during the chaotic years of the German Empire in a time when one could expect a revolution to unseat a ruling government any day. Wars broke out at the drop of a hat and devastated Europe.

Friedrich and Friederike's family of five children lived in Osterode, in the district of *Niedersachsen*, where Friedrich was a shoemaker. Friedrich, whom everybody called Fritz, was born in a backwater, Pomerania, then part of the Prussian Empire on the Baltic coast. He had told his children about his hometown, Pollnow, in the district of Schlawe (the German word for *Slavic*). Like all his children, Johanna understood her dad had escaped that "stagnant society of masters and serfs," as he described it. She thought her Vati was prone to embellishment and took the masters-and-serfs bit with a grain of salt. When he scolded them for something and compared himself and his ambition to the unwilling child, the children all knew and mouthed the refrain: "At age sixteen I left home to forge myself a better life in the west, where the bright lights of a modern society beckoned."

Sixteen years after Vati's departure from Pomerania, Johanna was born in 1881. From a young age, she noticed the many outlandishly dressed, different-looking people as she walked with her dad on errands through Osterode. Most of them were dressed in rags and begged for food.

"Who are those people, Vati?"

"*Ausländer, mein Mädchen.*" Foreigners, my girl. He wouldn't elaborate, but hurried to finish his business, looking grim.

Johanna wasn't easily discouraged. "Where from, Vati?"

"My former home, *Pommern*, in former Poland, or maybe further east, or south. I don't know. Come on, hurry, we should get home. Soon the guards will start harassing people."

It was unusual for her father to be so grim and silent. Johanna concluded that his anger must have something to do with the people in the streets, or else, the guards. His grimness didn't scare her off but made her thoughts return to a similar conversation she hadn't understood.

In class earlier that week, Johanna couldn't grasp the concept of the duties all Germans owed to their *Kaiser* despite her teacher's enthusiasm in the civics class. At age ten and more curious than most children, she had wondered about the *Reich's* entitlement to absorb other nations. Maybe because of *Meister's* insistence, she resisted accepting the Empire's manifest destiny. *Because I said* so he replied to her *why*. She had questioned out loud the fairness of the rich landowners and the nobility only having any power in the *Reichstag* — the government Chamber — but the teacher had nodded and asked her, his voice cool with a hint of derision, "Is your father Polish?"

"No, he is German," she had replied, but the question made her think, and her classmates also heard it. Her classmates had called Johanna *dirty Polak* more than once that week. She wondered if she should tell Vati about it.

As they walked , Fritz suddenly grabbed Johanna by her arm and pulled her sharply toward him, saving her from serious injury from a trap that suddenly appeared from an inner courtyard and turned into the street. "You need to always look into the alleys, child," he scolded gently as they recovered their pace.

"Yes, Vati." Grabbing onto Vati's coat for balance, she pouted, not distracted enough to drop the subject. "I hate my name. It's not German enough," she whined. "Your ancestors should have changed it more."

He looked down at her, a faint smile on his lips, when he said, "I thought it was all right, but you can change it when you get married, *Mädchen.*"

"What was your family name before the change, you can tell me," she asked, still curious.

Fritz quickened his pace, so Johanna had to run to keep up. "How come you know about a name change? Did I tell you already about it?"

"Yes, you did, Vati."

"Oh, I forgot. Anyway, my ancestors must have wanted to make it different from German. They replaced the ending to make it *sound* low-German with *-ske*, you know, the way to make a word into a diminutive, *little*, like Manske. In Pomerania, there are indeed many Manske families." He smiled at her.

Looking down to avoid tripping on the uneven sidewalk, she didn't see the smile on her father's face.

"But that isn't our name! You tricked me," she cried and grabbed her father's hand for more stability on the uneven cobblestones.

The streets became busy in the later afternoon, and it was getting dark. They weren't far from home. Fritz shifted the bag with material from one shoulder to the other and continued talking, as he shifted Johanna by her hand to his other side.

"Did you know that the Polish nobility in the olden days had the ending *-ski* to their name? In the Slavic language, of course. Maybe we are of nobility from way back when, and you are a *gräfin*, a duchess."

He winked at her. In a more serious voice, he added, "Your last name is something to be proud of, *mein liebes Mädchen,* my dear girl. My ancestors didn't Germanize it all the way. Your name connects you to your tribe, to all your relatives. Münzkes are different from Manskes."

He quickened his step again. Johanna weighed his answer and slowed down.

"Don't dawdle. Catch up, child." His tone had changed as if he was angry again, his mood suddenly changed. It made her stop asking more questions.

When they arrived home just in time before curfew, Vati pushed her through the door ahead of him. "All right, go inside and help your mother now." His voice was gruff, and it hurt Johanna, who wondered if it was her fault.

*** 

Several weeks passed until the teacher finally had enough of Johanna's curiosity. As soon as Johanna opened her mouth, he sent the inquisitive girl to the corridor as punishment for disrupting the class. Johanna — indignant, as she hadn't interrupted at all and had waited till there was a pause in between the teachers' words — got up and marched with her head held high out the door.

Standing in the corridor was no fun, and she caught on quickly how to stay quiet. As a person already tagged as less than desirable, she got the cold shoulder from her classmates, when she tried to make friends with the girls. They pinched her while lining up to go inside with the first bell. After the boys kicked her in the shins when she came close enough, she also absorbed the lesson that strength ruled on the playground. She cried silently at night in her bed so her sisters wouldn't hear her, and she didn't want to explain her humiliations.

In her history class, Johanna heard another lesson: many other nations had invaded and owned her Vati's Pomerania, stuck between Russia and Prussia on the east, and Germany on the west. If you didn't like this ruler, wait a few years, and another one would take over. But now it was part of the German Reich, as it should be.

That was not what the teacher said in class, but how Johanna summarized it in her mind. Her desire to understand her dad's lack of pride or loyalty to Germany kept her interested in the matter. His homeland became part of Germany in 1871, which made him German. On the surface, Vati remained neutral in political talks with the neighbors, but Johanna gradually detected his heart was with the Slavic people.

# Chapter 2

Johanna had become aware of the issue of their name on the first day of school when she was six years old through her teachers' reactions to her last name: their interest waned, or a nose would wrinkle, which only happened with some students. It made her feel less loved, of a lesser quality than the other students, and it saddened her. It took a while before she found out why. Not only was she a girl — unseen and better silent — she also had a Slavic-sounding name. Other classmates with similar names were also treated with contempt — a different, lesser breed of Germans. When she finally shared her misgivings with Vati after a couple of weeks of this, he told her how discrimination against ethnic Poles was common in the whole of Germany. She'd better get used to it.

\*\*\*

Those were big words, and she shirked away from them at age six. By the time she was ten years old, she had learned the word, *Polak*. She had become a doubter and didn't believe everything adults told her — even Vati. She was always full of questions.

Contrary to her eldest sister, Rieke, Johanna had a habit of joining Vati in the shop, watching him do his work and asking questions while Rieke watched the little ones. Mutti was not home yet. She liked having her dad alone to herself. She was surely special and tickled pink with Vati treating her as an adult. This afternoon, as she sat beside him on her stool in the shop, she finally found the words to explain her conundrum, which had been on her mind for a long time.

"Vati? Are we not German? Why do the teachers treat me like I am Polish?"

He pursed his lips, and his eyes went dark. In a grave voice, he explained.

"You are now old enough to know a bit more about my family. I'll tell you what happened in my hometown. When I was a child and Pomerania belonged to

Prussia, people had to move out of their homes at the spur of the moment to make space for the new immigrants: settlers from the west with German names."

He went on to tell her that those Germans were on a royal assignment from the Fürst with special privileges to settle in Pomerania, develop new lands, drain the swamps by the sea, and build new houses.

Johanna was afraid he would get angry, so she asked the next question with care, as she watched his face for changes. "Immigrants? What are those?"

"Newcomers. To us, they were *Ausländer*. The *Fürst*, the governor of the region, told the farm owners to hire the Germans. All landowners were ordered to send away their *Tagelöhners*, the farmhands, like my father, to make space for the new immigrants."

In a solemn tone, he explained that many Pomeranians were left to starve without jobs, while the newcomers had pieces of land given to them to develop. Other changes happened to hurt the Pomeranians. The King was embarrassed by the feudal system, a relic of the past, and changed it, so those farmers who had leased a bit of land to grow a few things had to now outright buy the land and were forced to pay higher fees for the interest on the loans. Instead of a tenant, they became deeply indebted to the landowner. As an owner, they were worse off.

Johanna gave a dismissive wave with her hand. Her father was just too pessimistic. "But that was in Pomerania, Vati, and a long time ago. We are in the unified German Reich now. It's not like that here."

Fritz, bent over the boot in his hands and ripping off a broken buckle, raised his eyebrows and grumbled, "Hey, how old do you think I am? It's wasn't that long ago! I still have a brother, Karl in the province of Pomerania." He wiped his face with his hand and looked at Johanna, wondering if he should tell her more. He had a pile of shoes waiting for repairs.

Rebuked for a second by his gruffness, she hesitated but excited by a long-lost family member, she asked, "Do I get to meet him? I don't know any of your family."

Vati's face softened at the thought of his brother. "I don't know. It's not easy to travel if you have no money, dear. Karl wrote me only a year after you were born that the Catholics and the Jews were expelled from Pomerania, and the Slavs and the former Polish had to go as well. The Germans called us *socialists and communists*. Anyway, not much has changed for me: I'm the newcomer here in Osterode, still thought of as a socialist."

He was finished with the boot, grabbed another shoe from the pile and started working on removing the split sole with a frown.

Johanna thought he had forgotten about her, or he was angry with her for the questions, which saddened her. She needed to cheer him up and she put a hand on her dad's knee and asked, "But your life is good here, isn't it Vati? And aren't you German, born in the German Reich?"

Fritz dropped the shoe without a sole on the workbench and patted her hand. As he got up to grab a new sole, he answered in a quiet voice: "Yes, I am a German, but am pretty sure I have Slavic ancestry, too. I have the paperwork and a birth certificate from the Prussian province of *Hinterpommern*, but I can't forget my former home and the Slavic people I knew there. We were all friends and worked shoulder-to-shoulder with them on the fields as a kid; our bloodlines were no issue."

He returned to his seat with a new piece of stiff, thick leather, picked up the shoe and clenched the sole onto it with one hand as he drew the outline of the shoe onto the leather with his other hand, then sat down.

Johanna was encouraged by Vati's willingness to share with her. She simply had to make him feel better. "What was so good about working yourself to death there, far away, for no money? Aren't you glad you left that swamp?"

He sighed and continued: "*Ach*, what would you know about such things, child? After the work was finished, we drank and belted out songs together in the bar on payday. I snuck in too, and, as long as my dad didn't spot me, I was okay. Our families married their daughters, and we intermingled. We all have mixed blood. There is no such thing as a full-blooded German Pomeranian."

Taken aback by this confession, she remembered her teacher. He was right, she had Slavic ancestry. "Oh, I didn't know, Vati. Does Mutti know?"

Vati stood up, took the sharp knife off the wall, and cut the sole to size along the drawn outline. "I don't know. We didn't talk about my old life."

He looked up. When he saw Johanna's shocked face, he added in a soft voice, "I liked it there, but we were poor. I wasn't going to wait till a rich girl fell in love with me," he laughed. "I didn't want poverty for my family, so I left."

He grabbed the gluepot and smeared some of the contents with a stiff brush on both the sole and the shoe. He looked at Johanna and smiled.

"Got to wait a minute or so for the glue to get sticky. It's smelly stuff, isn't it? Did you know it's made from horses' bones? Anyway, I got lucky. Before I was forced to leave, I arrived here in Osterode on my own accord. To answer your question, dear, no, I'm not so much German *at heart*. I don't know what I am. Do you?"

Vati's shoulders were slack, and his smile was sad, his eyes tired.

Johanna hadn't known much about the eastern provinces. Nobody in her family knew how bad it had been for Vati. All she could do was tearfully comment: "Oh, Vati, I didn't know, how sad that you miss your friends so much."

She put her hand on his arm again, but he shook her off by suddenly standing and walking to the wall cabinet, to get some tacks. On the way back to his seat he grabbed the heavy iron lest and placed it on the bench. The metal parts in the shape of mini feet of different sizes stuck out in every direction. He picked up his hammer, put the shoe upside down on the iron foot closest to him, and started pounding on the sole, as he shouted over the noise, "Go help your sister with the little ones."

***

That night in bed, unable to sleep, Johanna thought about her dad's conundrum, having left the country he loved without finding peace in his new world. She didn't grasp it all, except that life was misery for the Polish and the Pomeranians, even when they were Germans. Vati had confirmed for her what she had already suspected: his loyalty was with the old Pomeranians of mixed Slavic-German heritage.

Johanna decided then and there to get rid of all Polish identity, or Slavic, whatever the slur was. She wouldn't tell Vati about her decision, afraid he would think less of her if he knew. She *was* just German, just like all her brothers and sisters were, simply by their birth in Osterode.

But she couldn't forget about Vati's warnings about their name. *You mustn't talk about the name change,* he had said. *To tell the truth could be dangerous.* She still hated her name because it didn't sound German enough. She only yearned for status and for respect. But she listened respectfully to her dad's explanations. At ten, she was too young to know it all, so she used her time alone with Vati for the lingering, challenging questions.

From then on, Johanna intentionally used her time with Fritz to pick his brain, test her ideas, and gain more knowledge of the world. She realized her father had tried to educate her on their walks through town together, guiding her to make the right decisions. She loved her Vati but didn't want to disappoint him by being German. The secrets inside her were building and she developed a knack for hiding the truth.

***

Johanna grew up in one place. Because her father's business succeeded, the family didn't have to move to receive an income, which allowed the permanency in their lives. Never having been anywhere else, she developed a narrow frame of reference and couldn't understand everything her father told her. For decades, she had religiously followed his advice, and kept her mouth shut about a name change, extending it to include all subjects she had understood to be touchy, or controversial. On her sixteenth birthday, Vati had told her something else about her family, and she had pushed it deep down and filed it away as irrelevant information.

Now, a lifetime later, as she lay semi-conscious in her bed at ninety years old in a foreign country, she remembered. Vati had told her that his mother's parents were Jews. However, they had also registered as members of the Lutheran church — baptized and all — just like all Germans. She had always thought it was one of his implausible stories and such a nasty thing to make up because everybody in Germany already hated the Jews.

All her life she professed to be one-hundred percent German, an Aryan, and a Protestant Christian. In truth, she could never bring herself to believe in Christ, or a God in any religion. She had lived her life without it. Nobody cared now what an old woman thought or did. *She* didn't care. With eyes closed, she returned to her youth in Osterode.

# Chapter 3

Johanna adored her father. He was built like her: a squat person with a muscular body. His kind face with soft-grey eyes complemented a head of silky, medium-brown hair, so fine that it was unmanageable. But his real pride was the big mustache underneath his large nose that he spent a lot of time clipping with a pointy pair of scissors he had pinched from his wife's sewing basket. Johanna had the same kind of silky hair, but she only had a small nose with a slight bend — an aristocratic nose, Vati teased.

It was a different story with her mother, Friederike, with whom she didn't identify. Johanna didn't look like her mother — a tall, skinny woman with brown-blond hair, steel-blue eyes over high cheekbones, and a long, straight nose. Mutti didn't spend much time with the children, and Johanna didn't know her well. Mutti worked from early morning to late evening, with little time to spare for playing or reading stories to her children. In the mornings, she worked as a housemaid and laundrywoman for a wealthy family. Most afternoons, she also worked at the undertaker's, until late in the night sometimes. As a result, Johanna didn't see much more than a hard worker in Friederike.

"Why do you always work so much, Mutti?" Johanna asked one day, fed up with the long hours of helping Vati watch her little brothers and sisters. The younger ones relentlessly wanted her attention, especially when their eldest sister, Rieke wasn't around. It was a long night, and the children's bedtime couldn't come early enough when Mutti was with the undertaker and Rieke was out.

"Somebody needs to pay the rent, *Mädchen*," Friederike said with raised eyebrows. "Vati is not making enough money with the shoe repairs. We're lucky that he has the shop and can look after the children when I'm called at night to help. Satisfied, young lady?" She looked at her, still frowning.

Her answer raised Johanna's hackles. "But Rieke and I are watching the children. Vati never does," she protested. "Anyway, they are old enough. They can stay on their own now."

Friederike didn't tolerate any guff, especially not after a night at the undertaker. Her thin face looked even tighter than usual, when she said, "Enough, child, or should I give you something real to whine about?" It was just a threat, as Johanna was too old to be hit at sixteen.

Mutti took her shoes off in the way of having a backache: toes of one foot at the heel of the other, one by one, with both her hands pressed on her lower back. She left the shoes by the door and then disappeared into the bedroom, adjacent to the kitchen. She could at least have said thanks — what a thankless job it was to be an elder sister.

Everything was quiet in the house. Vati finished with his schnapps hours ago and had disappeared to the bedroom. She listened from the kitchen to his snoring, a sound like someone was dancing. Feet were shuffling rhythmically, starting with a sudden tap, then one, two, three counts of a raspy sound, one beat of silence, then two beats of a softer shuffle. Johanna smiled.

She climbed the stairs and snuck into her bed beside Rieke in the girls' bedroom under the eaves: three of them in one big bed — Hannah, the smallest, at the other end against the wall. The two boys, August and Willi, had their own room. She didn't think she would be cut out for having children and working from morning till evening. That's no life. How did her parents put up with it?

***

Granted, Johanna was proud to live on her street: such a pretty row of houses. The white stucco walls of the house were divided with black half-timbers in neat, geometric shapes. Her home was part of a whole block of the same townhomes located in the heart of Osterode. From there, it wasn't far to walk anywhere. Johanna and all her siblings were born in the house.

When Rieke was home too and had a handle on watching the kids, Johanna preferred to spend her spare time after school in the shop, watching her dad work. One afternoon she had asked, "Did you always want to be a shoemaker, Vati?"

Friedrich chuckled. "I'd have preferred to be a prince, but yes, it seemed like a good job. Did you know my grandfather, your Ur-Opa was a shoemaker, too?"

"No, I didn't. You only talk about your poor father."

"Well, now I am. It seemed natural to pick up where my grandad had left off because I didn't want to be just a *Tagelöhner* like my father: a serf to the landowner, toiling in the mud." He looked up and smiled at her.

She already knew he had left his home in Schlawe as an itinerant shoemaker, and in Osterode became an apprentice with a famous master shoemaker, Herr Knocke: the certificate on the shop wall said so. He and Mutti had to work ten years first to scrape enough money together for the year's deposit on the shop lease while he already was working with Master Knocke. From Mutti, she knew his earnings paid for the food and the clothes.

Vati told her when she was twelve, that his license for making new footwear was terminated because too many former Polish migrants settled in Osterode. The locals thought that the unfair competition from the recent immigrants offering cheaper work needed to be stopped. She was glad he even still had a shop. Johanna didn't wholly believe her father's interpretation of events. He saw things too negatively. He was a worrier.

Anyway, life wasn't all bad. Despite what she had told Mutti, she liked that Vati was home, one closed door away, although both Rieke and she were careful not to disturb him at his work. Sometimes he could unexpectedly get furious at them, and throw a shoe or boot in their direction, but always missed. She had to carefully prepare her time with him in the shop.

Mutti was out the door to her lady's home by seven in the morning. The children had raised themselves: the older ones looked after the little ones. On the other hand, if it weren't for Vati in his shop, things might have turned out differently, arriving late for school the least of it. Like most children, they might've been hungry all day, but for Vati. Only after he had given them their porridge and a cup of milk would he open the shop and send them on their way to school with a full belly.

***

In those days, when her youngest siblings were still little, the five of them walked to school, each child carrying their school satchel on their back with their lunches of a sourdough sandwich with lard and mustard. They had it better than most of their classmates and Johanna sometimes shared her lunch with a classmate, which helped her to make friends.

She thoroughly enjoyed that time of day, the hustle and bustle of the shops opening their doors and cleaning up their stone front steps. The troupe of children had to pay attention to avoid a pail of dirty water splashing over their heads, thrown through an open door into the street, or worse, the contents of the chamber pot. They avoided walking by their mother's workplace, not wanting to disturb her and incur her wrath later at home.

At that early hour, the carts delivered their goods to the shops, the guesthouses, and the miller. Sometimes a horse dropped its pile of horseshit, patiently waiting as the owner unloaded the grain or the sugar beets. The birds would flock down on the heap to pick at the undigested grains. Johanna didn't think that horse poop smelled all bad. On the other hand, when a stream of urine splashed on the pavement releasing a cloud of steam on a frosty morning, she would gingerly step aside to save her long skirt.

If lucky, one of the children would find an apple, which the grocer had just discarded into the street only slightly blemished. A few tasty bites were always left for the lucky finder, and the rest was fed to a waiting horse.

***

On this particular day, when she was thirteen years old, a nag with blinders pulled a funereal carriage with a coffin in its interior and passed the children on the road. The horse wore a black velvet cover over its back with a hood extending over its neck and face with ear tufts. It triggered her memory of a conversation with Mutti from the previous day, on *Allerheiligen* — All Saints Day. After the death of her second stillborn, Mutti had been home for a while, moping around the house, a quiet and sad shadow of herself. Her very last child had been a girl. During those days, Johanna frequently saw her mother standing in front of the sideboard, staring at two photographs. The photo of the baby boy had faded over more than fifteen years of exposure on the dresser. The other, more recent photograph was taken with a soft lens. Both babies had barely distinguishable facial features.

Johanna couldn't resist her curiosity when she caught her mother staring at the photos again. "Why do we have pictures of those babies on the sideboard, Mutti? I think taking photos of dead people is morbid." She swallowed the other cruel thought in time: *never alive, and nobody remembers being with them.*

As if Mutti read her mind, she quietly explained: "*I* have memories of them. The babies were living inside me for a long time until they were born. They were real to *me*."

Still curious, both now staring at the photographs, Johanna had pushed on, standing beside Friederike. "What do you think then? What about?"

Friederike wiped a hand over her face, gathered her thoughts, and then started speaking with a hesitant voice.

"I think about what they would look like now, today, how old they would be and, what they would have liked to become. Maybe a shoemaker, or a mother with many children herself, and then, then I imagine how you children would've gotten along." She stroked Johanna's cheek as she turned away to get on with her day, leaving Johanna wondering.

Johanna touched her cheek where Mutti's hand had been, thinking back about her mother's unusual gesture. She wished Mutti would touch her face more often. Mutti must not feel disgusted with dead bodies, she used to wash them at the funeral home. It dawned on her that maybe there's more to things than what one could see. She wondered what kind of a mother she would become, or if she would even reach the point that she'd want children. Suddenly, she remembered school in the middle of her daydreams, and called out to her siblings: "Hurry, let's run. We are going to be late for school," and she led the way, happily jogging the rest of the way to school.

# Chapter 4

On the first day of each school year, their teacher would test the children on what they still knew. They were asked to spell their names for the *Meister,* often a new person. Many had funny names she barely could pronounce, let alone spell, making Johanna curious about where these classmates came from. Strangely enough, she had never asked her mother the same question, assuming they came from Osterode and there was nothing interesting to tell.

After this All Saints Day and her conversation with Mutti about the dead babies, Johanna finally asked her — not the easiest parent to approach for personal questions — where her family came from, as she helped Mutti cook supper.

Friederike had answered with a serene expression on her face: "Vati's ancestors came from further east, or southeast, I'm not certain. Mine came from here, Osterode." That's all she wanted to say about that, although Mutti usually loved telling stories, but only if she was in the mood.

Sundays were her only days off from washing corpses and for the occasional story-telling time. After a long morning of sitting through the church service, Friederike had rested enough to talk with Vati in the parlor: the only break from work for both. Vati really liked his schnapps. Every day after closing the shop, he had some, but Mutti only joined him on Sundays. After their coffee, they'd drink from tiny glasses before Mutti started the chore of cooking dinner. Sometimes that would be a late dinner. Especially on winter days, Mutti enjoyed talking as the drink mellowed her. Vati listened to her tales but most often had a snooze in his chair. Which tale she would tell depended on the question the children would ask.

That Sunday, Johanna claimed the *stoof*— the wooden footstool for warming cold feet — to sit on. The foot-high hollow square with one open side had a few holes in the top cover. Vati removed the galvanized basin from inside the stool and put a few glowing coals from the stove in it with the tongs. He intended it for

Mutti, but when she was telling stories, she let any of the children use it. Johanna, with the longest attention span, often ended up with the stool.

Johanna's elder sister was named Friederike after her mother — Rieke for short. She would never join them at these cozy events, her nature too severe, carrying too much on her shoulders, and in Johanna's mind without imagination. Trying to change her mind, she asked Rieke on the Sunday after All Saints' Day, "Come, Rieke, join us and listen to a story. Just for once, we can be together as a family."

Before Rieke could answer, Mutti answered with Rieke's typically scornful voice. "Mutti is making things up. You can't believe any of it."

Johanna jerked her head around to watch her sister's eyes blinking rapidly, unsure whom to feel sorry for, Rieke or her mom, whose face was blank. She said to Rieke in a soothing tone, "I love Mutti's tales. It doesn't matter if it's all true. Stories aren't supposed to be real, dummy. You are allowed to embroider, make it fun, use your imagination."

Rieke lifted her head, nose in the air, her eyes challenging her, then haughtily walked towards the door, and scoffed: "Mutti just likes your admiration, Johanna. Who's the dummy now?"

Hurt by Rieke's rebuke and noticing the flash of sadness on her mother's face, Johanna quietly said: "Now, come on, Rieke. Be nice."

Rieke didn't reply and just stomped out of the house to check on their younger siblings. Willi, ten years old, was playing alone upstairs in the boys' bedroom, but Hannah and August were playing outside.

Wilhelm, Willi for short, was born after Johanna and could take care of himself. Nobody tried to boss him around, there was no need. He seemed to be much older than even Rieke and never did anything risky. Most days, he played nicely on his own with tin soldiers that a customer had left with Vati for him — the first son, born alive. But when he was younger, August tried to get his share of attention and grab a toy soldier. Willi could explode in anger and screech like a demon.

\*\*\*

Johanna felt rejected by Rieke, and absorbed the hurt vicariously for her mom. She wondered what Mutti had done to cause Rieke to have so little respect for her. Rieke was lately turning just as miserable as Mutti. Maybe she was just tired of being a second mom. Maybe she wanted to leave home, a year older than Johanna, fourteen. She was almost ready for a position as a live-in maid at fifteen.

After Rieke left the room, Friederike sighed. Then she said softly, "Rieke is doing a good job helping me with looking after the young ones. Come, tell me, what did you want to know today, my child?"

*** 

Before Mutti had even begun, Johanna's time with Mutti ended abruptly when the youngest kids, Hannah, eight years old, and August, aged five, burst into the kitchen and pushed Johanna from her stoof. Rieke followed behind, closed the door, and kept standing by the kitchen table. Cold from playing outside in the street, the imps were shivering and crowded around the cookstove.

"Where's Willi?" Mutti asked.

"Willi's playing upstairs in his bedroom. Settle down, you rascals," Rieke scolded and added, "Mutti, I'm going to see my friend Dora. I'll be back in an hour." She made her way to the door.

"Don't slam the door on your way out, dear child," Friederike replied softly.

Rieke slammed the door shut behind her.

"*Ach, Kinder: wie die Bilder, nur die Rahmen fehlen,*" Friederike sighed. Loosely translated as children are a great comfort in our old age and help us reach it faster too.

Mutti didn't need much of a nudge, and after two schnapps the most exciting story of how she and Vati had met came rolling off her tongue, when Johanna finally thought of asking that question.

The other children left to play their own games.

Mutti looked perturbed. "Are you going to listen all the way to the end of my story?" She looked at Johanna, who dutifully nodded.

"Sure, Mutti, I will. Go on then."

"The Empire of Germany," Friederike began.

Johanna's eyes glazed over, although she noticed the sense of pride in her mother's voice.

Friederike took a breath and concentrated on the next sentence, but Johanna jumped into the pause waving her hand to move her mother along. "Yeah, yeah, the *story about how you met*, Mutti, not about the German Empire. I take history class in school and have enough trouble with the teachers. Not you too, please."

Friederike sat up and frowned.

"But you need to know some history, child, as it explains why your Vati moved away and how we met. His parents raised their children with barely anything decent to eat, and many babies in Pomerania died of illness before they turned one year old. That's why your father left *Hinterpommern*."

Johanna interrupted her mother, again yearning for a tale of romance, not of misery.

"I heard all about that from Vati. We are all Germany now, Mutti."

"I know, I know. Just be quiet and listen. So, *my* family is from the free city-nation of Hannover in the middle of the German Empire. Your father didn't like the Prussians nor the Germans but decided to make the best of it after the unification of Germany when the whole of the mainland opened up. Your father moved into Hanover territory, leaving that backwater behind and poverty," Friederike empathically said, nodding for emphasis on the word poverty.

"So, good for Vati," Johanna said. She straightened her back, wondering if this is how family myths were born, by just repeating the story. She looked at her mother when she added, "I like the Germans."

Mutti's face beamed.

"You'll have to understand that your Vati traveled all the way across Germany from the town of Pollnow in Farther Pomerania. That undertaking showed guts and determination. I don't know how he did it, he was very young. His father had just died, and his mother with their four younger children had left him a few years earlier for another man. Fritz was all alone in the world. He earns your respect, child."

Johanna played with her thin, brown hair, and braided it loosely into one plait, to give it more volume. About to lose interest, she impatiently commented, "I do respect Vati. Mother, the story?"

With a sideways glance at her daughter, Friederike decided to ignore it and continued her story. "So, after Fritz arrived in Osterode, he started off on a job in construction. One day, when the tiles were wet from early morning condensation, one of the roofers lost his balance. Your father was in the yard and saw the roofer slide and yelled to him, but couldn't do anything to stop him from falling off the roof."

"Oh, no," Johanna gasped.

With a beaming face, coming to the climax of the story, Friederike said with aplomb, "The man fell to the ground and died on the spot of a broken neck."

"How awful for Vati to see that," Johanna exclaimed.

"Yes, it was, for him. His employer instructed Fritz to take the dead man to the undertaker. He spoke to a young lady who comforted him, a skinny, shy girl of seventeen. Her job was to wash and prepare the corpses for burial. Your Vati fell instantly in love, and only after a couple of dates asked her to marry him."

Friederike stared out of the kitchen window with a faraway look on her face. There was nothing to see outside: it was mid-winter, and the panes were frosted over on the inside with a beautiful damask pattern of white leaves. A small curl in the corner of Mutti's mouth gave away the emotion of her memory.

It took a few seconds before its meaning sunk in, and Johanna gasped. "No, it can't be. That was you?"

Friederike returned to the present at her daughter's questions and looked down at Johanna on the stool beside her. She took a sip from her schnapps. "It was me," she smiled.

Johanna looked with renewed interest at her mother. "I guess you weren't afraid of dead people, even when you were young. Vati must have been impressed. What about grandfather and grandmother? Who were they?"

"Well, my dear girl, *my* parents weren't very secretive about that. You know most of my family already. My last name just means *seagull*, so maybe my ancestors lived by the ocean at first and moved inland later. Fritz never visited his relatives, because we didn't have the money. You'll have to ask your father about his parents."

Johanna had tried that before but didn't get very far. All Vati replied to her questions about his family was that his ancestors came from further east from lower Polish nobility, he called it *Szlachta* — from a long time ago — and that his grandfather always used to wear a little black hat. Johanna never knew if that was true, as he winked when he said it.

Johanna shrugged.

"I tried talking to Vati, but he's not very clear. I don't think he knows either." She wanted to show her mom that she had been attentive, and quickly added: "I know the ending -*ski* of last names in Slavic languages is for men and -*ska* is for women. I should be *Münzka* in that case."

They both laughed.

"So, Mutti, if your parents were born here, but your ancestors were not, are you still German?"

Friederike thought for a few seconds, then replied, "I assume we all are Germans now from the day we became a unified German Empire. Of course, everything now *must* be in German, the language we all speak, and the names too. But I don't think your Vati agrees with that. When he arrived here, he had some friends, most were from the east with socialist ideas. Ask him."

Friederike's voice had become impatient. She straightened her back, bent forward, and pushed with her hands on the chair's seat to get up, relieving her aching knees from gravity's pain as she rose. "Except for your *Ur-Opa*, I never met any of Fritz's relatives. If your Vati doesn't want to talk about that time, you might get more out of *Ur-Opa*, your great-granddad. Bring him some schnapps, that might improve the flow. He's so quiet, I'm not sure if she still got all his wits about him."

"Thanks, Mutti," Johanna said with renewed interest in her ancestors' lives.

"Well, I'd better start on supper," Friederike exhaled, then inhaled deeply and walked to the kitchen, leaving behind a satisfied daughter on a mission for more stories.

# Chapter 5

When Johanna turned sixteen — the same age that her dad had left his hometown — Vati was finally ready to tell her more about his own youth. She had just returned home from her first day on the job as a maid for a wealthy trader. She brought Vati a fresh mug of tea in his shop and told him about her disappointing first day as a maid, not allowed to do much, and only having to watch the children. Then her father explained more about his adventure.

He appeared to be on a mission to teach her, in his words, *a valuable life lesson*. Johanna felt a lecture coming on when Vati started talking. Despite it, she stayed focused, as she was now much older and as an adult of sixteen, able to concentrate on him instead of on her own reactions.

He told her that her great-grandfather, Ur-Opa Heinrich had left Posen for Pomerania to start a family, just like he had left Pollnow after *his* Vati died. Back then, only German tradesmen were allowed to accept contracts, and many locals left Pomerania then, looking for work elsewhere. Many others emigrated to America and Australia. His family didn't have the money, so he had settled in Pollnow.

Heinrich's son, Ferdinand, worked all his life for little money as a farmhand on the estates of the wealthy landowners in the Pollnow region without a chance for advancement. His wife, Philippine, left Ferdinand when she got a better offer and so, broke his heart. That got him really into the bottle. Vati said his dad drank too much. "That's why my parents agreed between them that I should stay with him, to keep him company, and maybe to watch over him."

"Oh, how awful for you, Vati." Johanna wasn't sure if she wanted to hear it all, suspecting there were reasons he had been so secretive for so long.

Fritz continued slicing the excess material of a sole he had just glued to a man's shoe before he continued. "I was eight when my mother left him. I couldn't look after him, I failed him. I often found him unconscious, passed out in the shed, or on the floor of the kitchen. He had a hard time accepting everything and drank his sorrow away."

Fritz wiped a hand over his face and looked at her with sad, watering eyes.

The revelation moved her to tears. She grabbed his arm, and whispered, "Vati, it's not your fault, you were a child yourself. It was unfair to make you watch over him." Then she let go of his arm.

He grabbed the rasp and started smoothing the edges of the sole. Without looking at Johanna, he spoke in a soft voice about how he hadn't come home one night, years later. In the morning, Fritz looked for him and found him on a field at his employer's estate, frozen to death. He suspected it was on purpose.

This was the first time Vati had talked about his parents more elaborately. The truth was worse than she had anticipated, and her heart ached.

"Vati, how *schrecklich*, awful. How did that happen?"

Fritz wiped a hand over his eyes, then lifted his head and met Johanna's eyes, and told her how his father left on a winter's day from his job at the estate, dead-tired. People said he was to stop by the tavern in town. But he never arrived there either. It was in the week before Christmas.

With the confusion visible on her face as the truth of his cryptic words didn't sink in, she asked, "What do you mean, never arrived? Where were you?"

Fritz shifted his gaze and focused on the shoe in his hands, as he curtly said, "I was inside, in the tavern. I had looked for him at the usual spots, but I was too late. The next morning, I found the bastard under a blanket of hoar frost, frozen solid."

He said it hadn't been that much of a surprise to him, as his mother had left his father years earlier for his drinking and for his anger. Vati's four siblings, all younger, had already happily lived for several years with Philippine, his mother, and her new husband. Ferdinand's parents were heartbroken about his death.

"After my father's death, I wouldn't stay one day longer in that stinking hole-in-the-ground. I packed my rucksack and left the next day. Didn't even attend the funeral."

She had to say something but didn't know what, her throat full of tears, sad for her Vati's hardship at such a young age — the same age she was now. She laid her hand on his arm again and softly mumbled, "Oh, Vati, how awful for you."

He looked back at her with a bitter little smile. However, his eyes were still kind when he spoke again.

"Yeah, I was sad, and angry at the same time, no, *livid* at him, for messing up his life and mine, not thinking about anybody else but himself. But nobody can promise you that life will be fair, sweetheart."

He grabbed her hand from his arm and squeezed for a second, then released it. "I know political parties make big promises, but don't believe them. For a while, I believed in socialism and communism." He went on telling her he read many books after he arrived in Osterode and made some friends who encouraged him to make his own luck by going after what he wanted.

"Keep your wits about you as you take your chances. There's no other way. I guess my father forgot that. He got sad and sought escape in the drink."

Vati's stories about the Eastern Provinces were so very different from what she learned in school. What would be the real story, she wondered? After a long silence, becoming ever more uncomfortable, she said, "Vati, my teacher said that most Slavic people had already left eastwards and only German people lived in Pomerania when it became the Empire."

Fritz bent over and patted her on her head, for which she really was too old at sixteen, so she grabbed his hand and held it for a while as he continued talking, perched on his high stool behind his workbench.

"I see. Of course, they would teach you that. Germans can't accept they're a mix of ethnicities."

He told her that his ancestors likely came from Minsky, but he didn't know for sure. *His* dad told him that Slavic names had to be changed into German-sounding names, against their will. Those who didn't want to submit to that humiliation, left for the east, Lithuania, Russia, and Belarus.

"So, in a way, your teachers are right. I believe all of that oppression drove my father to drink, which caused my mother to leave him. It killed him, in the end.

Don't let them ever break your spirit, my dear, even if you must submit to their rules."

Johanna saved her father's pain in her heart and internalized the message as her main principle to live by and resolved to n*ever let anybody rob her of her identity.*

# Chapter 6

When Fritz was born, his grandparents, Heinrich and Ludovike lived in Pomerania and he knew them well as a child. Heinrich still made an income as a shoemaker in Pollnow. It was almost enough to feed himself and his wife. Occasionally, the parish church gave the elderly couple a small amount from the Sunday collection: a very welcome gift.

When his wife died, Heinrich went to live with his eldest grandson in the western part of the Empire. Heinrich joined Fritz in his shop in Osterode at the unusually old age of ninety years old, when Johanna was maybe six or seven years old. She distinctly remembered Ur-Opa's arrival from another province with his belongings loaded up high on a small wagon. Vati had sold the horse afterward, because they didn't have a stable, nor money for horse feed.

Friederike had never met Heinrich before, and at first grumbled at the idea of another mouth to feed. She quickly dropped her resistance after Fritz reminded her that their example would show the children the importance of the duty to care for one's elderly relatives, and Heinrich could make himself useful with small jobs in the shop.

Only Fritz and Friederike knew at the time that Heinrich was included in the planned mass deportation. The German government wanted more Germans and fewer Slavic citizens in their newly acquired Prussian lands to speed up the "Germanization." Ludovike's death and Fritz's invitation just happened to coincide with the deportation order. When Heinrich got the approval to move to Osterode, Johanna just assumed Ur-Opa was lonely after *Ur-Omi*'s death and wanted to be with his family.

Ten years later, in 1897, Heinrich was bent like a willow tree, and his fingers were gnarly, like the stumps on a willow tree after the annual harvest of its twigs for making furniture. Ur-Opa looked like a sorcerer in the Grimm stories, bald, with a beard, and a large nose. Most of the time, he wore a woolen cap and he kept a warm shawl around his shoulders and chest. A silent man, he shuffled with tiny steps while holding on to the walls.

He lived in the converted storage room behind the shop. Vati had emptied a large, oak wardrobe for his things, which became a scary place for the children to hide in their hide-and-seek play. Johanna's job every night was to fill up the hot water bottle and slip the metal container in a sock, to prevent burning his thin skin, and under the feather bedcover. After closing time, Vati opened the shop door wide to heat the bedroom from the shop's fireplace.

Like everybody else, Ur-Opa had to go through the shop for the outhouse in the court behind the house to do his number two business, but he peed in a copper pail, kept between the wardrobe and his bed, and covered by a solid copper lid. Early in the morning, the tanner would arrive to pick up the piss with his horse cart, already loaded up high with bloody, fresh cowhides. He would pour the urine into a large vat attached to the back of the cart, wedged between the still-hairy skins and the cart's slatted-wood hatch. In exchange for the trouble, the tanner would give Vati a rebate on the price of leather. Vati wasn't supposed to make shoes. Johanna knew that he still made boots and riding pants for some select, wealthy customers and guards, who always arrived after closing hours.

That night like all others, the family ate their meal in stages because they didn't have enough chairs: usually the eldest three children — Rieke, Johanna and Willi — and Vati in the first sitting, with Ur-Opa, Mutti, Hannah, and August in the second.

Supper consisted of sauerkraut and potatoes with a meagre helping of *speck*, bacon and a generous dousing of lard-based brown sauce. Before setting the table, Johanna sneaked into the shop as Vati took his shop clothes off in the bedroom. She rummaged through the drawers, to find the bottle her dad always kept there to offer an outstanding customer a drink for sealing the deal on a lucrative order.

Searching for the bottle, she recalled what Vati had told her about Ur-Opa, once a young whippersnapper, crafting his fancy shoes for the daughters of the Governor, Prince Radziwille of the Grand Duchy of Posen. Ur-Opa had insisted that his son would baptize his first girls with these names, as a favor to him: Fredyryka and Johanna. Fritz had said, "We liked the names, so we did name you and Rieke after them."

At the time, she had doubted the story's veracity and replied *hard to believe that*, but Vati had not scolded her for her callous comment doubting him. It added to his *Weltschmerz*, his world-weariness, and his face showed his pain, when he replied, "You can't judge a book by its cover, *Schätzchen*. Your Ur-Opa tried to make it, against all the difficulties put up for us, and he did pretty well."

***

Johanna was still on her errand to find the bottle, intent on getting more out of Ur-Opa and reached far into the drawer of her dad's workbench. Yes! There was the bottle. She pushed her hair out of her face and tucked the loose strands behind her ears, lifted one of the two shot glasses out of the drawer, and rubbed it clean with her skirt. She picked up the two extra quilts she had retrieved from the chest and draped them over her arm. It would be cold in Ur-Opa's lair. She walked through the shop and knocked on the door at the far end, on a mission and excited to find out the truth from the horse's mouth.

"Ur-Opa, time for supper. Are you coming, *bitte?*"

Nothing happened. Johanna vigorously rapped on the solid wooden oak door a few times before she opened it wide. After a couple of minutes, the bent figure of Ur-Opa opened the door a crack, a woolen nightcap on his head, and his shoulders wrapped in a heavy horsehair blanket. When he saw Johanna, the suspicion melted from his face. Beaming, he opened the door wide.

"Come in, my sweet girl," Heinrich whispered. "I was just about to prop the door open to let the heat in."

"Yes, that's good. Ur-Opa. It's time for supper." She put her load on the stool beside his chair, grabbed his arm, and led him to the kitchen. She said to her youngest brother, "Trade places with me, August. I want to sit with Ur-Opa tonight. You'll get my Sunday dessert."

***

Sitting beside Heinrich at the table, Johanna hung on to his every word, as her Ur-Opa chatted after some encouragement. Johanna asked if it was true about the princesses in Poznan and that Rieke and she were their namesakes.

"Yes, certainly. That's true."

He told her he believed the princesses were in love with him, and he mentioned their full names: Eliza Fryderyka and Wanda Johanna. Heinrich sighed, and with a self-deprecating smile he added, "Although I *was* a good-looking lad, if I dare say so myself, they loved me probably for my hands making them whatever shoes they desired, and in any color, they could think of."

Mutti's eyes lit up and she looked at Ur-Opa with a big smile.

Ur-Opa smiled too, his eyes sparkled, and he exuded energy, defying his wrecked body and his age. He looked more like a friendly troll, popped out from under a bridge. Johanna immediately felt guilty for thinking of that unfair comparison. Ur-Opa was almost a century old, a milestone reserved only for the extremely hardy. Who knew what she would look like as an old woman if she even reached that number? For a moment, Johanna closed her eyes and imagined Ur-Opa as a young man, eager and capable with supple hands and a creative mind.

Mutti was surprised but quietly listened to Ur-Opa talking away, while Hannah wasn't interested, and just quickly emptied her plate to ask permission to leave the table. Soon, dinner was over, and Ur-Opa stood as Friederike cleared the table.

"Mutti, I'm going to chat some more with Ur-Opa," Johanna whispered. Mutti just nodded.

In Ur-Opa's room, Johanna unwrapped her package, wrapped a blanket over his knees, and poured him a drink. "I would like to hear some more about those days. Are you up to it, Ur-Opa?" she asked with her sweetest smile as she handed him the glass.

"Always," he said. "Ask me what you want to know, child."

Ur-Opa didn't need much encouragement now. He continued talking, his nearly blind eyes with the bottle-thick glasses staring in the distance. "*Schenk noch mal rein,*" he said after a while, nudging her for another drink.

She admired the effect of a bit of alcohol on an old man and wondered if she should pour him the next drink. *Der Alte* seemed tipsy already, and Vati might get mad if she emptied his bottle. She decided on half a glass.

"Sure. Mmm, that is good. My Ludovike always said I loved the bottle too much, but I think one schnapps a day keeps my blood flowing. Where were we? Oh yes: shoemaking."

His specialty was color, the reason that His Excellency hired him, he suspected. He used soft calf leather in bright colors, pleasing the ladies of the Radziwill family. His certificate as a royal provider allowed him to obtain the rarest pigments for the leather dyers. He bragged about having the finest calfskin in any color the ladies wanted. "After my designation as a royal shoemaker, I had no lack of customers."

He stopped talking, his gaze focused on the distance, his glass empty.

"And then, Ur-Opa," Johanna nudged and gently took the empty glass from him.

Heinrich shook his head and focused on her.

"Yes. Where was I? Oh, yes. Prince Radziwill, the royal designation." He went on about this member from a famous royal family, an important man: the *Reichsfürst* of the Grand Duchy of Posen in the Holy Roman Empire, who had reigned over Lithuania before he became the Duke of Posen before it became part of Prussia.

"The Prince, as a patron for the arts was famous for the concerts of all the great composers of the times at his other palaces in Berlin and in Antonin." He ended by saying, "Alas, my time at the palace ended when the war with France was lost and the Prince was thrown out of his position." He closed his eyes.

Johanna saw that Heinrich looked very tired and considered not pushing him further.

"What a shame," she said softly. Remembering Ur-Opa's deafness, she spoke louder. "That's too bad, Ur-Opa. What happened?"

Heinrich opened his eyes, opaque with cataracts, and exhaled long and audibly. He tried to push his shoulders straight, but his scoliosis-affected spine prevented that, and he sagged back into a crouch.

"I was out of a job. It had been so wonderful. I still dream about it sometimes." Heinrich's eyes filled with tears as a smile played around his mouth.

Johanna didn't want the story to end. She put her hand on his knee. "What do you dream about, Ur-Opa?"

Eagerly, as if he had been waiting for her encouragement, Heinrich continued.

"Well, Prince Radziwill hosted many famous and important people. Did you know that Chopin composed his Piano Trio Opus 8 for him?"

He proudly told her about the premiere as if it had been yesterday and not seventy years ago at the palace on October 2, 1828, and he had cried. It was so beautiful.

"Princess Eliza wore my red shoes that night." Heinrich's eyes watered.

Johanna wasn't sure whether it was sentiment or his plugged eye ducts causing his tears, but she could imagine it was grief for missing it, if it was all true. Regretting she had waited this long to see a tip of the veil lifted, she said softly, "How wonderful you have that memory, Ur-Opa."

Heinrich didn't hear her, and after another deep sigh, continued talking, his voice fading to a whisper with another story about Ludwig van Beethoven, who had composed a work on assignment from the Prince, and that Goethe wrote parts of Faust while at his palace. She doubted the veracity of *der Alte's* memories: a shoemaker attending such a high-class event, tempted to believe her Ur-Opa was another fibber or just an embellisher, just like her dad.

"At least, that's what the Princess told me. She allowed me sometimes to stay at concerts, if I stayed in the back at the bottom of the server's staircase in the basement, so nobody could see me."

Chastised for her earlier doubts, Johanna's heart ached for her old Ur-Opa, once a vibrant young man. She wanted to distract him from the heartache of lost youth and fame, and asked, "Ur-Opa, how did you meet your wife? Did you find her in Posen or after you settled in Pollnow?"

"*Ach, meine Liebe*, that's another story. We were thrown into poverty in Posen — we called it by its Slavic name: Poznan. It had been a marvelous time, but it was all over for me. I immediately left Poznan and went north-west, to the coast with more trade and business opportunities, closer to the Baltic Sea, and ended up in Pollnow."

He took a deliberate breath, which sounded like a gasp, then rubbed his head.

Johanna took the opportunity to seek his answer to one more question.

"Ur-Opa, your wife. We were talking about your wife." She unfolded one of her extra blankets and helped him tuck it over his knees.

"Thanks, dear, I was a little cold. Oh, yes. That's right. I met my sweet Ludovike in Pollnow." His face softened and his eyes went unfocused. A smile appeared. He had spoken in a voice permeated with love. Johanna hoped to have her future lover speak about her with that much longing — *Sehnsucht*.

He explained that his Ludovike was staying in a *Gasthaus* in Pollnow with her brother, David, who tried to get into a university in Berlin, but she changed her mind when they met and stayed with Heinrich instead.

"She had this beautiful, long hair the color of dried hay turned liquid, and large eyes, like the sea. I could look into those eyes forever and let myself drown in them," he chuckled. Embarrassed, he smiled, shook his head as if to purge his yearning, and then continued. "We settled, and our two sons were born. After she passed, there was nothing left in Pollnow for me. Everybody had moved away."

He expressed gratitude for Fritz and Friederike, letting him stay in Osterode with the family. "After my sweet Ludovike passed away, I didn't care if I lived or died. Your Vati is a good grandson," he nodded in confirmation of his words. "I would've died there, broken-hearted, just like my Ferdinand."

It was quiet. Johanna looked closely at his face, difficult to distinguish in the scattered light. Heinrich's eyes were closed. A trickle on his chin from his mouth shimmered in the light of the candle inside the lantern. She pulled the blanket up over his raspy chest and draped the other one over his shoulders, rather than waking him up to crawl into bed. She quietly slipped out of the room, keeping the door to the shop open wide. She threw another log into the hearth. Shaking her head about the wonderful fairytale she had heard, she climbed the stairs to the girls' bedroom.

# Chapter 7

As soon as the opportunity arose a couple of days later, Johanna asked her dad what he knew about that time. He smiled indulgently.

"My, you are persistent." He confirmed that Prince Radziwill was related to the royal families of Europe and that the various rulers did each other favors and gave away possessions as a peace offering, or as a reward in a battle. The Prince got the Duchy, but he blew it by favoring the Polish. The Prussians who ruled the area hadn't like that. Because Radziwill belonged to the Slavic nobility, he naturally had sympathy for the defeated Slavic Poles — the underdogs — and he had vehemently opposed the Prussian Germanization campaign.

Johanna didn't get much of the politics. She was just not that interested, but she knew what *was* necessary for families and children on a human scale. She wanted to be liked, and life would be very tough for the Slavs, and to be so hated would be for her, too. She had asked him what was wrong with the Polish.

Vati denied any good reasons for it, and that it was all right for the Polish to want a country of their own just as they had previously, and that it mostly was a political thing about territory. The area was strategically too valuable for risking the Polish suddenly siding with the enemy after they became independent. That was the reason for the Germanization. They should forget they were Slavic. He scoffed as he said that and sounded bitter.

She didn't like this Vati and wanted to change the subject, but wasn't sure if she understood his words' meaning, so she asked, just to be sure.

"What do you mean with that Germanization, Vati?"

"In plain language: melting into German society — becoming Germans — and that means it's forbidden to speak a native language or learn your own history in school."

He said the Polish in Germany couldn't enter university or get a decent business going and that it wasn't the ethnic Poles' fault that they couldn't amount to anything. They were actually *kept* down. In Pomerania, they were only allowed to be subservient laborers on potato farms, with no other choice than to be servants in Prussian households of the nobility. After the factories and the shipyard started to make others rich, the wealthy also bought large estates in Pomerania and hired the locals.

"We were already there for ages, as the owners of small businesses, a shoemaker, a blacksmith, but we were only allowed to earn peanuts." His face was distorted, full of hate even, and his voice compressed with a different tone, low and growly.

Startled, as she had never seen him this much aggravated, Johanna thought of the logical conclusion: "Was our family involved at all in a rebellion, Vati?"

He paused for a few seconds, then slowly replied, "Well, no... or maybe... I'm not sure of anything. I think some of Ur-Opa's in-laws might've been active during the uprising.

Johanna chuckled. "Really? That sweet old man had a rebellious wife? I can't believe that, Vati."

Fritz threw the boot with force into the corner. With barely suppressed anger, he looked at her. He barked: "Believe it or not, but the result was that things in the eastern provinces have always been so much rougher than here in Osterode."

Johanna recoiled, chastised, and stood up from her stool. In a meek voice, she said, "Oh sorry, Vati, I didn't mean to make light of it."

Fritz softened, and with both hands spread in an apologizing gesture, said with a voice full of tears, "We had no choice but to become part of the German Empire."

***

Not long after their conversation, Mutti tried to raise Heinrich in the morning with his usual mug of tea, but Ur-Opa didn't wake up. It had been a simple, sober funeral march to the outskirts of town on a day with a watery sun, but luckily without wind or rain.

When Mutti had called the children earlier to say goodbye to the body in the front room, Johanna didn't know how to behave. "Give him a kiss," her Mutti told the children, but she just couldn't. At the gravesite, Johanna was full of regret. She couldn't rid the picture of Ur-Opa in his coffin from her mind. She should have been more generous with her time, more interested in her great-grandfather while he was still alive. She was sad about the fact he was gone, and with him, part of his history. One day he was here, the next moment gone.

She knew about death, but now she had seen his lifeless face, this hull of a body with his personality gone, it was shocking, so final. His lifeless face was not him: he was so obviously not there anymore. She feared she'd always see this image of him as a dead corpse instead of his sweet face full of emotions.

Watching Ur-Opa being lowered into the earth, and her family members throwing a handful of dirt on the wooden coffin — one by one — before they left the gravesite, she stiffened, and her heart hardened. She didn't want to cry. She dug her nails into her palms inside her coat pockets to distract her thoughts. And she yet hadn't gotten an answer to the many questions about her ancestors. She didn't know anything about their lives.

As grief tried to overwhelm her she switched her thoughts to practical questions to cover her ache. Walking home from the burial site, she formed her intent to ask Vati once more, or even maybe Mutti, but only after her Sunday schnapps. And what was this doublespeak of Vati about being Jewish on his mother's side? Who was his mother, this Philippine Weisen, or whatever her name was?

# Chapter 8

Fritz had promised Friederike that as a member of the Shoemakers Guild in Osterode his shoe business would be protected from the anti-Polish actions. He was wrong. When he saw a copy of the new rules delivered by an errand boy to the shop, only four weeks after his grandfather died, his anger rose. He was no longer allowed to own a business as an immigrant and had to find a new owner for the business. Another restriction that caught his eye was that no ethnic Poles were allowed to hold any official government position. After reading the entire announcement, Fritz cried out, "Goddamn, those Germans."

Johanna came running to see what caused the yelling and stood watching her father's meltdown, helpless to do anything to help him, hurting for him.

Friederike threw up her hands, startled by her husband's outburst. "Shhh, husband, keep your voice down," she admonished. "The neighbors will hear you."

Fritz complained loudly as he paced his shop floor. He was having none of it.

"What am I supposed to do now? Sell my business? Work for the new owner? Or what else, go to work in a steel mill? At my age?" He uttered a string of curses.

Friederike hung onto his arm with a worried face, pleading. "Come, dear man, let's calm down and have a drink. We can talk about it. We'll find a solution, we always do."

They disappeared into the front room, only meant for Sundays and special occasions, and with the door closed, they stayed there for the next hour. Their voices went up and down, flaring up, and then subsiding to a whisper. After the younger children had come home from school it was still too early for Vati to stop working, but he didn't go back to work. It was only afternoon.

Johanna's mind frantically looked for solutions as she paced the floor, waiting for them to come out of the front room. What could she do? Her dad always looked after them. Now it was time she'd step up. She was the age she could work somewhere. Tomorrow she would look for a job. Her heart broke for her dad, not even allowed any longer to repair shoes, let alone make new shoes, reduced to a burden to his family. The meal was late that night, and all ate in silence.

***

A week later, a government official busted Fritz in his little shop with a customer after curfew. The inspector asked him all kinds of questions, and also questioned the customer, but since the latter was a wealthy landowner, the inspector waved Fritz's portly customer out of the shop. Johanna watched it all with trepidation, upset but ready to jump in and defend her dad, but the inspector left, finished with his questions.

The next day, three guards from the Reich's office arrived. They were still arguing and questioning Fritz when Johanna came home. The Prussian guards with their pointy helmets took away all tools and Fritz's inventory. When the captain ordered him to vacate the premises, Fritz sunk to his knees onto the cold floor and cried with his hands covering his face.

Johanna rushed to him and pulled him up by his elbow. "Vati, don't let them crush you, stand up."

"We'll give you till tomorrow to clear out," the commander barked, standing wide-legged in the entrance, his musket slung over one shoulder. The ostentatious plume on his helmet waved with his head's movements, like a peacock.

Friederike, just coming home, needed only a second to understand what happened. Pushing them aside as she got through the door, she faced them after closing the door. Her face beet-red, she screamed at the captain: "Aren't you ashamed of yourself, kicking an honest guild member to the curb, who never did anything wrong but work hard for his family?" As Friederike spoke, the peacock lifted an eyebrow, and turned his back to her. His two sidekicks kept staring at Friederike.

Johanna, still pulling her dad's elbow and trying to raise him to his feet, was crushed for her poor dad and absorbed his humiliation. She wanted to rush at that commander, beat him with her fists, spit in his face, and yell at him to leave her dad alone. They would lose their home; without it, Willi, Hannah and August would have to be raised by Mutti's relatives while Mutti worked. Johanna would go into service with a family, her parents didn't have to worry about her.

As she held on to the heavy weight of Vati's body, she wondered whether that guard knew he looked like an oversized parrot. The man's fancy feathers on his helmet distinguished him as the higher-ranked. When he left, his two apes without feathers followed him out the door into the street. Johanna looked at Mutti, now kneeled beside Vati on his other side, sinking to the floor. Both were crying. Johanna let go of her Vati's elbow, and he slipped prone to the floor, where he lay sobbing, covering his face with both hands.

With the guards gone from the house, the cold hand on her heart disappeared and released her from having to be strong. Unable to fix the situation, she broke down crying as well and kneeled beside her dad, caressing his head.

"You shouldn't have kept records," Friederike muttered between sobs. That didn't help, and Fritz sobbed louder. His wailing induced Friederike to stop weeping, and she cried out: "Ach dear, calm down. Don't let the bastards break you, Fritz. We can start again."

Johanna, startled by her mother's outburst, stopped crying and let go of Vati's head.

Friederike grabbed his shoulders with both hands and drew Fritz into her chest.

"No, I can't," he sobbed, "I'm so tired, I need to rest. I can't get up. Help me." He stopped weeping.

"Come, Schatz, I'll help you." Mutti grabbed his elbow and told Johanna to grab the other arm as she got up and attempted to pull Fritz to his feet. "Let's take him to bed for a rest."

It was as if Johanna's body vibrated with anger. She could've kicked somebody, but whom? Not her dad, this wreck of a man, reduced to becoming an old man in the course of an hour. Her disgust overcame her, and she grabbed her father rather impatiently by the other elbow trying to haul him onto his feet, but the color of his face startled her. It was grey. "Mutti, look at Vati," she urged in a low voice.

"Och, Du lieber Gott," Friederike cried. "He's ill, get a doctor, sofort!"

Johanna let her dad's arm go. Her Vati's limp body sank back to the floor, his eyes closed.

"Go. Go, right now." Mutti screamed, waving her arms.

Johanna grabbed her coat and ran out of the house. As she ran to the doctor's office in the main square only a few blocks away, she pulled her arms through the jacket sleeves. Her dad could not die, he had to stay, he was too young for death. She repeated the mantra *don't let him die, don't let him die* all the way to the doctor's office, moving her lips as she phrased the words, tears now streaming down her cheeks, which she didn't even notice. The panic moved her legs faster than ever before.

\*\*\*

Johanna's run for medical help was in vain. He was making her wait, until he had finished with his patient. By the time she came home with the physician in tow, Vati had died. She found Mutti sitting next to him on the floor, holding his head in her lap, sobbing so hard it made her shoulders shake. The doctor couldn't save Fritz and told her the verdict after his quick inspection. Mutti stopped weeping and focused on the doctor.

He concluded, "It was a massive heart attack, must have had poor circulation. Did he have bad news, or an especially strenuous time maybe?"

"Oh, you don't know the half of it," Johanna grumbled, tears blinding her vision. "Thanks for coming, but you better leave now."

Her dad was gone. *They had not been fast enough*, was all Johanna could think.

How was that possible? She blamed the doctor for not leaving immediately, then herself for not being forceful enough. She had been too slow. She had failed. It was her fault. Grief hit her hard and stunned her.

The doctor grabbed his hat off the table where he had thrown it on his arrival. He replaced it on his head as he said, "I am so sorry I couldn't help. You can pick up the death certificate tomorrow. I'll send you the bill in the mail. That will give you a few days delay."

Johanna nodded and closed the door after him, the words *thanks for nothing* on her mind. With the upcoming eviction, there was no hope for a forwarding address for sending a bill. She had no illusions about her future. The world was a dark place.

***

A couple of days later, another funeral took place and another march through the narrow streets to the little cemetery, too soon after Ur-Opa's burial. This time, Mutter accepted a generous church member's offer to lend her his horse and cart. There was no money left for anything fancier.

Johanna was seething without a target for her anger, like a trapped animal, with no home and no income left, her beloved dad gone, her mother turned into a sad wreck of a woman, and two of her young siblings not yet able to stand on their own feet. She had no tears left for public mourning. Her chest was constricted with loathing for the German *occupiers*, as her Vati saw them, having crushed his spirit — the cause of his broken heart, and of his drinking. She realized he had been one of the last to speak the language, the universal language understood by all Slavs in the eastern parts of the Empire. With him, all knowledge of their culture was gone from her family. With the law forbidding it, Fritz had not dared to teach his children the language. It was not right. She had always thought Vati exaggerated, but she had to admit he had a point, now that he was gone. *Sorry Vati, I was wrong, I didn't believe you and now it's too late,* she whispered, walking behind the cart with his coffin.

Friederike — mute — was riding on the cart's seat up front, unable to walk a far distance. Johanna's mother had turned into a silent widow. With Fritz's death, their income was decimated, and the eviction made them homeless. The financial troubles added to the Empire's moral debt, owed to her family, for which Johanna would make the Germans pay. She hated them right now, the guards, and the doctor, who wouldn't leave quickly enough, the anti-Polish laws and the government, and even Vati's rich customers, who knowingly paid him for illegal work.

It had been the Prussians who had first destroyed her father's life in Pomerania, and the Germans took what was left of his life in a hostile land. Like Fritz, she blamed them all for *his* father's death. Why did his parents even name him *Friedrich Wilhelm*, after the Prussian king? Her childish wish — to become wholly German — severely faltered then.

***

Her eldest brother Willi, who called himself Wilhelm now, didn't feel that way: he had already left home to enlist in the army and had not returned for the funeral. Rieke was married now. She had found herself a good husband, a butcher. Rieke was pregnant and walked with her husband behind the flatbed wagon, together with Johanna, Hannah, and August. The day of Vati's death, she had talked Mutti into moving in with her and her husband, relieving Johanna from worrying about them. She only had to find a roof over her head for herself.

Rieke had told her that morning: "Hannah and August can move in with us until they find an apprenticeship, or a position and work for a living, but you'll have to find yourself a live-in housekeeping job."

It had not been unexpected, but to be rejected by her own sister hurt her deeply, nevertheless. "Fine," she had replied. "I want that, anyway."

When Vati was still alive, she had wanted to start a service job and lie about her age. It was real now. She could beg Rieke and offer to sleep on the floor, it didn't matter. She would make do, but the words wouldn't come. Pride forbade her. She hated her life and hated Rieke.

# Chapter 9

The new century had come with great promise for the German Empire. Three years into the 1900s, at age twenty-three, Johanna had burned through many jobs. Her independent mind and her brash demeanor meant conflicts with her mistresses would follow as soon as she opened her mouth in protest. Within a couple of months after being hired, she made that self-fulling prophecy come through: she was not suited for subservience. She hated being a live-in maid but had no options. She hated her life.

The masters of the house believed that paying her salary meant they had access to all of her. In addition to Johanna's brash personality and her rebukes of anybody within the household approaching her for sexual favors, the competition from others with more German-sounding names just proved too much. The odor of the Polish clung to her, and her assertive mouth always led to dismissals.

She learned to keep her lips permanently pursed into a thin stripe for fear she would speak in protest and lose her current job, and then be without a roof over her head. She wished her name was Hohenzollern, something royal like that, or even plain Müller would have been better. As an in-house maid and general servant, a *Dienstmagd,* cleaning their homes, only the well-do-to could offer her employment. When the burgomaster's wife offered her a job recently, she accepted the prestigious position despite the many limits on her freedom and one day off a month, working daily and staying awake until dismissed by the mistress sometimes past nine in the evening, bathing once a week, sharing a room, and getting up at five.

Not that there were any high standards required for the behavior of the employer. No, that was only expected from the staff. Despite herself and her experiences, and desperate for an income, she accepted the job with trepidation, hoping that at least a burgomaster would know how to behave.

The mayor's mansion was in the heart of the city in a fancy, three-story block of buildings. Johanna shared her room in the attic under the eaves with the lady's maid. Like most of their kind, the burgomaster and his wife kept separate sleeping quarters on the second floor. The three children slept in two additional rooms off the same corridor.

One of Johanna's jobs was making the beds for the household members. On one disastrous morning, she bent over the end of the master's bed to tuck the sheets under the mattress when someone grabbed her hips and shoved her face-down on the bed. She hadn't seen or heard anybody come into the room, but as he whispered to her, she recognized the master's voice. The bastard panted as he tried to pull up her skirt: "Come on, little Polish girl, give it to me. I know you want it too."

Johanna froze, then struggled to get him off her back without effect. He was too heavy. She started screaming, "No, no, no." The master didn't like her resistance and growled, "Be quiet. I am your master. *Polnische Schlampe*. I own you. Lie still."

She had never been called a Polish slut to her face or back. She became as stiff as a plank, keeping her body as heavy as she could, pressing her feet and legs together. A hand pushed her face down into the pillow. She could not scream. It was no use: the solid mass of the much larger man pinned her down on the bed, and a strong arm grabbed her skirts and pushed at her legs as he mumbled dirty talk.

She was helpless. Her heart thumped as if it would explode, and she tried to scream again. She was livid, realizing she shouldn't have counted on any man's decency, mad at herself. Damn all men, animals, they are. She was being raped, and anxiety shot through her, fearing a pregnancy, and shame. Suddenly, the door flew open and smacked hard against the wall. A high-pitched shriek filled the room.

"Ahhhhh, Jesus and mighty God, Karl, you, *Schwein*. Get off her."

The weight lifted and she was free to move. She scrambled off the bed, breathing a sigh of relief. The burgomaster fumbled with his pants while standing beside the bed. He straightened his clothes, then stomped out of the room without a word, brushing past his wife. The mistress stood by the door with a distorted face, full of hate, and she seemed to weigh how much Johanna was to blame. The elderly woman's balled fists, held close to her chest, shook slightly.

Johanna thought *those hands would prefer to strangle her husband.* She stammered with a red face and a still-frantically beating heart, "I didn't hear the master come into the room, Frau Burgomaster. I was attacked, I didn't invite it."

As Johanna tried to leave the room and passed by her mistress in the doorway, the woman smacked Johanna's cheek, took a deep breath, paused for a second slap, and then instead, shouted: "*Raus, verschwinde,* disappear. You are fired!"

Johanna walked out of that mansion never to return. She was relieved it had ended like this. She knew of other girls that had been whisked away, pregnant by the master, and their children whisked away to a different family or an orphanage. That would have ruined her life completely. She swore under her breath as she walked to Rieke's house. Rather than taking another job as a Dienstmagd again, she'd beg Rieke to take her in.

***

Hannah had married recently and moved in with the in-laws. Rieke had been hired at the funeral home, taking over her mother's former job, and let Johanna stay at her place until she found a job. After her narrow escape with the Burgomaster, she became even more vigilant, ensuring she never was anywhere alone with *any* master or any *man.* But this wisdom came at a cost. The words *dirty Polish whore,* and *little mongrel hussy,* now seared in her heart forever, froze her with their contempt. As soon as she gave her last name, rejections followed, often came with slurs about her ethnicity, so she contemplated changing it. If she changed it, she would do exactly what her father's ancestors had done: Germanize. It still wasn't a German name.

Her earlier wish to be wholly German gnawed at her. Maybe she had been smarter as a child, and she should change her name to a solid German name. *Munster,* maybe. She said the name out loud, tasting its flavor. Not bad. *Munster.* Monster.

***

A week after the assault, Johanna was out in the streets looking at ads nailed to the noticeboards outside the guesthouses and at the town hall. She was the only one in her family who seemed to lag and had trouble finding a husband. On this glorious day, she saw an advertisement that caught her attention. *Wanted: a capable person with self-confidence to run the convenience shop for a railroad construction project.* She jumped at the chance and walked to the office of HBS, the company that posted the advertisement, and she put in her application. She hurried to Rieke's home to tell Mutti about it, still living with Rieke and her husband since the eviction.

"But you will have to leave Osterode for that job," Friederike gasped. She managed to get up, pushed her fists into her waist, and with her lips pursed tightly, held Johanna's stare. "You can't leave us. Your family needs you here." Although her eyes were light-colored, they shone, no, virtually *glowed* with anger, willing Johanna to back down.

"Mutti, you can't demand that of me. I have no home; I need a decent job. I can't sponge off Rieke forever."

Judging from her mother's demeanor, Johanna realized leaving town wouldn't be easy. She was surprised and pleased with Mutti's reaction. She thought Mutti wouldn't care if she left. It must be because of the family's dwindling numbers. She cleared her throat, and in a low voice, she tried to reason, throwing in a white lie or two.

"But Mutti, I haven't even applied yet. They probably have a man in mind. Don't be cross with me. I need a good job. Rieke and Hannah are secure in their marriages and August and Wilhelm have steady jobs. You are taken care of; you don't need me. I might never marry, and I need an income."

Friederike just stared at her. Then she said, "You are leaving me, just like your Vati."

Finally, Johanna lost her temper and screeched, "That's not fair. Nobody needs me here. I resent you for saying that."

She glanced away and looked at the door, hoping Vati would come through and side with her, but the wall between them and the street didn't move, and Vati was dead. Oh, she missed him dearly. If he were still alive, leaving Vati would have been the hardest part. Maybe a good thing he was already gone.

Her anger dissipated as she moved into the kitchen towards the rattan basket with the day's ration of potatoes. The day after she was kicked out of the Burgomaster's house, she got a new job as a server in *Gasthaus Am Platz* in the village square, but she had little to do. The boss demanded she would stay late after all the other servers were gone, and she had flat-out refused. He fired her on the spot within the same week she got hired. She could at least say she had experience serving food now.

She quietly asked, "Can I help you with making dinner, Mutti? What did Rieke get you to cook? Can I peel the potatoes for you?"

Friederike sighed and let her arms drop alongside her body as she replied, "Sure, Johanna, if you like."

# Chapter 10

"Our company was the first state railway in Germany," Müller, the HBS railroad company's personnel manager bragged. The company was called the Duke of Brunswick's State Railway, the *Herzöglich Braunschweigische Staatseisenbahn*.

"Already in 1838, we constructed the first section of our line from Brunswick to Bad Harzburg at Wolfenbüttel. Railroad lines are an absolute necessity for our country's expansion."

The middle-aged man in his tight uniform, its cloth stretched beyond the size the seamstress had intended, looked at Johanna with a stern face, unaware of his own pomposity. He wasn't done with his speech yet. He told her that the project would build a railroad net all over Germany — the biggest company project in decades — and she'd be working on the *Ostbahn* — the eastern part. He confirmed her experience handling money at the Gasthaus and serving people was a plus. Then he said something that made her ears perk up.

"I expect you to go out of town with the company to run the concession shop."

"Oh, that's no problem," Johanna quickly replied. "I am not married and am free to take the job." Remembering the assaults, she added, "As long as I have a space for myself that I can lock." She fiercely stared him in the eye; head held high. She wasn't going to let her chance at a good job pass her by because of the men. She had to grab this chance to see the world, get out of town, and make a living. Her dependency on Rieke was killing her.

The man in his rail uniform behind his large bureau averted his gaze, smiled, then continued his intended speech.

"I see you've got spunk. You'll need it."

He told her that the concession would be in an empty carriage and follow the workers to the construction site, wherever that was. She'd had to bake bread at times when the project would be in the middle of nowhere. Other times the project would be close to a town.

Suddenly he paused, looked intently at her and asked, "Aren't you concerned to be the only woman among those rough construction guys?"

"I know how to handle men, sir, and I am careful with my own safety as well, Herr Müller, as long as I have my own space," she replied, straightening her back in the chair. Was she allowed to sleep in the cantina car, for safety reasons? Yes, she was allowed. He would make sure there was a good lock on the door.

He smiled indulgently.

"Well, in any case, I will instruct the superintendent of the project to keep an eye out for your safety. We need somebody now."

He explained that they had no time for delays, as the project was already behind schedule since the amalgamation with the Prussian Royal State Railway, division Magdeburg. The new factories in the Ruhr region relied on rails to export their goods across the German Empire. People needed to eat and were dependent on the food from the eastern fields from Pomerania."

The fat man sat back and studied Johanna, sitting on the edge of her chair with a straight back as prim as a soldier standing at attention.

"That is fine with me," Johanna responded without hesitation. She had to have this job, and she was so delighted to work at something real within her grasp, if only she acted confidently enough. "I have no responsibilities in Osterode and could leave anytime. I'm up for the adventure, if the pay is decent."

She didn't tell him she couldn't wait to get out of town, excited by the adventure ahead of her.

"Good to hear it. You can start tomorrow with setting up the kiosk."

He clarified how the company would advance the money for the inventory, and installments be taken off her bi-weekly salary until all paid off. During the construction, she would stay in her separate work carriage with the concession booth, but all would travel to the start of the project together: the engine crew with the superintendent in the caboose, a couple of extra wagons for the laborers, and all the equipment on flatbeds.

"Your wages will be the starting wage of a laborer with a pay raise after you pass the trial period. So, you'll take the job?" He looked at her with searching eyes, expecting a barrier of some kind.

"Absolutely," Johanna beamed, got up, and offered the man her hand across the desk. The man smiled broadly and grabbed it. "A girl to my liking. It's a deal."

They went over a few more details. Müller decided on the amount the company would lend her for an inventory and how much to deduct from each paycheck.

An hour after entering the office, Johanna practically danced to Rieke's home to tell them all about her marvelous new job.

# Chapter 11

Three days later, Johanna spent her first day of March, 1903 traveling east from Osterode by carriage to a designated village. The caravan would travel from there to the end of a line, where the work would begin. It was spring, so the crew could take advantage of the long season. On her arrival at the village, she could see the waiting wagons on a side line behind a steam locomotive and many men in coveralls, loading what was left of the pile of rocks beside rails, needed for the project. She saw flatbeds stocked up high with freshly tarred railroad ties, other flatbeds with just steel rails, and several closed industrial cars.

She had to cross a large field with stubble which pricked her feet in her fancy Sunday shoes. One of the crewmembers walked with self-possessed air and a raised chest in her direction. He introduced himself as Wilhelm, the second in command, and offered her his hand for support on the walk across the field, a large, calloused workingman's paw. He showed her the facilities, then told her to come back the next day and report to him at 5:30 in the morning for the departure. She spent a restless night at the guest house Wilhelm had recommended, half an hour's walk away. Instead of walking, she took a cab to the worksite in the morning, paid for by her advance. Within minutes of her arrival, the train had taken off east at six in the morning as the shrill whistle blasts woke up the town.

Johanna had utilized her first burst of energy to set up the equipment as the train moved through the landscape to the end of the line. Everything she had bought the day after she landed the job was still wrapped up in wooden crates with straw: several large kettles for tea and coffee, a stove, galvanized washing basins, a washing board, an icebox, large bowls and pots, tin cups and plates, and a new mattress. The preparations lasted only a couple of days, enough time to say her goodbyes. She had been unable to hide her joy, so Friederike had commented: "You can't get rid of us fast enough, can you?"

Johanna refused to feel guilty, and only had replied, "Ach Mutti…." Her voice trailed off without finishing her sentence. It seemed so long ago, and that was only yesterday.

She set up her concessions in the empty passengers' carriage. She made a small display of razorblades, brushes, shaving soap, socks, and a whole box of soap bars on one table. The car looked pretty fancy, with windows and curtains, and a few benches were left in it for seating her customers. The food that needed cooling had already been stored into the icebox in the tiny kitchen adjacent to the dinner car: beer, bread, sausages, cheese, lard, and milk. The tea, coffee, and sugar went into a cabinet overhead. She needed a stool to get to it with her short stature. The back door led to a partition with a toilet: a seat with a hole in the floor, and she could see the railroad disappearing underneath her.

Then she turned to her sleeping quarters. The railroad car was divided into two parts with a partition between the public dining section and the sleeping quarters with the beds. It had two wall beds, one above the other, which could be let down for sleeping and flipped up when not needed. She stacked her personal effects and two suitcases against the opposite wall, where the bunkbeds had been removed. After Johanna was satisfied with her work, she stepped back, nodded and smiled. Her adventure had begun, she was ready for anything.

*** 

On this first day, the small locomotive pulled the caravan-on-rails, behind it the passengers' car converted to sleeping bunks for the permanent crew, and next Johanna's concession carriage, then the flatbed cars, stacked high with building materials and equipment.

After five hours of travel, the train stopped. Johanna had been ready to put the kettle on the coal stove as soon as the wagon would stop. It was lunchtime. Miracle of miracles: only a couple of days after the interview, she was here, in the middle of nowhere in a dream job as an entrepreneur, busy preparing lunches for the crew. She was bursting with joy, as well as a feeling she hadn't experienced before in her life: pride.

***

The tea was ready, and Johanna was busy spreading lard on slices of bread for cheese sandwiches. When she looked up, a handsome man she guessed was in his late twenties or early thirties stood in front of the open window, watching her.

"Good afternoon, *Fräulein*," he said with a smile, taking in all of her, or as much as possible from behind the open window.

"*Guten Tag, mein Herr*," Johanna replied, red-faced from all her hard work. "What can I do for you?"

He guffawed loudly. "Ha-ha, that's the most polite offer from a *hübsches Mädchen* I've had in a very long time."He waited with a big smile.

Her face turned an even deeper red, and she was at a loss for words for a few moments after being called a pretty girl. Then she recovered.

"I am sorry, I should've first introduced myself. My name is Johanna, and I run this concession stand. Would you like tea and a sandwich, or would you rather have a beer, sir?"

The man grinned and with a twinkle in his eyes said: "Hello, Fräulein Johanna. You are right, I'm sorry too. You are looking at Hendrik Zondervan, the superintendent. Nice to meet my concession manager. You don't know how happy my men are we even have a concession. Welcome to the crew."

He stuck his hand up through the window, chuckling, and she grabbed it for a quick shake, and said, "Oh no, and I treated you like you were a common laborer. I'll get you the best sandwich ever. What will you have?"

"Well, no harm done, I still am a common laborer, and you can give me two of your best sandwiches then, and my thermos filled with tea, please — *bitte*."

She hurried to grab this order for her first esteemed customer, embarrassed about the beginning, but nevertheless elated to be working with this handsome, nice man. He wasn't even an easterner — her euphemism for Polish — judging from his foreign accent. Excited about her luck, she hoped *Herr* Zondervan wouldn't see how inept she was. About to hand him his order on a metal tray through the window, she changed her mind and put down the tray on a table. All recovered from her shyness, she opened the carriage door wide with a smile.

"Wouldn't you rather eat in, sir? I have a few seats here."

"*Sehr gerne. Dankeschön, Fraulein,*" he said with a wide grin — very good, thank you, miss — and climbed inside.

She gestured to his meal, waiting for him on the table. "Guten Appetit, sir," she said. "I would like the tray back when you're finished, please."

Johanna watched the man as he took a seat. He was not tall, but stocky and powerful in his chest, shoulders, and arms. He had kind eyes, brown, with an open look, and a head full of dark-blond hair. But what would catch everyone's attention was his big mustache.

He wasn't finished inspecting her either, and his eyes didn't leave her face as he took his first bite. "Sofort, mein lieber *Fräulein* Johanna," he replied. Then he took a short break to chew and spoke to her again, still the only other person in the car.

"We'll be working for years on this line, if you don't run away first from the attention of my bunch of rough construction guys. Thank you for taking the job, Fräulein Johanna. I will protect you from any unwanted attention. Feel free to tell me right away of any problems." He twirled his moustache, the only sign of insecurity.

"Oh, no, you can't get rid of me that easily," she beamed. "I wouldn't know where else to go anyway. I have nothing left in Osterode, sir, but I will call in your help when I need it. Herr Zondervan, thank you so much for the job. I am so looking forward to working for you."

***

After that first day, with the thirty-plus men all fed and watered for the day, Johanna sank down on her bunk, dead-tired, but happier and more hopeful about her future than she remembered ever having been. She had made sure the lock on the door was secured. She fell asleep as soon as her head hit the luxury, down-and-feather pillow, purchased from her advance.

# Chapter 12

HBS put Johanna on a trial period of three months. Thanks to Hendrik's positive feedback to head office, she got the job permanently after the mandatory time had passed. She made simple, one-pot meals, always served with thick slices of dark bread. Some days it looked more like soup than a stew, and those were days when nobody had been able to get to a nearby town to buy supplies, so Johanna had to make do with whatever she had.

She met each day with Hendrik at the evening meal. He was the last of his crew to eat, a sign of his sense of responsibility and generosity, making sure that none of his crew would go hungry. Soon she found out that Hendrik had arrived in the German Empire a decade ago as a young, eager worker from Holland with a measure of technical knowledge. He had worked his way up with HBS to *Schachtmeister*, crew boss in no time at all.

Johanna understood in the *Deutsche Reich*, the Dutch were considered tribal relatives — fellow *Germanic* people. Consequently, Hendrik had more inherent status than the newcomers, mostly mixed Slavic-German immigrants, whom the government relocated from the east to work in the burgeoning steel industry. It was not hard for her to like Hendrik. She was pleased when he showed an interest in *her,* and she didn't hesitate to let him know that she felt the same way about him.

She savored their daily flirtations, made him extra tasty lunches, and gave him the odd complimentary beer. His quiet but cheerful nature was immensely attractive. After a couple of months on the road, they couldn't resist the temptation any longer and their relationship progressed. Johanna already had decided that Hendrik, six years older than she, was all she could wish for as a future husband.

Hendrik was protective of Johanna. He watched the men like a hawk, living up to his promise to protect her on the project. Alas, he could not wholly ward off his men's attempts to get closer to the pretty Johanna, even more attractive because of the crew's isolation. It was nearly impossible for them as strangers in these towns in the boonies to find brothels or a bar with willing girls.

During Christmas time, many of the men left for the closest village to try their luck. That Christmas Eve of 1903, one of the crew came back to the worksite after an unsuccessful foray for love in the adjacent hamlet, very drunk, and desperate to shore up his ego. His eye caught Johanna, just closing shop. She had put the garbage outside and raised her foot to re-enter the carriage when strong arms grabbed her from behind and pulled her toward the ground.

At first she assumed it was Hendrik, pulling a bad joke on her, but the man's rough grab and his sour smell that enveloped her in the next second told her it wasn't Hendrik. She screamed, and her high-pitched screech for help carried across the quiet worksite. "*Hilf mir, hilf mir. Ahhhhrrrr. Jemand, hilf mir.*"

Although it seemed much longer, it wasn't more than a few seconds before she felt him let go of her skirt, which he had managed to push halfway over her behind, and the man dropped to his knees behind her. She quickly turned and straightened her skirt.

Hendrik stood there, seething with anger, a wooden club smeared with blood in his right hand. "Are you all right, *Liebling*?" He didn't wait for her answer, grabbed the slumped man and bent his arms behind his slack body, and told her, "Quick, get me a piece of rope before he wakes up."

***

As Hendrik left, hauling the semi-conscious man with him to another car, Johanna made coffee and savored the word *Liebling*, beloved. Hendrik must have been watching her as she cleaned up, or he couldn't have been there so quickly to rescue her. The nature of the attack wasn't anything new to her, but her legs were still shaking. Although she had been scared, she realized she was less troubled by the assault than Hendrik. She hadn't told him about her past experiences. It was better for him — and her — to see her as a resilient and practical woman, and unblemished. She couldn't risk having his mind infected with the German view of her as a mongrel.

When Hendrik returned, he seemed to have regained control over his emotions. As he sat down at one of the tables, Johanna pushed a cup of coffee toward him. In a calm voice, he said: "I locked up the man; he can't harm you anymore." He smiled at her.

She smiled back. "I am so grateful, Hendrik. Thank you so much for your quick action."

He got up and took her in his arms, held her tightly for a second or two, then caressed her shoulders, arms, and face. "It's my fault for not having been alert enough to prevent it from happening."

Johanna held his eyes, and with a quiet voice, replied, "Don't blame yourself. You saved me. I'm alright." On a lighter tone, she added, "Dear man, but you can let me go now. Drink your coffee."

***

Hendrik kept the assailant locked up in one of the railroad cars, so they'd have a quiet Christmas Day together. He had bought a gift for her: a beautiful, silver brooch, which she immediately had him pin on her dress. In turn, she cooked an extra delicious meal for him. A few days earlier, she had managed to buy a couple of fat fowl from a local woman, looking for customers. She had offered her the partridges for a reasonable price.

***

The next day, Hendrik went into the town to report the assault and brought back the Imperial Guards, who took the sobered up and remorseful crewmember to the station's cell block. He told Johanna that he had fired the perp, just to make sure he wouldn't come back in case of a release.

"I sent the report to the company's head office in a telegram, so they'll know what you have to endure on the job."

"Oh, Hendrik, I'm not sure that was wise. What will they think of me?"

"That you are a courageous and loyal employee, of course."

# Chapter 13

After ten months of traveling together, Johanna was just finishing up cleaning at the end of the day, putting the dishes away, when Hendrik cleared his throat, so she'd look at him. He had dropped on one knee beside her and popped the question.

She threw both hands up in the air, and the tin plate in her hands dropped to the floor. It overwhelmed her that her wish had come through. Hendrik was all she wished for, this calm and decent man loving her was a gift from heaven. She gushed, "Hendrik, *ja, ja,* of course, *ja. Mein Liebster,* I'll follow you anywhere, even to Holland." And she meant it then.

From that day on, she allowed him to sleep in the cabin with her, but she insisted he would find rubbers, as she couldn't get pregnant during their travels. Getting pregnant would mean the end of their adventure, and she wasn't ready to settle, be stuck somewhere in some town as Hendrik moved on. But she wanted children like any decent woman, and soon, as she was getting on in years at almost twenty-four.

***

Soon after Christmas, the construction work stalled, because the locomotive needed a complicated repair, which could last a few days. They had arrived near the town of Celle. Hendrik came to the concession cabin to tell Johanna about the delay. He undid his well-exercised body from winter jacket and headgear, leaving a puddle on the plank floor from his snowy boots.

Johanna decided to address the issue that had preoccupied her for days as she poured Hendrik a mug of coffee.

"Hendrik, dear, what would you think about taking advantage of the break, find the town office in Celle, and get married?"

His head jerked up, and he stared at her, then a smile spread across his face. He threw up his hands in wonder, then exclaimed, "Oh my, you are a practical woman indeed." He shook his head at so much initiative, then added, "Why not? You didn't have any second thoughts?" He pulled her onto his lap.

She smoothed out his big Kaiser's moustache, curling the ends with the tips of her finger and thumb.

"Well, I asked *you* now, didn't I," she chuckled. "Are you having those doubts?" He shook his head. "No!" She kissed him and stood up. He followed her. Through the window, they saw laborers coming to take advantage of the break and buy some of her merchandise. One of them was Jan, Hendrik's younger brother, who had joined the crew some months ago.

"We'd better hurry then," Hendrik commented.

Johanna quickly got her coat, scarf, and hat, and dressed for the cold. "Dear Hendrik, I'm not giving you a chance to back out," she laughed."

As they left the concession cabin, she called out to Jan and the approaching workers with excitement, her face radiant: "Sorry. *Enschuldigung*! The kiosk is closed. We are getting married in Celle."

***

As the snow fell in the middle of January in 1904, Hendrik and Johanna got married in Lower Saxony. Jan was Hendrik's witness. A random man who happened to be at the town hall became the second witness. There were no rings to exchange. No matter, she had her man.

Married in Germany to a Dutchman with a good job and his baby growing inside her, in spite of the prophylactics, Johanna was more than satisfied: her dream had come through. They'd make it work somehow *with* a baby. She couldn't stop kissing him that day. Hendrik seemed as happy with her as she was with him, something she hadn't thought possible when she lived in Osterode.

***

Shortly after the wedding, the news reached the worksite that Pomerania, the birthplace of Johanna's father, was placed under severe measures. The government had established a colonization commission for this eastern province and implemented its recommendations that the Slavic locals no longer be allowed to own any businesses in the eastern provinces. The only jobs left for them were on the farms, not an avenue to wealth for those indebted farmers. Not only that, but the government demanded that the priority for all agricultural activities must be the greater German Empire and its products sent to central Germany first.

"I guess this leaves little for the locals to chew on," said Hendrik after reading it out loud to Johanna as they had a quiet moment, seated after the evening meal in the cozy dining carriage. All the workers had disappeared to their bunks on this dark February night.

"Oh, no, how cruel," she sighed. "I am only thankful *Ur-Opa* and *Vati* didn't have to live through that anymore."

She had understood the Germans considered her father's ancestral lands backward, and its ethnic peoples an inferior sort, just like the Jews; both types of citizens deemed unreliable, if not seen as dangerous heretics and rebels, possibly even socialists, or communists. The area had become even more destitute by the year. Not a place Johanna would like to explore for her family's future. A sense of relief knowing she had escaped that fate almost overwhelmed her.

"Hendrik, I read in an older newspaper that our Chancellor Von Bismarck has extensive property in Pomerania. I suspect that my grandfather must have worked on those estates. I'm never going back there." She remembered the horror of his death as told by her Vati.

"You don't have to. Bismarck made the commission's Germanization policies apply here too, my Mädchen," said Hendrik mildly. "These rules apply in *all* of the German Empire, not just the eastern regions."

When she and Hendrik were in town for the marriage registration, she noticed an increase in the numbers of police officers hanging around on just about every street corner. Now it made sense: they were there to enforce the new, anti-Polish rules.

"Oh, no," she gasped. It then it dawned on her that it didn't apply to her anymore. It was too late for further Germanization of her name anyway, as she had considered after the Burgomaster's assault. Her father's last name had become inconsequential. She got up from her chair, walked over to Hendrik and planted a kiss on his head. Her marriage to this Dutchman had saved her. "I am so happy I married you," she sighed, so appreciative of his proposal to marry her, and not backing out.

Not long after the wedding, the Office for German Culture began its work, and the *Kulturkampf* started: the battle to wipe out all other influences and leave solely *German* identities in the minds and hearts of its citizens. It couldn't hurt Johanna anymore and she wore her status of the wife of a Dutchman as a knight's armor, invulnerable, looking forward to the future as Hendrik enjoyed all his benefits as her husband.

# Chapter 14

The form the *Kulturkampf* took was hard to imagine. Still, Hendrik kept Johanna apprised, mostly in conversations at dinnertime, when he told her about his experiences on his weekly requisition trips into the towns. Most of the time, Johanna didn't go with him, as she had bread to bake. This last time, the butcher in town told him that the German police were picking up Polish workers in the eastern provinces and brought them here to work in the factories. He told Johanna he saw people protesting with placards and handing out pamphlets against the minorities this morning.

"That worries me." Hendrik commented, more agitated than usual, shifting uncomfortably on his chair. With a frown of distaste, he said, "They say the ethnic Polish are flooding the country from the east: *overrun by the mongrels*, the sign said."

"How rude," Johanna said softly, looking at him. Not that she wasn't concerned for those easterners, forced to leave home, but she had distanced herself from the east, convinced she should stick to her childhood promise after all: be all-German. She put down her fork to listen.

Hendrik didn't agree with that recruiting method, but saw its benefit for the industry, and considered himself fortunate for not having any vacancies. Johanna knew he would hire his workers regardless of their ethnicity.

"It's also illogical," he replied. "They can't just steal cheap workers away from Pomerania and further east, and then despise them once they're residents, and stop them from using the resources that were meant for everybody. Germans are already saying that the Polish are taking their jobs away. Where do they get that idea? Poland hasn't existed for ages: it was divvied up between the German Reich and

Russia several wars ago. And those Germans don't even want to work in the factories at those low wages they pay the easterners. If the government passes more laws
against the *former* Polish, there will be trouble."

Johanna nodded, surprised Hendrik had acquired a political opinion suddenly.
He reminded her of Vati, whose anti-German attitudes had made things hard for
Mutti. She had not seen it that way before, but now she understood that life with
him hadn't been easy on Mutti. She had thought a lot about her predicament in
the last weeks. After a pause, she slowly took up the challenge and explained the
complicated Germans to her foreign husband, using her dad's words.

"I think the Germans hate the Pomeranians because they collaborated with the
French in the war with France and would rather be under the French than the
Prussians, especially in Stettin, which the French left last. They are still being pun-
ished for their disloyalty to the German Alliance. I'm not sure how *I* feel," she said,
then quickly added: "as a German."

"What's happening to my wife," Hendrik teased, eyebrows raised, a big smile
on his face. "You're becoming political?"

Johanna straightened her back and stuck her chin out. "What? Can't a woman
have an opinion on public policy? I have a brain. I can think for myself."

"Of course, dear, glad to see it," he chuckled.

***

That night after making love, Johanna told Hendrik about her decision as she let
down her hair from the daytime bun and brushed it. Confronted by the current
hate propaganda, she had been shocked by the German hostility against the ethnic
Poles. Aware of Fritz's grumblings, she had always assumed he exaggerated, and
maybe he hadn't. But he is dead now. Life goes on. She must choose her loyalties
using her brain, not her heart. She snuggled up next to Hendrik on the bunk,
raised herself on an elbow, and looked at him.

Hendrik was dozing beside her in their narrow bunkbed. It was July 21, 1904,
a date she wouldn't ever forget: the day she and Hendrik both knew they would
become a family.

"Dear husband, I want to tell you of my decision that I no longer claim to be a part-Polish descendant, but only German. I am sick and tired of the slander and abuse, and the bad reputation of the Poles. Anyway, my relatives are solid Germans. Rieke has already moved to Hanover with her husband. She wrote me that Wilhelm had been fighting to put down rebellions of the natives in the colonies, doing his bit for Germany. He earned his stripes. We were all born in Osterode anyway. It's settled. We are one hundred percent German."

"Hmm," was all he replied in a mild voice with his eyes closed.

"Don't you care?" she asked.

"Dear wife, I love *you*, not your nationality. We're going to Holland anyway, and then you can become Dutch. Nationality or ethnicity doesn't mean anything to me. We are all just humans." He opened his eyes and stared at her; his brown eyes sincere.

"All right. I don't mind becoming Dutch," she admitted. "But I want to talk about something else: children."

She stopped talking and listened for his reply. It was darkening quickly in the cabin as the night advanced. The last stretch of the construction had been too far from any town for buying rubbers, so they had used the rhythm method. She stared into the darkness, weighing the words to broach the issue. Hendrik seemed mellow, if not half-asleep. Now would be the perfect moment for the conversation.

"*Liebest*, I think I'm pregnant," she said softly.

"Hmmm," he answered.

Johanna sat up and shook him. "Wake up, you dufus, don't pretend you're listening."

Hendrik startled awake and sat up. The faint beam of light coming from outside fell on him, and she could see his face, eyes wide. "Wait, what did you say?"

"I'm expecting, Hendrik." She searched his face for anger or disappointment, but all his face showed was his delight.

"Really? Are you sure?" His hand touched her face, and he caressed her cheek.

Johanna put her hands on his chest and lightly pushed him backward, her heart thumping fast. "Of course, I'm sure."

With eyes wide and a big grin, he replied: "Are you crazy? Of course, I'm happy. Now you must stay with me because we'll be a family. How wonderful." He lifted her off the bed and carried her around the cabin, singing over and over *we're going to have a baby*, as tears of happiness rolled down Johanna's cheeks.

# Chapter 15

Luckily, the work on the railroad progressed well. Hendrik's crew was scheduled exclusively for the northern Saxony line, so Hendrik and Johanna would stay in the central part of the German Empire. Since the Prussian decisive victory in 1815 against France's Napoleonic armies, the empire was a safe and prosperous nation. Furthermore, in 1871 it absorbed the German city-states and Prussia, as well as other states to the south and became one large nation — the largest empire in Europe — with lots of resources. Johanna's mind was put to rest about her future family's safety.

For many families, it was a different story.

Her younger sister, Hannah had written of their brother Wilhelm's return home from battle in the colonies, safe and sound. Although there was peace in the country, his family was poorer than ever. Released from the army, he had no job.

Johanna thought of what Hendrik had said. Like many Germans, she wanted to blame the poor for staying poor with their lack of initiative and willpower, *not* on their lower wages and disadvantages. She remembered the battles of her dad and his tale about his grandfather Ferdinand's struggles with booze — whom she'd never even met — and who had got himself frozen, a suicide. She wanted to believe that he lacked the willpower to stop drinking and pull himself by his bootstraps out of the mess. *That* was the cause of their misfortune.

A memory of Vati's pain and anger, her grief when he died — too soon — gnawed at her conviction. His gentleness was what she remembered most about him, their closeness, their conversations. Was there a point where people give up fighting and start agreeing with others' low opinions? But Willi had nothing to be ashamed of. He had been in battle, he was honorable, he would find another job. She shook the sense of responsibility for her younger brother aside. She had her own life to live.

Johanna van Zanten

The depressed economy without the prospect of a quick turnaround led many residents to leave Germany for America and Australia. The ships were loaded with thousands of migrants — poor easterners and others seeking their destiny outside the German Empire.

When Vati was still alive, Uncle Karl from Pomerania had traveled to Hamburg to emigrate to America with his family, and his still-single brother, Uncle August had joined them. Fritz realized he would never see them again, and Johanna had never even met her uncles. Nevertheless, she completely understood their desire to escape poverty and the constant discrimination. She was pleased with their initiative to fight themselves free from poverty and their entrepreneurial spirit. Johanna was sorry Vati hadn't been able to send them off on the quay in Hamburg for lack of money to travel.

*Pommern.* Pomerania. Although she'd never lived there, her father's homeland figured in her life through him. Suddenly a skipping game song popped into her head:

*Maikäfer flieg,*

*Dein Vater ist im Krieg,*

*Deine Mutter ist in Pommerland,*

*Pommerland ist abgebrannt.*

*Maikäfer flieg.*

June bug, fly,

Your father is at war,

Your mother is in Pomerania,

Pomerania burnt to a crisp.

June bug, fly.

The song only now became meaningful. It reflected the losses many must have experienced in the eastern territories. The rulers had started wars but offloaded the actual battles on their indentured workers. As the crops remained unharvested or not seeded in, everybody starved.

How were parents supposed to feed their children when there was no income and no food? Now that her first child was on its way, Johanna grasped the stress her parents had endured, barely making a living in Osterode with two parents working. She hadn't shared all this history yet with Hendrik.

***

Hendrik and Johanna stayed informed about the political divisions in the interior. Johanna wanted to understand what was happening, what her tribe was up to, but she saw that the news meant something completely different for Hendrik. He filtered the news for a certain result, although she didn't realize which news her husband anticipated. As the resentments grew among ethnic groups in Germany, Johanna didn't understand that Hendrik tried to determine when it was time to leave the country.

Johanna read with increasing alarm how social unrest escalated, seemingly infectious, spreading to other nations, especially in Austria-Hungary to the south *and* its neighboring countries, priming Greater Europe for another rebellion. Remembering Ur-Opa's story of the downfall of Poznan, she became frightened.

Despite what trouble might be brewing, the traveling couple had more immediate problems: bringing babies into the world, and they pushed the rising international tensions to the background. The first signs of labor came way too early in the winter, in mid-January. Although Johanna had become as large as a house, her compact body almost square, she knew she hadn't reached the ideal number of weeks for the unborn's maturity. As the pain in her back wrecked her body, she called out to one of the workers nearby to tell the supervisor his wife needed him.

Within a few minutes, Hendrik stomped into the cabin, out of breath from his sprint.

"Is it time, Johanna, dear?" he breathed, as he grabbed her arm to support her while she stood bent over, hanging on to the backrest of a bench.

The already-strong contractions made her pause every few minutes, as she shared her worries, her brow in a frown, a glint of panic in her eyes.

"Hendrik, I am in labor, but it's too early. I am afraid for the baby. Go get a doctor or a midwife from town. Quickly."

As she paced, and then paused with each contraction, hanging on to the upper bunkbed, she wondered if she had everything ready for delivery. Water was always boiling on the stove in the cabin. She grabbed all the towels and the biggest basin. Too bad they only had the single bunks, but in case of an emergency, she could lie down on the floor on top of a blanket.

She'd hoped to avoid giving birth in a railcar but stopping Hendrik from traveling had been impossible. She had tried her utmost but couldn't convince him to move into town. Wasn't that always the way with men: the job comes first, the wife, second. She'd felt disappointed, but then told herself Hendrik was a typical man, and no prince. "Damn you, stubborn Dutchman," she grumbled. She slowly folded her body onto the lower bunkbed and waited.

*** 

Within an hour, Hendrik was back with a midwife from the small town at the end of the tracks. It wasn't far from the city of Celle, where they had been married. Johanna was worried but also relieved when the contractions stopped soon after Hendrik had left. The pain was gone, but what was her baby doing? Did he die? The midwife sent Hendrik away. "You can come back in ten minutes," she instructed him.

The midwife checked Johanna's cervix' dilation: not enough. She put her big megaphone to Johanna's swollen body, and then poked and pressed down on her abdomen. She stepped away, looking surprised.

"There are two babies, did you know, Frau Zondervan?"

"What?" Johanna exclaimed. "No, I had no idea, but I sure am big, aren't I? That would explain it. Why has the pain stopped? Are they still alive?" Her anxiety sounded through, although she tried to stay calm.

"Yes, don't you worry. I heard two heartbeats. It's good that the contractions stopped. Maybe we can keep them inside you for a few more weeks. The longer they stayed in the womb, the better." But she also insisted Johanna couldn't deliver them in the cabin and had to move into town, due to the unknown period it might take the babies to mature till birth. Another reason she quoted appealed very much to Johanna: they'd have more chances to be born and stay alive with a professional around. "I could help you find temporary accommodation in Altenhagen, my town, closer than Celle."

When Hendrik came back into the cabin, he was not happy hearing the midwife's condition for Johanna to move into town and he seemed confused about the news of the two babies. Upset but powerless to do anything about it, he stepped outside and paced as he decided how to respond to this new problem. Johanna had told him her mother lost two babies in childbirth. He realized her life might be in danger, too. The thought chilled his heart. He returned to the railcar. Inside, he took her hand as she rested on the bed.

"*Ach*, Johanna, we won't risk the babies' lives, or yours. We will welcome two babies with joy, and we'll go into town and find a place to wait for our children. That's the least we could do. The railroad can manage without us."

"*Danke schön, Liebster.* Thank you, dear." Offered a solution, Johanna suddenly became aware she had been upset. She allowed herself to break down, and overcome with relief, she wept long and hard, as Hendrik patted her hand, looking shocked.

# Chapter 16

Hendrik's crew was accommodating. Although sorry to see Johanna leave and going to miss her excellent food, they assured the couple they'd manage without them. Hendrik assigned a deputy, and one of the crew had his wife take care of the concessions for a while.

"I don't think it's going to be for long, maybe a month at the most, we'll see," Hendrik assured the young man backfilling for him. The men wished Johanna all the best.

Through the mediation of Frau Mattias, the midwife, a horse-pulled sled pulled up on the road across the field the next day. Hendrik supported Johanna by the elbow, as he carried her valise with necessities in his other hand. They made their way toward the road and the waiting sled through a foot of snow, anxious, excited, and full of love.

***

At the recommended boarding house in Altenhagen, Hendrik had rented a room, and another two uneventful weeks went by. A fortnight later, Johanna's labor pains resumed. Five hours later, with the help of Frau Mattias, Johanna gave birth to a tiny premature girl. Frau Mattias cleaned and wrapped up the baby girl, as Johanna, half-upright, rested on an elbow and watched her like a hawk. Finally, she handed the bundle to Johanna.

She unwrapped the top part of the wrap and with tears in her eyes studied the tiny hands, the mouth, the head and the child's open, dark-blue eyes. She then kissed the head and chuckled through her tears, "Everything is there. She's perfect. Thank you so much." She gazed some more at the quiet, swaddled child. After a few minutes, the anxious Johanna, still pumped with adrenaline, asked, "Should I start walking to speed it up?"

"No, no, you rest. The other child lives, I just heard its heartbeat. In due time it will come. They're fraternal twins and have separate placentas," assured Frau Mattias. The quiet baby was tired, not making a peep. The midwife took her back and laid her for now in the basket. She called Hendrik into the room to let him have a peek. He just stared at the baby with eyes full of tears before he snuck away again.

*** 

An hour later, a rather well-formed baby boy entered the world with significantly more work and pain than his sister. "Isn't that just the case with guys: always wanting the attention," Frau Mattias joked, but Johanna was too exhausted to reply. She immediately fell asleep and had a nap. Frau Mattias took the two babies, all bundled up, to Hendrik in the living room, and nestled them toe to toe inside their rattan basket next to him.

When Johanna woke up, Hendrik sat on the bed beside her, beaming, as he held her hand.

"*Liebste*, you are a *tovenares*." He used a Dutch word, and she didn't know what he said.

She smiled back. A second later, her face clouded over as she hesitated over the word. "What did you call me, just now?"

"A sorceress. You made two wonderful babies, both healthy and sweet. I would've been delighted with one, but you do one better: one baby of each gender." He kissed her, flushed from excitement.

She was refreshed, energized after the nap, sat up, ready to get off the bed. She softly pinched Hendrik in the bulge of his biceps. In a playful voice, she replied: "Oh, husband, don't sell yourself short. You had something to do with it. I'm just grateful we had these extra weeks for the babies to mature more." No, not to term, but at least a little longer, and she was delighted that both infants were breathing and healthy. She had feared that one would die, which happened more often than she wanted to know.

Never having given birth, she feared her mother's fate would hit her too. A stillborn baby was different: as if the child didn't want to be living, had rejected the mother. The child perfectly developed, but lifeless. She shuddered thinking about the photographs on her mother's dresser, full of sorrow for her mother she'd never experienced before now.

Hendrik looked at her as they held hands. No other words were needed.

After a while, she spoke again.

"You name the children, Hendrik. Your family names are good enough for me. It might help them if we ever end up in Holland."

"Of course, we will get there. Thank you for your generosity, dear."

Hendrik proposed to call the little baby girl Elfriede after his mother. She was born first, setting the pace for life; an eager little girl, he argued. She'll be strong, like his mother. The boy got the name Johan, one of the names of his father."

"They could be German names as well," she smiled.

She struggled to feed Johan, and a frown of concern appeared. "I'll leave you be now," said Hendrik and quietly left the room.

***

Little Johan was slow to latch on and didn't seem hungry at all. His body was slack, his movements quite apathetic. Although he was built more robust than the skittish Elfriede, Johanna feared her son might not survive. She had been too soon in assuming all was well. Now she had seen him and already loved him with all her heart, he just could not die. She talked quietly to him, little words like *my baby boy*, alternately with a soft humming, hoping to seduce him into a strong sense of life.

She turned to the midwife and squeezed out her questions with a hoarse voice, "Frau Mattias, is there something wrong with him? Am I going to lose him?"

Frau Matias said not to worry, that he was just tired from being born. She was going to leave and return later that night to see if things had changed. "Give it a few hours," she said as she left the room with an encouraging nod and a smile.

As recommended, Johanna put Johan in his crib and tried to nap herself. She fell asleep for an hour or two despite her worries, until she was startled awake by a weird sound, and realized Johan was crying. "Oh, he is hurting," she feared, and carefully lifted him out of the basket to inspect him. When he felt her body against his, he stopped crying and made rooting movements, searching for her breast. She tried again to feed him. This time he was hungry. She sighed loudly, and a new relief from feeding her child, her capacity to provide nutrition, the satisfaction, and the intimacy of it overwhelmed her. Tearful, she enjoyed the first feed, until Johan was full of milk and fell asleep in her arms.

\*\*\*

By the evening of that second day of February 1905, the babies and Johanna were getting used to one another. When Frau Mattias dropped by, Johanna was lying back on the pillows, smiling. She had fed both children — her milk had come in — and even Johan had a good feed. She had been up for a while, was exhausted but very happy, and it helped even more that Frau Matias approved, finding everything in order, and left with the promise to drop in the next day again.

Hendrik sat by her side with Elfriede in his arms, while Johan rested on his mother's chest. He looked at Johanna, but then looked away when their eyes met as if he needed to gather courage. Johanna knew right away he had something on his mind.

Weary, she softly whispered, "What's the matter, Hendrik? You want to tell me something?"

He looked guilty as if she'd caught him in the act. "Well, dear, yes, you got me. But we can talk about it tomorrow."

She searched his face, but he had wiped off any emotion.

"Good, tomorrow we'll talk. Please, put the babies in the basket for me, dear."

\*\*\*

The next day the children got an emergency baptism in the Lutheran church. Emergency, because the usual announcement procedures didn't apply. It was the thing on Hendrik's mind the previous night he didn't want to talk about. Johanna objected and wanted it delayed, but Hendrik was pushing her to speed things up. It was Sunday, and Hendrik had told the minister that the babies would move away in a couple of days. It was now or never.

"The only alternative is we don't baptize them until later if we get a chance," he told her.

"That's not fair, Hendrik. Only yesterday I feared Johan wouldn't survive. Yes, we should baptize them, but can't we wait a week?" She was nearly crying, trying to hold herself together as they argued in their Gasthaus room.

"No, we can't stay another week. The minister of the Lutheran church has already agreed with my request. We can't back out now. Or you can stay here on your own for another week if you like, but I must go back to work. Sorry, dear."

She had given in to the pressure, still concerned about Johan's health.

As Johanna and Hendrik looked on, the babies let themselves be baptized without a peep from either of them. Johanna made sure they wouldn't catch a cold, and their heads barely peaked out from the clothing inside the cold church. She dried off the water immediately afterwards and tucked the woolen blankets over their heads. The rest of that day and into the evening, she kept a close eye on the babies, checked for skin color frequently, feeling their heads for signs of a raised temperature.

The end of their short vacation from the railroad came too early for Johanna. The next morning, Hendrik went to the townhall and registered the babies, picked up another basket and then loaded everybody on the hired sled. Silently, and stressed, Johanna mounted, with more blankets and two baskets for the children. With the extra supplies Hendrik had bought during the wait before the birth, they returned to work.

***

At the HBN site, the crew cheered on their arrival. Hendrik gave all crew members a free beer with their lunch, and in the evening, he got his bottles of schnapps and poured everybody a good measure. The men slapped his back and made jokes about his fertility: two in one shot. Henrik's sense of guilt — which turned out to be about speeding up their return — completely disappeared as soon as they arrived back on the construction site. Happy and a proud father, he snuggled at the end of the day up to Johanna.

Throughout the day, she had watched Johan and checked him religiously, even when he was asleep in his basket. She made sure she was ready for him when he woke up, hoping he'd be hungry. With Elfriede, things fell into place more naturally, and this lively child had no trouble making her needs known.

She was still awake, worrying about the babies' health and whether she would be able to cope. How she would simultaneously care for two babies and the job was a task she could not oversee right then. Hendrik had promised he would help in the evenings after work. He already made the concession purchases for her from a list Johanna made for him. She would also have extra help for one week from the woman that had backfilled for her. After that week, she wouldn't have anybody to look after the babies during the busiest times. There was no other option but to just do it, one step after the first, and on.

# Chapter 17

In the meantime, Europe's political situation deteriorated quickly without having any impact on the happy couple, continuing their slow trek across the country's north. Hendrik was more than content in his job of building the rail line with the luxury of his family nearby. He was the silent type, but as far as Johanna could tell, her husband was satisfied. His work was rewarding and left him with enough energy to enthusiastically play with the healthy tykes in the evenings and help with cleaning up.

Johanna didn't have much time for him, busy with washing, making meals for the thirty-odd men, nursing babies, changing nappies, and even more laundry. It was exhausting, but she was very happy for the moment in their mobile enclave with the children gaining weight, catching up on their missed in-utero month, and even Johan put on the baby fat that made dimples in his cheeks.

Hendrik had constructed a gate of wooden slats to allow Johanna some space, away from the babies, but able to still see them. Elfriede, whose name had turned quickly into *Frieda*, and Johan reached the four-month stage. When the customers were at work, the babies freely attempted to crawl off their blankets to explore the carriage, Johan always trying to catch up to his quicksilver sister. At other times, when the barrier between the private and public areas of the car was up, they peeked around the gate's slats to see what their mother was doing, or just had a nap.

Johanna took great care to have them locked away as she changed water kettles and poured the hot water to refill the coffee kettle. The toddlers with their sunny temperaments greatly appealed to the customers, and the workers often volunteered to hold the tykes and entertain them after work.

It was challenging to find help, as no in-train accommodation for a live-in maid was feasible, so the couple made do with what they had. The children's presence at the worksite significantly improved the general atmosphere among the crew. Although the rather permissive leadership style of the boss was gossiped about, the laborers also appreciated him. Johanna noticed a general atmosphere of sweetness; with gratitude, she was also proud that she and her beautiful twins contributed to it.

Before spring arrived, Hendrik had constructed a collapsible, indoor/outdoor, two-child playpen to quickly set up at the next location on their travels when the train stopped. It relieved the workers from holding-the-baby duty, while still able to watch these handsome children grow up and start to walk: great fun for everybody. The children functioned as a substitute for the crewmembers' own children, left behind for the job. The tikes thrived under all that attention.

*** 

Soon enough, Johanna was pregnant again. It was mid-August when she was certain, and this time, she told Hendrik right away. The construction work had steadily progressed towards the west, and the site was now located southeast of Bremen. She knew her juggling act was going to be more difficult with more children, and she wasn't sure how she felt about it as she looked at it from all sides. Like the first children, this was also unplanned.

The night she meant to tell Hendrik of — what she hoped was — the good news, she sat down on his lap with Johan on her arm, as Hendrik was stuffing a pipe, and in her sweetest voice, said, "Dear Hendrik, do you have any idea when we've saved enough money to buy our farm? Germany needs more farmers now. We're not spending much money, so our savings should have grown quite nicely, no?"

When she felt Hendrik's body turn rigid, she got up and concluded he wasn't elated with the question and placed little Johan on his lap. She picked up Elfriede off the floor and settled her into her arms for a feed. The sweet baby, with her eyes turning into an indeterminable color, stared at Johanna, contently making suckling noises as she hungrily fed from Johanna's breast. Her nervousness about Hendrik's reaction turned into an overwhelming feeling of contentment with her children as she held Elfriede's eyes with hers. Another one wouldn't change that.

"Oh, yes, I considered quitting many times, Johanna, *lieverd*, darling," Hendrik replied. He laid his pipe down, grabbed the whittled little locomotive from his pocket, he had made for Johan and gave it to him now. The boy fingered it, put it in his mouth, gumming it, soaking it on all sides.

Johanna looked up from Elfriede and turned her gaze to her husband. She knew Hendrik liked his work, and that he wouldn't stop the job without a lot of pressure. In a neutral voice, she replied: "Since we're having our third child soon, I would like you to consider it seriously now before the baby is born."

He looked away and continued playing with Johan.

After a long pause, he said without looking at her, "When are you due?"

"If all goes according to plan, I calculated mid-April, but you know things don't always go as planned." She was nervous about the lack of enthusiasm in his response. Her voice had sounded more strident than she meant to convey, so she hastened to add, "But don't worry. You don't have to be with me for the delivery. I can move into a town, just like last time, but stay there by myself. I know what to expect this time. It will be all right if you stay working. It was just a thought." She felt like apologizing, but then pushed that idea away. After all, Hendrik was as responsible as she was for their babies.

Hendrik was visibly gathering his thoughts, a deep frown on his face, and then said: "I would like to save up more money to buy a farm, but not in Germany."

"Why not, dear?"

Hendrik, speaking slowly in search of the words, explained — trying not to hurt her feelings, but he did anyway — that he'd like to leave the country soon. He said he had no confidence in the German ability for abiding by a peace treaty. He called the Prussians and Germans, war-hungry, and that they had no talent for a truce.

"No intention to offend you, dear, you taking on a German identity and all, but I'd rather leave this wretched country today than tomorrow."

"Oh, Hendrik," she gasped. "Will you return to Holland soon? I didn't realize you hated my country that much." Disappointed, she felt like crying. This was the harshest he had ever spoken about Germany.

He elaborated on why he wanted to go to Holland and painted a picture of his relatives, their lifestyle, farming and small businessmen, and how they could help them create a life, going to the same church, and having family celebrations together. How he would select some land with the advice of his brother, who knew the area well and told him there was lots of farmland for sale. His younger brother Jan, now with him on the railroad, would return home with them. Then he added he was going to quit when the line got close to Oldenburg. "I promise I'll quit then, and we'll cash in."

Relieved it was not as immediate a change as his words let her believe, she replied with trepidation audible in her voice, "As long as you don't start hating me, a German."

She had finished feeding Elfriede, who had fallen asleep in her arms. Johanna got up and nestled the completely relaxed child in her wooden box that functioned as her crib, as the babies had grown out of their baskets. "I'll have Johan now. I feed him last because he isn't as demanding as Elfriede," she explained.

"I could never hate you, darling," he said with a big smile, as he handed Johan to his wife. "And I'm delighted we'll get another baby, dear," he beamed.

It was the answer Johanna had waited for, and she smiled back, accepting that her husband would first look at the practical sides before he allowed his emotions in.

*** 

The company seemed to really want to cover the country with iron, but Hendrik didn't want to travel outside the Hanover area and *Niedersachsen* before the birth of the baby, so he declined offers to move to job sites elsewhere. A week before the due date, Hendrik had hired a caregiver to look after the twins and another woman for the concession shop, for the time being. He supervised both ladies and his crew.

Johanna moved to the town of Wulfsen a week before her third child's expected due date. It had been perfectly planned and everything went accordingly. She had weaned the twins and they ate what they all ate on the train, just mashed finely. The couple's second boy was born on April 19 in the spring of 1906. After the new baby's uneventful birth, the midwife sent a message for Hendrik to pick up Johanna and the child.

Hendrik was visibly proud that Johanna gave him another son, like a pro, and he showed this generosity toward his wife later that day. Back at the concession carriage, Hendrik was exceptionally affectionate, touching her frequently, caressing her cheeks, and patting her bottom. After Johanna had spoon-fed Elfriede and Johan, he presented her with the gift of an eighteen-karat gold chain.

"This is for you," he said with a shy smile. As Johanna held the newborn, Hendrik laid the delicate chain around her neck and fiddled with the clasp in the back, then kissed her neck's the soft spot at the hairline. With misted eyes, he admitted to her he had been worried.

"There is always that moment one realizes a woman could die giving birth, even someone as strong as you. I wouldn't know what to do without you, dear. This time you should name our new baby, Johanna. Give him a German name to preserve your heritage in our children, or a Polish name, if you like."

Johanna, taken aback by the comment, studied Hendrik's face and body language to search for an intent to mock her, but he was apparently earnest. Of course. How could he — a born Dutchman — be aware of the full impact of a Polish-Slavic heritage, and more importantly, its consequences? On the other hand, he didn't care. She envied him for his Dutch heritage, and his lack of sensitivity to identity, his lack of shame, his undiluted self-confidence.

"Let's call him Heinrich, my father's second name, and the name of my Ur-Opa, and of all the men in my family for three generations back or maybe more. I loved my dad very much."

She had to blink away the tears welling up in her eyes. More emotional than usual with her hormones out of balance, she shared the meaning of names, and how she had as a child discovered German sentiments about her last name. She talked about her father, who was proud to be part Slavic and spoke the language as the last of her family. That she would be betraying his ideals by giving their son a German name, but she was never taught the language, as Slavic was already forbidden when she came around. She told Hendrik how her father had done his best to protect them and Germanized his children, although he was conflicted about it, too, as his heart was with the Slavs. She ended her string of confidences with, "You're so lucky to be Dutch, a full-blooded Germanic tribe member."

She pushed her hair out of her face. Her braid was undone, and her dark-brown hair, devoid of shine now, stuck to her face.

Hendrik's face remained blank.

"I never looked at being Dutch that way," he answered, putting his arm around Johanna and baby Heinrich. "Sorry it was so hard for you," he whispered. Elfriede and Johan stood by Johanna's knees on wobbly legs, barely a year old, both staring at that wrinkly thing in their mother's arms, wrapped in cloth. Hendrik took the baby from her and squatted beside the toddlers. "Look at your new brother, isn't he adorable?"

The twins didn't understand. As Johanna sat down on the bench, Johan stretched his finger to the wrinkly red face of that wriggly *thing* and Johanna grabbed his hand before he could do any harm.

"Gently, or baby Heinrich might get hurt."

Elfriede didn't show a lot of interest but seemed glad her *Mutti* was back, and held on to her, both little arms wrapped around Johanna's legs. "Come, sweetheart," she said and lifted Elfriede on her lap beside Heinrich, her heart bursting for so much grace and love in her life. "I'm glad I weaned the twins," she added as an after-thought.

Hendrik lifted Johan and sat down on the bench beside Johanna. "We're a lucky bunch, aren't we," he whispered in her ear.

# Chapter 18

As their life on the railroad kept moving forward, Hendrik received a promotion. He was a manager now, which allowed him to hire somebody to take his place as his deputy. That left him more time to spend at night with his family, take some time off for a real lunch break, and cease work at a decent hour.

By October of 1906, Johanna knew she was expecting again. It was too soon after baby Heinrich, and she wasn't happy about it, blaming Hendrik this time. She had often asked him to buy some rubbers, but he always had some excuse, such as he couldn't find any in the nearest town. Abstaining from having intercourse and taking her temperature to pinpoint her fertile days instead of rubbers already proved to be an unreliable method. She should've known better.

After mulling over her discovery for days, she shrugged off her worries, realizing the advantages. It would be better to have all babies close together. Then she would be out of diapers within a couple of years and *stay* out of the endless laundering for good. Regardless, she was stuck on the construction site with her babies, so if staying close to home and on the train meant it would get Hendrik the farm he wanted sooner, so much the better. Their freedom would be built on her sacrifice, and she anticipated that their enjoyment of their future farm would be its intrinsic reward. Something to look forward to.

Beyond prepping the meals for the laborers and looking after the children, Johanna found time for reading in the quiet hours in the carriage. Since hearing Ur-Opa Heinrich's story about the Radziwill family, she had become interested in knowing more about the Empire's rulers and the rest of the nobility. She had found out that the province of Pomerania was dotted with many estates and castles, almost a thousand of them. Like her father's relatives, thousands worked as serfs to maintain the rulers in their lives of luxury, which included the current prime minister, Otto von Bismarck. That man must have kept a lot of people in poverty to wring profits from those depressed agricultural lands, like her grandfather, who had died on the fields.

Johanna's hunger for information turned her into an avid reader of any publication about royalty she could get her hands on. As a result, doors opened to new knowledge, which led to an addiction to reading about anything else, too. Hendrik knew how to get her to smile: by bringing her back books and magazines from his weekly foraging trips into the nearest town. Even Hendrik's workers knew and took advantage of that knowledge by occasionally bringing her something to read in exchange for a free beer.

Reading provided her with the education she never realized she had been missing, until now. Her parents had expected their children to work after their school years. Like her father, she would've had an uphill road to attend university without her family's financial backing. The well-known Pomeranian universities were closed after the last transfer of power. The best her Vati could hope for was an apprenticeship. For the women, a good marriage was the ticket out. It was impossible to attend a university outside Pomerania without a sponsor or rich parents, in a German city or abroad.

Vati had told her all about great-uncle David, the bachelor. He had moved away from Pollnow to pursue his university degrees, first in Breslau when it was still allowed, and later in Berlin. According to Vati, his mother used to sigh: *If only you could've followed in your Uncle David's footsteps.*

Johanna had protested then, fighting her dad's pessimism. "But you don't have to get a university degree to be successful. If Ur-Opa had been able to keep his successful shoe business, he could've saved for a study fund for you, Vati, and for your brother too." Alas, the anti-Polish measures in all the Empire had torpedoed that. Besides, the family had no money, and he had just accepted their restrictions as a fact of life.

As an unintended side effect of the simple act of absorbing all she read, Johanna found an interest in politics. It was a hot item in the press of the day, judging by how much was printed about socialists and communists. She read that all former-Polish nationals were banned from the German universities for their dangerously rebellious nature. She had become aware of the discrimination against others as well, Serbs and Bosnians. Their demonstrations often turned into riots and fights with the guards in the German Empire, but also in the neighboring Austrian-Hungarian Empire.

The increasingly violent actions against Jewish citizens everywhere seemed acceptable to most, and the newspapers warned their readers most of all about the dangers of socialism and communism. The two often went together: socialists *were* Jews. Although she didn't precisely understand the problems these people and their ideas presented, she was glad she wasn't one of them, considering the general hatred heaped on them.

One night after dinner, she turned to Hendrik for more details. As he held Johan on his lap, and Elfriede played with Heinrich on a blanket on the floor, she asked:

"Hendrik, what is all that with the Serbs and the Austrians? I read they are very unhappy."

"My darling wife, don't you bother with politics."

After she pushed for answers, he told her that her meddling in politics would only bring them misfortune. "I'm still a foreigner and don't need to attract the attention of the authorities, or I might be kicked out. I really don't know the details of what is going on." His frowning face spoke volumes and his eyes avoided her. In a stern voice, he told her, "Anyway, my wife shouldn't publicly commit to any political opinions for the same reason." He closed the door on further debate with the comment, "We'll be out of this country before you know it. Sorry, I can't help you."

He rolled one end of his large moustache between a finger and thumb, then the other side, and with both hands from the center under his nose out across his upper lip, finally looking at Johanna with concern.

True to her nature, she wasn't going to let it go.

"I found out more things about my relatives." She told him that although the former-Polish were subjected to harsh measures in Posen and Pomerania, the Jews got it even more, and harsher. They weren't allowed to live in a lot of villages and cities. Her father had hinted at it sometimes, but she hadn't known enough to take in what it all meant, until reading up on the background. "Maybe the Serbs feel oppressed in the same way, like the Polish here in Germany. Could that be possible?"

A shadow of annoyance flashed over Hendrik's face. Still, he patiently answered her a second later with his usual kindness, apparently hoping she wouldn't dig any further.

"It might be, my dear. I don't know anything about that. No good can come from speculating about it. You're driving yourself crazy. Let it go, please."

Johanna wasn't discouraged by her husband's apathy. She knew her kind husband was a peacemaker and an apolitical soul. She had to tell somebody. At the very least, he could be her sounding board. With a sad face and a loud sigh, she continued speaking about her newly found truths.

"Christian artisans and vocational guilds severely limited the Jewish colleagues. I only realize now that my father, as a member of the shoe-makers guild in Osterode, unwillingly might have been responsible for shutting down the Jewish businesses in town."

As she spoke, she became more upset. "My Vati may have been part of it, but his guild didn't do him any good, as he himself became the victim of discrimination against the Polish. I cried my eyes out when he was evicted, and then I witnessed him dying on the floor of our shop."

Thinking back about those days with eyes full of tears, she was ashamed, feeling so stupid that she only now realized her father might have been a party to this racism *and* a victim of it.

Hendrik put Johan on the floor, walked over to Johanna, and put his hand on her shoulder in a tender gesture, his face full of worry.

"Dear wife, you cannot know what all happened. Don't worry so much, it wasn't your fault. You were just a child. How could you know? Your father is resting in peace now. It is over. Isn't it the children's bedtime? Let's put them to bed together."

His voice turned enthusiastic, as he kissed her on her head. Gently, he picked up both twins. Johanna picked up Heinrich, and together they put the children through their bedtime routines. Focusing on the children calmed down Johanna enough to put her grief aside, for the moment. Hendrik was a great storyteller, and so patient with the children, who loved him as much as they loved Johanna. She realized how fortunate she was.

# Chapter 19

Time flew by. Railroad construction had been a priority for the government: it had bought out the private companies to form one national super network. As a result, Hendrik's state-owned company HBS of the Duchy of Brunswick had been absorbed into the State Railways. No costs were spared to get the secondary lines built regardless of the weather. Even in winter, the crews had to keep fires going to thaw out the ground as needed.

As the railroad passed over the northern part of the interior progressing toward the western border, Johanna and Hendrik were simply focused on their family. Pregnant, Johanna could stop worrying about birth control. Exhausted, she rolled into bed at night.

Another set of fraternal twins was born in the town of Hankensbüttel in the fall of 1907. Inspired by Ur-Opa's romantic story of the princesses and listening to concerts at the palace of Prince Radziwill, Johanna assumed the right to pick the babies' names. Since her own name created a connection with Ur-Opa, Antoni Radziwill, and the German culture, inducing images of romantic love in her, she wanted names to similarly reflect the fairy tale of her own life's romance. She named her younger twins after Robert and Klara Schumann, the famous composer and his pianist wife. Theirs was the incredibly romantic story about two artists creating an exceptional success of their lives as a team. Hendrik let her, happy to grant her this silliness. Only he would know; Johanna would never divulge that romantic notion to others, afraid of ridicule.

It became crowded in the caboose with all those babies and toddlers. Johanna was now always exhausted, not just at the end of the day. It seemed her whole life was feeding children, laundry, and cooking, and she had little time or patience for Hendrik. She asked Hendrik to inquire about a wet-nurse on his purchasing trips in town, but these were hard to come by. She desperately wanted to see her relatives, her sister, her mother. She would just have to *make* time. At her only moment of the day for sitting down — after all men were fed — she brought it up with Hendrik.

"I'm happy we're staying in Hannover. It allows me to visit Hannah's family. I want to go as soon as the rains stop," she said to Hendrik.

He looked at her, smiling, as he said, "Sure, dearest. Go. I'm not stopping you."

She threw up her hands, and exasperated, said, "But how can I go? Will you get someone to run the concessions? I think I'll stay overnight, if Hannah wants it. Would you hire a buggy for me?"

He wiped his mouth and mustache with a napkin. Calmly, he said, "Of course. How else will you get there with five babies? Are you sure you want to do that on your own?"

Hearing that answer from Hendrik, relief overcame her, as if the shackles came off. She had worried too much, kept it all inside her without good reason. She got up and gave him a big kiss. "Thank you, I needed to hear that. Do you want another beer? I think I'll have one too."

As the two youngest simultaneously began to howl for their dinner right that moment, she hastily finished her meal; Hendrik got another beer for himself.

***

Some days after that visit to Osterode, Johanna overlooked her brood one afternoon, contemplating her *current* life, a thing she never took the time to do. Life wasn't quite as satisfactory anymore and seemed to be one long rut of laundering, feeding babies, cooking and feeding men, and nothing for her mind to do. It dawned on her to do something about it. In the evening, she brought it up, while Hendrik was eating his apple pie, *apfeltorte*.

"I hadn't planned on having five babies within three years, Hendrik. It's time we stopped; don't you think?"

Apples were in season, and he had picked up a nice basket of large Golden Reinettes on his last trip. With his mouth full of pie, he put his fork down, suspicion all over his face. He finished chewing before he protested.

"What do you mean, stop?" He sat back on his bench, all attention on Johanna.

She hated what she had to do next, but did it anyway with a red face, taking a deep breath before she started talking. She pushed her hair back and tucked the loose strands in her neck under her hairnet.

"I mean, we cannot have more children. We're not set up for it. I refuse to make do any longer. I'm now always working hard for the company and looking after the children in these primitive circumstances. Menial things I don't care for, and I've had enough. We must find a solution." Her voice had risen, and she was nearly screaming by the end of her sentence, startling herself, let alone Hendrik, who stared at her, wide-eyed. As she lost control over her voice and broke down in sobs, Hendrik's expression turned to fear.

"Really? I thought you were happy," he said quietly. He looked down at his pie, his appetite gone.

Johanna, regaining control and wringing her handkerchief in her hands, admitted: "I was, honestly, but it's all getting too much, dear," looking at her red hands with the cloth in it, swollen from all the laundering.

Hendrik wiped a hand over his eyes and exhaled, then said, "But how can we? If you stop the concession business, it'll take us much longer to scrape the money together for the farm. When you move into town, would that really be a solution? I would miss you very much besides having to hire another operator for the concession sales. Is that what you want?" He looked up, and searched Johanna's face for signs of doubt. There weren't any.

Johanna sighed. "I also meant to say that we cannot have any intercourse, or you'll have rubbers," she said blushing. "I am sacrificing too much; I'm getting old before my time. We must change how we do things."

"Oh, you meant that kind of stopping," he breathed, visibly relieved.

Her mouth was set to a thin stripe. Then she continued, "Well, not only *that*," she grumbled, then softened again. "I'll think about it for another week, but I think it's time we stopped this crazy traveling. I would love to have a real bath with some privacy. All this hassle with pails and kettles and heating water on the stove is too much. I want a proper, private bathroom with a real tub."

She didn't bring up the newspapers with pictures of a washing machine, a wooden tub with a motor attached, which moves a tripod agitator around its center to clean the clothes. That was another dream she might fulfill, once she lived in town. Imagine having one, and no longer having to ruin her hands on the washboard. How lovely. She would still need to haul pails of water around, but at least her hands wouldn't be sore all the time. She would wait a while and give Hendrik time to let her demands sink in. For now, he had seen her exasperation, and he loved her. He would do the right thing. It would be alright. Relieved, she sat back and stuffed her wet hankie away in her sleeve.

"Thank you, *lieverd*," Hendrik replied, and he came over to kiss her, then slipped away from the caboose and Johanna for a walk, his shoulders slumped.

# Chapter 20

A couple of days later, Hendrik left the caboose in the morning as usual. He walked to the far end of the line to inspect the new ties in their gravel beds before the steel rails were to be laid down, for attachment with heavy bolts.

Johanna had been up for hours. With an apron dusted with flour, she prepared the baking pans for lunch bread. The dough was rising on the table under a few tea towels. The babies — *Klara and Robbie* — still slept in their baskets behind the gate. Elfriede and Johan played on the floor in the dining car on this side of the gate. They kept little Heinrich happy, stretched out on his back on his quilt. It was not very tidy in the prep-and-dining part of the car, but such is life.

Suddenly, a loud clanging on the iron door announced an unexpected visitor. Johanna opened the door, wondering who would knock first.

"We're not ready for lunch yet," she said in a clipped voice, opening the door to the impeccably dressed man standing before her in a railroad uniform. She looked him up and down, guessing his age to be about forty. "You'll have to come back later, eleven will be all right."

"Good morning, Frau Zondervan," the man said mildly, not moving an inch from the entrance. "I am the inspector with the State Railway to do an evaluation of the worksite. Would you know where I could find *Herr* Zondervan?"

He peeked past Johanna into the cabin. Johanna only then noticed the briefcase in his hand.

Three-year-old Elfriede checked out the unknown visitor, already standing in a smelly diaper behind Johanna, not potty-trained sufficiently yet. Johanna had planned on changing her after the dough was in the bread pans. The tyke now pushed past her mother before Johanna could grab her, and the stink wafting along with her. The word *trouble* flashed through Johanna's brain. She should've at least put the children behind the gate.

"Hendrik is at the far end of the line, inspecting the work," she replied. Realizing she should be friendlier, for Hendrik's sake, she added, *"Mein Herr."*

She pointed in the right direction, to the west, as she tried to put wayward her locks back under the hairnet with one hand and held Frieda back with the other.

The inspector tipped his cap, his face unreadable, then turned away from the caboose, and walked towards the direction she had indicated.

Johanna picked up little Elfriede and told her in a hushed voice, "Frieda, honey, Mutti is getting you cleaned up." After having changed the protesting toddler, she gave Johan the same treatment, then it was Heinrich's turn. She put the clean children together in the playpen and gave them a hard biscuit to chomp on. The babies were still sleeping, thank God. She hoped they wouldn't wake up before that inspector was gone.

She rushed to tidy the cabin, the dining area of the caboose and the family's sleeping quarters, then mopped the floor. At a frantic pace, she shoved the bread dough into the oven. She put water on for a fresh kettle of coffee. Then sat down and waited anxiously for the inspector to return with Hendrik, to drink her good coffee. She worried; he might have gotten the wrong impression of her from his sudden appearance earlier. When he would see the clean carriage and meet her lovely family, he would change his mind. Dear Lord, what did this sudden inspector's visit mean? Before today, nobody checked up on Hendrik or her.

\*\*\*

An hour later, Hendrik entered the carriage with a beaten-down demeanor, moving slowly and carefully, head bent like a freshly broken-in horse. Johanna almost couldn't wait for him to speak, but Hendrik stayed mute. Finally, she couldn't stay silent anymore and burst out with her questions.

"What did he say to you, Hendrik? Come on, tell me, don't stay *stumm*. I can take whatever the verdict is."

She already knew by his demeanor that the confrontation with the inspector had been nasty. It wasn't easy for Hendrik to acknowledge a mistake. His obviously expanded, but unauthorized private involvement on the worksite with the concession worker — she, Johanna — would have consequences. Besides, married women usually didn't work, and certainly not in the same place where their husband was the supervisor. She could afford to stay at home and just be a *hausfrau*. It didn't look good. Johanna hoped he had chosen for *her* and not the company, if there was a choice to be made. She pushed a mug with coffee in his hands as he sat down in the dining section.

"Didn't that inspector want to come in for a coffee?" She stood beside him with her hands on her hips, ready to defend him against anybody.

"No. He didn't want coffee," Hendrik grumbled, and paused, took a sip, then spoke again. "He came from Hanover and wanted to get back right away. The fact that I have my family here insulted him. Very un-German, that mess, he said. He meant here, in the concession car. Damn, Johanna. Couldn't you at least have the place tidy before he arrived?"

He sat back and put the coffee mug down hard in front of him on the table, splashing its contents.

Johanna sucked in a deep breath, anger flashing through her, and retorted in a thin voice cracking with tension, "So it's my fault?"

"I'm not saying that," he grunted and swallowed the rest of his words.

Johanna bristled. "Yes, you did. Didn't head office know we got married? But the man who hired me knew I was living in the concessions car. What did he damn well expect to find?"

Hendrik was silent.

"He should be glad you're not running a brothel," Johanna scoffed.

Hendrik moved around as if on a hot stove and his buttocks were burning.

"Well, uh, not really, dear," he stammered.

"What? What did you say?"

She stared at him, afraid of what he would say next, her anger making room for the fear he had done something stupid.

"You know, I didn't let head office know we were married, or when we had the babies. It's a private thing in my opinion, and none of the company's business.

Anyway, I was afraid I'd be deducted wages if they knew. That our salaries would be combined, and we wouldn't be paid the same earnings as a married couple. I know, I know. I was stupid. He'll let us know after the board's decided. He said it was fraud." He nodded his head a couple of times, grabbed his coffee, and began slurping the hot liquid.

Johanna could hold back no longer. "Damn it, Hendrik. Was this worth it?" She stood up, her fists pressed on her hips, glaring at him.

Hendrik kept his lips on his coffee mug, avoiding her eyes.

After a few minutes, Johanna said with a frown, but calmer, "Alright, nicely done, husband. Now what?"

She turned around when no answer was forthcoming. She had to get busy with the lunch for the crew very soon. The bread was ready, and she took the pans out of the oven and turned the loaves out to cool. Then she sat down across from her husband.

"Will we get fired?" Her voice was soft now.

Hendrik sighed, put his head in his hands and mumbled, "As the manager I was expected to inform them of all changes." He looked up. "I withheld the changes in my own situation. That inspector called it fraudulent conduct. But I really think he had it in for us, a Dutchman taking a German's well-paid job. The mess in the dining car. Oh well, that wasn't the main thing, Johanna. I just hope I won't lose my job over something this stupid."

"I hope so too," she said quietly and got up to finish her work.

***

A few days later, an agent delivered a formal letter in which the board informed Hendrik of its decision. Hendrik's unauthorized use of the concession car for his family was understandable, but the family had to vacate the premises, nevertheless. The space was not suitable, and the worksite too dangerous for small children. It would be Hendrik's decision whether to hire a new concessions operator or to keep Johanna on without children. In any case, children were not allowed on the worksite. That was it.

Hendrik was not fired. That's all that counted in Johanna's view. After the lunch break when the crew had gone back to work, she and Hendrik had some time to talk.

"Oh, Hendrik, that's not bad, is it? Neither of us is fired. We were going to change things anyway," Johanna placated him and tried to suppress the glee she felt about the company deciding on their move into town.

"Well, I am glad *you* are happy," he responded with a sour face. "I guess you will lose your job. I can't see how else we could manage it now. You see another way?"

Johanna understood that she hadn't fooled Hendrik. She couldn't contain herself and let out a deep sigh of relief. The company would have lost their excellent superintendent, had they been so foolish to fire him, never mind the inspector's prejudice.

"Alright, it's decided for us. I will move into a house with the children. Maybe now I can finally get a bath in a real tub," she said, staring out the window, imagining the luxury feel of that. "One bath a year after every delivery is not enough. I can't wait," she beamed.

Hendrik sat back and looked at her with an expression of surprise. "It's not all that bad then? You won't feel abandoned alone in a town with the children? Frankly, I was more worried about how you'd feel. I don't care about what that jerk thinks. They need me more than I need them," he chuckled.

# Chapter 21

Hendrik figured it would be another couple of years before the railroad line would be complete, so they would look for a decent rental in town. He asked her for her permission to stay on his job, as they needed a bit more money for their dream. Moving into town, with neighbors — and more help, and space for the children to play: it was a miracle. What could she say? Johanna liked this new adventure.

In the days following the board's letter, Hendrik took some time off work for house-hunting and rented a one-horse buggy. He tucked all the family into the padded interior and drove the rig himself, seated on the perch. Off they went to the town of Zeeven, located between Hamburg and Oldenburg, not far from the border with Holland.

It was lovely weather, that fall. Johanna, thoroughly happy, had brought a picnic basket for the trip and demanded frequent breaks as they checked the vacant houses to keep the children happy with a snack. They had lunch in a park. The children loved it, and although they were a handful and wanted to walk into the pond, it was a lovely family day, away from the confined spaces of the construction site.

At their picnic, seated in the grass on a blanket, Hendrik confided something to Johanna.

"Do you know what the inspector said to me, when I protested his description of the mess in the car?"

She braced herself but put her face on neutral.

"Don't get mad, it just shows the guy was a jerk, but we knew that already. He asked if you were the Münzke woman, then accused me of failing to inform the personnel office I had hooked up with a Polish baba." Hendrik chuckled.

Slurs were nothing new to Johanna, but the words still stung, and her heartbeat accelerated as she blurted out in anger, "What an ass. Did you defend me?"

"Of course, I defended you, calm yourself, *lieveling*. I told him that you're head and shoulders above any full-blooded Dutch or German wife I ever knew, smart, and hardworking, and sweet to me," he laughed. He looked at her with Klara and Robbie tightly in her arms, each on a side as they sat on the lawn of a park.

When she looked back at him, she noticed the sparkle in his eye. She refrained from commenting on the sweetness of it, but saved every word of it in her heart, and loved him for his cheekiness. She sneered with audible resentment, "I bet he's one of the old guard Prussians, who think they're better than anybody else."

Back in the carriage on the way home, she kept Heinrich on her lap. Elfriede didn't want to sit and stood at her knee. "Frieda," she admonished her daughter, "come, sit down on the floor, sweetheart. It's unsafe to stand when the carriage is moving."

"Listen to your mother, girl," Hendrik admonished. "Do what Johan does."

"Papa," Elfriede said, and tried to get closer to him, just as the carriage pulled up sharply through a rut and veered sideways.

Hendrik stretched an arm backward and down, catching her in time by grabbing her sweater. "We'd better extend the trip by another day; everybody is getting tired."

It was a good thing they were close to a Gasthaus.

\*\*\*

After two days of searching, they located a lovely, two-story house with a backyard for the children on a side street in a decent neighborhood. It even had a separate bathroom with a clawfoot tub, off the kitchen, and a flushing toilet. With a cheery voice, Johanna allocated the space upstairs: one bedroom under the eaves for the children and the other across the landing for the adults.

Looking at the reaction on Johanna's face, Hendrik hesitated to say the words, but she smiled at him. Her happiness couldn't get *kaput*. "I might not come home every night, dear, you realize that, don't you?"

\*\*\*

Everything was a lot simpler in town, and it allowed Johanna to stay up to date on the latest news as well. The vastly decreased number of daily activities without her work on the train quickly turned into an effective, new routine with much time to spare. She read and took a rest when she could when all the children were napping. Life was terrific with hot water coming out of the bathroom tap for baths.

The hot water supply was an experimental thing *to try out*, the owner told them. The water collected in a large tank in the cellar was heated by its own burner. She had to start the coal burner and take her bath when the water was hot enough, so she only turned it on when she was planning to take a bath. It happened once a week — a great improvement from once a year, and all the children went in after her. For dishes and laundry, she just put the old kettle and the large pot on the stove.

The house had running water from a municipal water system, which was a miracle to Johanna. No more stopping and filling the water tank every few days from a reservoir along the line. The landlord had advised them to boil the water before using it for food, drinking, or facial washing. After the Hamburg disaster with cholera, spreading from the tap to thousands of households some years back, the municipal government would not be held liable if citizens didn't follow its advice, he said.

Beyond looking after the children and doing laundry, and the meal prep in a much-simplified manner, her time was her own. She could have been the wife of a duke, and not be happier. *Gräfin* Zondervan didn't sound bad at all.

Hendrik only came home on the Saturday evenings to leave again on Sunday nights, and the odd night in between, when he had not much to do and could leave the supervision to his subordinate. Since their move into town, Johanna had demanded only protected sex, so with Hendrik gone most days, and her life filled with the children, no more babies were born.

# Chapter 22

Time flowed almost unnoticeably in her comfortable life, and before she realized it, Johanna found herself making the arrangements for her eldest children, Johan and Elfriede, to enter primary school. Then a year later, it was Heinrich's turn. Another year later, her youngest two were ready for school. Klara and Robbie complained they each wanted their own satchel. Johanna sat down at the kitchen table, wiped a hand over face, and said to them, "Are you really that old, my babies?"

"I'm no baby," Robbie protested.

When Hendrik came home that Friday, she reminded him in the bedroom, alone together. "Our children are now in school, all of them. You know what that means, dear, don't you?"

As he undressed, he looked tired, his back quite bent, and he hardly could keep his eyes open. "Not now, Johanna, please. I'm exhausted."

"I just wanted to share with you that our little ones are moving on in years. *We* are also getting older." She reached for the covers on Hendrik's side, grabbed his elbow, and helped to lower himself down on the edge of the bed, dressed in his underwear.

"Tell me about it," he grumbled, as he pulled his legs onto the bed, and fell back into the pillows, closing his eyes immediately.

Like she had done with her children, Johanna pulled the covers over his shoulders, and tucked in her husband, disappointed he was unreachable to her, but also aware he needed to recover from the week of work before they could have a conversation.

***

The next day before the children got up on this day off from school, she ran out to the store, curious about the rumors the neighbors had passed on to her. Since the first time the neighbor had shared his views, she began buying the newspaper every day, anxiously scanning the news columns for any signs that the German government would close the borders. When Hendrik finally got out of bed due to the children's loud arguments, she was reading the newspaper.

In the Kingdom of Serbia, south of the border, anti-government protest demonstrations had turned violent. The Serbs were unhappy with their government's apathy in reclaiming the lost Bosnian territory and accused the cabinet of a lack of courage, calling the King a coward. The paper printed the government's call to its citizens not to go out in the streets unnecessarily — a place to avoid. In the German Empire, many foreigners and jobless were roaming the streets as well, with frequent riots and clashes between groups of people.

She remembered Ur-Opa's story of a rebellion, which had caused the end of his thriving business and his life in Poznan to his great regret, his dreams squashed, and he had not even been involved in politics. She feared a similar disaster could easily happen to her family. Hendrik could be kicked out — a foreigner. When she told him about what she had read, he just sighed and shook his head.

"I am tired of this, Johanna. Don't tell me about what you read. I can read the newspaper myself, if I want to."

Hurt, she turned away. Hendrik was frequently not himself, when he got home at the end of the week. She worried about him, hoping he would quit his job, but keeping her thoughts to herself from then on.

***

As the battles between demonstrators in the Austrian-Hungarian Empire made the country ungovernable and even spread beyond its borders, her anxiety became a burden, even more because she couldn't share it with Hendrik. Most days, she fired up the water heater as soon as the children were off to school and took frequent baths with dried lavender to calm herself down. When Hendrik came home the next Friday, he saw the bill of the coal deliveries: unusually high. He frowned but didn't comment on it.

The powder keg went off not long after Johanna began to take daily baths. The rumor reached her in the bakery shop that the crown prince of Austria was assassinated. On Saturday, a few days after the assassination, she got her hands on a fresh magazine and read a reporter's details in a special report on the assault on the crown prince and his wife. She read with shaky hands, afraid for its fall-out.

Since the assassination, she had hoped the perpetrator wasn't a German national. The report of today had the answer. She needed Hendrik, she must speak to him about the danger to her own family, to him, and about leaving the country with him. Fortunately, it was Saturday, and he was home, puttering outside in the backyard.

She hurried out the door to find him. As she ran towards the spot where he was chatting with the neighbor over the hedge between the two properties, she called out.

"Hendrik, it was a Bosnian Serb who shot Crown Prince Franz Ferdinand and Princess Sophie."

As soon as she was close enough, he grabbed her arm, and pulled her back into the direction of the house, unusually bossy for him, and he groaned, "What are you doing, where are the children?"

As he forced her towards the backdoor, she replied. "They are still sleeping, but listen, this is bad. The Serbs wanted them killed, innocent people. This is terrible, but at least it wasn't a German." she said and pulled herself free.

He grabbed her by the elbow again and pushed her through the door, a frown on his face.

In the kitchen, Johanna struggled to understand her husband's strange actions and her own anxiety. She dropped herself on a chair and attempted to control her breathing, so she could speak. Her anxiety about Hendrik's refusal to listen to her and not taking her seriously made her want to cry. His rudeness in the company of their neighbor hurtful. Why was he like that to her?

He looked angry, a scowl on his face, eyes fiery.

"What are these people to you? Getting upset about those political incidents is a losing battle. Stay out of it. You'll bring misfortune to us. Your job is to look after the children, and mine is to save money so we can leave this wretched country. Soon, we'll be in Holland and safe."

Standing in front of the stove, she burst out crying, upset he was such an ogre, so dismissive of her.

"Why are you so mean to me?" she managed to get out between sobs. "Is it because I don't bring in any money anymore?"

Hendrik exclaimed, "Oh no, not you too," and sat down heavily on a kitchen chair.

Johanna tried to get her feelings under control. Minutes went by in silence until Hendrik spoke again.

"I'm sorry. I didn't mean to be so rough with you. I had a terrible week; my deputy gave me a hard time and wants to quit. I mean to say you'd best not to worry about politics, Johanna. We have no power. It's all decided behind closed doors by the parties involved. I bet you that the assassin was paid by someone to cause trouble, maybe even a relative. Stop finding a reason to get so worked up, and stop taking so many baths and wasting money, please. We will leave soon for Holland."

She had stopped sobbing and wiped her face. Although not ready yet to forget about his outburst, she remained reluctant to accept his words, even after his apology.

"That's what you keep telling me, but *when* will we leave? The children are already growing up and in school. It will be too late to leave after they close the borders. I want peace for our children. They shouldn't grow up in a war."

He stomped his foot on the floor once and demanded: "Stop talking about it." Then he turned and disappeared into the living room. A minute later, she smelled the pipe tobacco.

Although now angry with him, she didn't follow him thinking it better for him to calm down on his own. He had slammed the living room door shut behind him — unusual, self-centered and rude behavior. Something was going on. His deputy leaving was not it. She had to get to the bottom of it. Why was he not duly concerned about her, his family, and the children possibly getting caught up in a war?

\*\*\*

The next day, their neighbors initiated a chat as they lingered on their doorstep, their leaving for church coinciding with Johanna and Hendrik's departure. The wife was an uneducated *Hausfrau*, but the man worked in the *Standesamt*, the townhall. He seemed an intelligent man judging from his views about the international situation.

"The Russians are in cahoots with the Serbians," said the civil servant. "It's clear they want to divide the land between them and are looking for a reason to invade, but Austria-Hungary won't let them pull them into a war. I wonder what side our government will choose, and if the *Kaiser* is already having nightmares." He chuckled.

Judging from his sarcasm, Johanna concluded he was obviously not a loyalist, but she was relieved somebody was thinking along the same lines as she and hoped that Hendrik would pay attention. As the man talked, apparently liking the sound of his own voice, Hendrik and she listened.

"The Russians have strong allies: France and even Great Britain might join them in a war. The Balkans are a tinderbox. We'll see *when* it explodes, not *if*. I'm surprised the Austrian-Hungarian Monarch hasn't declared war on Serbia already for killing his son, ending the dynasty with this assassination. I guess he first wants to see who will turn out to be their ally and join them in the battle. Germany will no doubt join the alliance."

The man looked important, his hands clasped each other behind his back, his bent elbows on each side emphasizing a broad chest. This man would suit a uniform.

Hendrik provided the ideal audience for the neighbor, accepting his predictions without a word.

Johanna was still angry at him and found it necessary to emphasize the neighbor's point to Hendrik and repeated it. "Oh my, did you hear that, dear? It will explode, he said." She hoped Hendrik remembered that she'd told him of her fear for exactly that, and for the safety of their children, and take her words more seriously.

"Come, Johanna, time to go to church. Let's get the kids," Hendrik grumbled in response.

***

In his sermon that morning, the minister mentioned the threat of war and urged his parishioners to stay calm and to let the government take care of them. His sermon didn't calm Johanna. Everybody knew the Serbian army was mobilized and stood ready at the borders. The talk of the town was the Monarch of Austria-Hungary, who would surely send an ultimatum to Serbia with impossibly harsh terms, making it almost impossible to accept for Serbia. That would turn into a war. Then the dominos would fall across Europe and another useless disaster would demolish the continent. Johanna was desperate to find a way to reach her angry, uncommunicative husband for some reassurance.

Not long after his monologue to Johanna and Hendrik, the neighbor was proven right. The day the Austrian-Hungarian Monarch declared war on Serbia, Herr Müller lingered outside on his porch. He looked around, hoping to see somebody to talk to about the unavoidable disaster *he* had predicted.

Johanna stood in front of her window and saw Herr Müller coming home in the middle of the week. Hendrik was away at work. As usual, the neighbor smoked a cigarette on his front stoop, before he'd go inside. She raced outside and asked him, "What's new, Herr Müller? Do you have any news?"

Herr Müller shared his news, as Frau Müller jealously joined them on the stoop.

"Oh, *mein Gott. Dass bedeuted Sturm.* That means mayhem," Johanna said.

Her deepest fears were becoming reality. What was Hendrik going to do? They had to leave now. She had heard enough about the hardship of war to want to escape it and leave the country. She had to confront him, find out what kept him so closed off.

What kept him here was making money. They must have saved enough by now. Maybe he needed her to insist they'd leave now. Taking hot baths to settle her frantic mind didn't do it for her anymore. As long as the shadow of war threw its shadow over everything, she'd remain panicked.

Her Müller nodded, as his wife slapped her hand over her mouth in terror. Silently, he grabbed his wife's arm, and they disappeared into their home.

***

Another European war had begun. Johanna cried the day the declaration of war was announced, July 28, 1914. She had not been able to find a way through Hendrik's armor yet. He would not come home until several days later. The treacherous Russians had indeed changed sides: Russia, Belgium, France, Italy, Britain, and Serbia lined up as the Allied troops against Austria-Hungary and its ally Germany, joined by the Ottoman Empire and Bulgaria, the Central Powers. Holland was not mentioned. If this meant Hendrik's country would still be an option for them to settle, they should leave now.

She considered renting a trap and driving to Hendrik's worksite, but the thought that he likely would be rude, and angry with her, withheld her. She fired up the coal burner for a hot bath. Damned the diminishing coal stash.

# Chapter 23

One week later, on August 4, 1914, German troops crossed the border into Belgium. Before that day, the German Army had mobilized the troops. For weeks on end, Johanna had seen the many soldiers on the roads. She hadn't needed the neighbor or Hendrik to tell her something was up. She feared her brother Willi would be called up as well. How long would the Dutch border stay open? Probably not for very long.

That day, Hendrik came home in the middle of the week just for a couple of days. After hearing the news at the worksite, he realized Johanna would be worried, so he decided to see how she was doing. As he told her later, he had deliberated during the ride home about keeping the news about the invasion of Belgium from her, as her nervousness would increase. But with the chatty neighbor next door, and Johanna often picking up a newspaper, it was a moot point.

When Hendrik arrived, indeed, the pompous man next door came outside, and jubilantly announced the German *initiative*, he called it. The neighbor-in-the-know had the latest info from a colleague with "inside knowledge." Even if he had wanted, Hendrik couldn't stop the man. He hadn't even greeted Johanna yet.

"The troops went for the town of Liege on their way to France. Our army has the newest and most powerful weapons in its arsenal. They can take that city in one day, thanks to these enormous siege cannons, and the Kaiser knows what to do with them," Herr Müller bragged.

"Is that right," Hendrik mused. It sounded impossible. Everybody knew that Liege was heavily fortified from the wars with the two Napoleons. Just then, Johanna joined them on their porch. This time, Frau Müller didn't join them.

"Are you signing up for the army, then?" Hendrik asked Herr Müller.

"Oh, no, I have my family to care for and got my notice of exemption. War is for the young, and for the generals of the standing army, and I'm no general," the fat man chuckled, then asked, "And you? Are you volunteering?"

"No, I'm Dutch, I don't have to fight, fortunately," Hendrik replied, throwing his hands up in relief with a smile.

Just to show off her relatives' sense of obligation in front of this braggart, Johanna announced with pride, "My sister's husband joined last week, and I already have two nephews and a brother in the army." She turned to Hendrik. "Dear, please come inside."

"Good for you," Herr Müller said, then quickly disappeared inside his own house.

Johanna and Hendrik turned away to go inside. "What a typical bag of hot air, living vicariously through the army, while he is too much of coward to sign up," Johanna scoffed. Hendrik walked behind her, grabbed her arm, pulled her close, and hissed in her ear.

"Shhh, *vrouw* (wife), he might hear you." He let go of her and quietly added: "Don't make any enemies needlessly. By the way, you're one to talk with your relatives in the military."

Johanna shrugged, not caring what the neighbors would think about her. Happy that Hendrik had come home unexpectedly, she only wanted to be out of there now and be on the road to Holland.

*** 

Inside, they found Robbie and Klara waiting behind the door, curious to know what had made their parents talk to the neighbors. The two youngest children had been inseparable since Johanna's instruction to Klara, not even three years old then, to watch over Robert. Back then at the construction site, when Johanna was hanging out the laundry on a sunny day, she had permitted them to play outside and roam about a bit where she could watch them. The handcar operators hadn't noticed the tiny boy by the tracks. Robbie barely escaped a fast-moving handcar nearing the carriage. Now, years later, Johanna had to admit that the inspector had been right to evict them from the worksite. It *had* been unsafe, and she didn't have eyes in her back.

As the chatting children followed her into the kitchen, Johanna started supper, contemplating her children's natures. Since birth, Klara had been quicker to catch on to things than Robert, hence Johanna's instruction to the more mature of the twins. Johanna always had believed the pressure in the womb — too small for two — was to blame for this difference in acuity, this lag in development. Of course, the authority she'd given Klara over Robbie could have persuaded him to leave things to his sister, making him passive, but she didn't want to believe that. At age six, it was clear that Robert hadn't caught up yet to his sister.

Elfriede and Johan showed a similar pattern between them: the girl seemed brighter than the boy. Her middle child, Heinrich had escaped that situation altogether, and he seemed the smartest of all. He already was an independent boy, quite cheeky, with a talent for manipulating everybody around him into giving him what he wanted.

"What happened, Mutti?" Klara asked.

"Nothing for children to worry about, *Schatz*," Johanna replied. "Your school is the only thing for you to worry about. We'll have to check and see that you two have got everything you need, rucksack, pencils, your good shoes, and the uniforms. Are you excited?"

She had hoped to already live in Holland, so the children could gradually integrate into the Dutch school system. No such luck. Her train of thought changed to the evening when the children would be in bed. She'd have the conversation with Hendrik about leaving Germany.

\*\*\*

Earlier, she had accused him of not caring, of treating her like a dumb housewife. He had completely changed from how he treated her when she was his concession manager, she charged. "Is it all about the money then?" she had asked, and he had been dumbfounded. That night, they finally talked.

He sat on the edge of the bed and stared at her. "Is that what you think about me?"

She fired back: "No, is that what you think about *me*, is the question." She stood firmly in front of him, about to burst into tears, but not willing to let him off the hook.

Hendrik explained patiently to be afraid that the Dutch neutrality would be breached, and his country be caught up in the war. In that case, as a Dutch citizen he probably would be called up for military duty. But if they stayed in Germany, he was not available for military duty. He apologized for his rude reaction to her earlier, and added there was trouble among the workers, who were on opposing sides and started fights, which made it hard for him, and he had to reshuffle them and change the crew shifts.

He assured her he did not respect her any less, and seeing how wonderful she was with the kids, and had settled with living in town, he thought that was worth the cut in pay. He just had a lot of worries. She forgave him that night.

***

A week later, having had time to reflect, she wanted to talk to Hendrik again, talk through all their options. With a war in progress, their plans for a move might be stalled forever. That couldn't happen. At the time, nobody believed that civilians would be involved. It was just a war for soldiers. Of course, she didn't want to go through all that misery of war with dead children or a dead husband. But Holland was still neutral.

***

A few days later, with Hendrik back at the construction site, Johanna ran to the tobacco shop in town first thing in the morning before the children went off to school for a fresh newspaper, just in case the papers sold out later. She asked Frau Müller to watch the children for a bit. If Hendrik were around with his preference of ignoring the facts, he would stop her. Denial was his great strategy for coping with disaster, but not hers. She had to be informed.

Within days, German troops had penetrated deep into northeastern France and ended up within thirty miles of Paris. That first week of September, the German army wreaked havoc along enemy lines, leaving many soldiers *and civilians* dead in its wake. French and British forces confronted the invading German forces and mounted a successful counterattack, driving the Germans back through Belgium, where they got stuck.

Johanna read the updates of the battles each day that week with increasing alarm, afraid that the German troops would cross the Belgian border into Holland. But the Russians didn't sit on their hands either. Johanna got excited when she read about her grandfather's people — the Slavic and former Poles of the Eastern Provinces–joining their Slavic neighbors, the Lithuanians. Instead of joining the German soldiers, they became allies of the Russians. She didn't know what to think of this. It confused her.

The newspaper called them traitors and reminded the readers that in the previous Franco-Prussian war, these very same easterners had formed an enormous army that included Moravian, Wallachian, Tatar, and Czech fighters in the battle with France — *on the French side*. Their powerful resistance had siphoned German troops away from the western front to beat this army of easterners at the eastern front. Napoleon's troops had held out the longest in Pomerania, delaying the German victory.

Vati had told her all about it with glee, it seemed centuries ago now. In his mind, these Pomeranians were heroes, loyal to their folk, and they saw the French as liberators from oppression. Their resistance to Prussians and Germans was in his eyes an ongoing struggle against the *colonizers*, going back centuries.

However, the German advance didn't end in a quick success. Its failure to consolidate in Belgian territory meant the end of German plans for a speedy victory in France. The fight stayed put in the mud of the Nord-Pas-de-Calais region of France and turned into a trench war without an end in sight. Holland did see no need to get involved. Johanna was so caught up in the news that she forgot to speak again with Hendrik about the move and how to plan their departure to Holland, until he came home on Saturday. The good thing for them was that the fight taking place in another country allowed them to carefully plan their departure, keeping their family safe — in Germany for now.

Hendrik and Johanna mirrored that entrenchment of the troops in the trenches with their own lives. They stayed put, separated from each other in their own worlds. Like the so-called Western Front, they didn't make a move.

***

In the second week of September, Hendrik came back for a brief overnight layover midweek. He had been missing Johanna, he told her. As soon as the children were in bed after their tiring first week in school, the couple sat down with a bottle of schnapps.

"Oh, Hendrik, I am so glad you're back," Johanna confessed, remembering her worries, which seemed to be strongest when in bed alone, unable to sleep from worry. "I'm very concerned about this war. Can we plan how we should leave Germany now?"

They agreed it would be impossible to predict how long this war was going to last. They also agreed they wanted to raise their children in a peaceful country, and not expose them to hate and ethnic strife, poverty, and suffering.

Johanna quoted what she had read in the newspaper about the previous thirty-year-war, and its result: two million Germans killed then, and much of Europe thrown into poverty and misery for decades. If this war was going to run along similar lines, the outcome would be a disaster.

Hendrik shook his head, sorrow on his face, and his mouth slack. He observed her quietly as he was looking for words. Then he spoke.

"Dear Johanna, I'll have to disappoint you."

He then told her about his worries of the last few months but not shared them with her until now, because she was already such a worrywart. The company promised him substantially more money for finishing the line and the pressure was tremendous for the crew to keep up. The army needed to transport people and materials, especially for the war in the trenches. It would be advantageous for them and their goal of buying Dutch land to stay for a couple more years.

"I promise, we will leave as soon as this part of the line is done. I truly promise. You can trust me."

"Oh, Hendrik," she cried out. "You can't be serious. Why? Money isn't everything. Our children's safety is worth more." She finished her drink in one big gulp, reached for the bottle, and poured herself another.

Hendrik's expression changed from kind, and she saw a flash of impatience in his eyes. With a frown, he said: "Sorry, I have decided."

A rush of anger took over. She jumped up. In front of Hendrik with clenched fists, she hit his chest in rapid blows, to no effect. Hendrik just stared at her. Seeing the impact, or lack thereof, she burst out in sobs and sank to her knees in front of him. Her hands grasping his knees, she managed to speak through her tears. Exhausted by this yoyo decision-making process, Hendrik had just decided for her.

"I can't do this anymore. I've done everything you wanted me to do. Why can't you for once do what I want? It's not for me, it's for the children. Don't you get that? I hate war, I hate it."

Hendrik put his hand on her head and caressed her hair. "I hate it too," he whispered. "Come, sit with me." He lifted her head, then gently took her hands, and pulled her on his lap.

# Chapter 24

Life in Germany for the Germans deteriorated, but in Hendrik and Johanna's life, the status quo continued, as the shops got emptier. The war demanded even more lives; neighbors and parishioners exchanged whispered condolences. Johanna found out from the shopkeepers whenever a relative had died, as they put a photograph and a black ribbon in their shop windows. There were many, many wounded with horrible injuries visible in the streets, and the homecomings were sad affairs. "The modern equipment caused all that," knew their neighbor, Mr. Müller.

Johanna's brother-in-law was wounded. Rieke came to visit Johanna, breaking down in tears as soon as Johanna opened the front door. After Rieke told her about her husband's fate — probably going to lose his leg and be maimed for life and cared for in a military hospital — the sisters sat together in silence as Rieke wept without making a sound. Johanna remembered having a childhood rivalry with Rieke, but now she only felt sorry for her. What Rieke went through reflected her own fear of harm to her children.

After a while, Rieke recovered and quietly said, "It isn't fair. We have two children, who still need a father. What can my Johann do without his leg?"

Although conscription was the required sacrifice for the country, Johanna wasn't sure whether a country's war was worth the gift of anyone's life. Angry about it, she nevertheless wouldn't say that out loud to her sister. Instead, she softly said, "Yes, it is so unfair. I would offer to help when he comes home, but with my five it would be hard, unless Hendrik is home to look after the kids."

She put her hand on Rieke's, inert on the table next to the plate with the untouched sandwiches. They had never been close, as children. Rieke, as the eldest, was Mutti's right hand, but all that petty sibling stuff had disappeared. Johanna silently acknowledged they had both grown up.

"On a weekend, then, when Hendrik is home, that would work for me," Rieke said in a flat voice as she squeezed Johanna's hand, and then let it drop away.

Rieke was not sure if Johanna could help at all. They agreed that it was a good thing Mutti didn't have to go through this all, as she had died a few years back, before the children were born. "Let me see how it goes. I will write you if I need you to come." They said their goodbyes, and then Rieke left for the return trip to Hanover.

That night Johanna worried more than usual. She considered herself lucky to have married a Dutchman. His country was peaceful, rational, and sensible. But things in life can change on a dime. *That*, she knew, too.

***

The Russian troops and their allies on the eastern front were unable to break through German lines. Defeat on the battlefield made the Russian people impatient with the war and the Czar, blaming him for the failure. The economic instability, the scarcity of food, and everything else to sustain a decent life — especially for the poverty-stricken workers and peasants — made things hurtle to a breaking point.

Johanna completely understood the Russians' refusal of making more sacrifices for the Czar and she agreed with the reporters' predictions that Russia was ripe for a revolution. Her royalty mags kept her updated, not only with the war — albeit in a superficial, gossipy kind of way — but also with the intricacies of the lives of the wealthy royals all over Europe.

She learned about the British, the German, the Austrian, and the Russian monarchs. She found them unremarkable men, who were all related and looked alike, and had their pictures taken always dressed in uniform with immaculately trimmed beards and receding hairlines with some beautiful princess on their arm. In her magazines, these glorious people lived their lives in isolation from their subjects in unimaginable wealth, not giving a damn about who was subject to their whims.

Despite her yearning to read about royalty fairy tales, Johanna wasn't blind to the exploitation of their subjects — the enduring, terrible inequality of the people in Europe, and she thought back about her Vati's complaint. The glossy pictures and superficial stories only functioned as escape literature, providing a few minutes of relief from reality.

After reading the royalty rags, the newspapers brought her back to earth with their descriptions of the ordinary people's suffering. She needed both in her life: the good and the bad examples. Without either, she wouldn't have had any ambition to do better. She wished she had been older, so she'd have been more of a support to her father in his bad days. She hated poverty but wasn't ready to become an activist, like her dad had in his bachelor days. The examples in her life had shown only crushed rebellions, death, and bad treatment of those, who had resisted the enduring discrimination of the Polish Slavs.

***

Hendrik had long stopped buying Johanna the magazines and questioned her about the reading materials as they sat in their living room after dinner. "Why do you even buy that trash?"

She ignored his negativity, and in a sincere voice, asked him, "Why can't the grandchildren of one family together not make peace happen in Europe?"

He had no clue what she was talking about and, distracted by her question, looked at her in wonder. "What do you mean, one family? How could they?"

"Well, Czar Nicholas, our Kaiser Wilhelm, and King George of Britain — monarchs who rule our world — are cousins. They even look like triplets. *That* family."

Hendrik scratched his head, amazed how Johanna sometimes came out with something crazy she obviously had thought about. Hendrik quickly retorted: "Stay out of his relatives' business, I'd think." Her specific train of thought just was so vastly different from his, like two railroad cars moving in opposite directions.

He wiped his face, then thoughtfully brushed his emperor's mustache with both hands. He imagined his German wife and the unavoidable conflicts arising between her and the rest of his relatives back in Holland if he ever moved home.

Johanna knew Hendrik couldn't care less if somebody was of royalty or a pauper, as long as someone was honest. She tried to explain her thoughts, sat back, didn't reply to his terse comment, but persevered on her subject. "I heard that in Russia the poor have started demonstrations against their Czar and his unpopular German wife, Alexandra. What is the Kaiser going to do about saving his cousin's family?"

After she explained it this way, she didn't sound that mad anymore.

"Do you remember the prophetic words of our neighbor about the tinderbox in the Balkans? It did happen as he said. Looks like something might happen in Russia soon too."

Hendrik had other worries, which became evident to Johanna when he spoke again. "I bet the royals' deepest wish is to get out of the country," he said with a sigh.

"Just like you," she said without missing a beat, hoping that was true, but her cynical thought was that he could leave anytime he wanted, currently. "Why don't you, Hendrik?"

He ignored her remark and replied by explaining his conundrum.

"More than half of my workers bought a ticket to America, and I lost a few to conscription already. I could lose the bulk of my workers in the next three months. If they got permission from the emigration office to leave, they'd all be out of here in a flash. Luckily for me, my brother has committed to staying for as long as I do."

"Why do *they* want to leave?" Johanna said as she put a fresh cup of coffee for him on the kitchen table.

She liked Hendrik talking to her about his problems in the cozy space of the kitchen. The children were spread over the house and the yard, doing homework, or playing somewhere, the youngest two already seven years old, almost eight. She savored these moments of grown-up time, just her Dutchman and she, talking quietly. It made her feel so mature and wise, and vital, in the prime of their lives, occupying their places in the world. She could delude herself thinking she was a *somebody*, not just a *Hausfrau* or a mother.

"Well, some of my men told me their reasons." He elaborated what these were. Although America was neutral, like Holland, the Americans may eventually become involved in the war, taking the British side. If that happened, the would-be emigrants would be stuck in Germany, because the Americans wouldn't admit any enemy Germans into their country, and the German emigration office would stop them from leaving, to fight in the war, or to work, keeping the country going. "So, they are in a hurry to leave while they still can,"

She sat down across from her him with a coffee of her own.

"Oh, how smart of your men. Wouldn't you want to emigrate to America, dear? Some of my uncles went. I remember my Vati secretly feeling sorry for himself because he couldn't go. I saw him breaking down crying at their announcement. Mutti was rather cruel, and told him if he wanted to leave, he should go too. He never replied to her." After her own recent battles with Hendrik, Johanna only now understood how her parents' marriage had gone stale over holding different expectations, disappointments, and unfulfilled promises.

Although Hendrik could just imagine that situation with his wife, avoiding his responsibilities was not like him, he assured Johanna. "My intrepid days as a young man are over," he added empathically. "I have my eyes set on non-so-far away Holland, the best country I know. *My* adventure was moving to Germany," he added in a self-deprecating drawl, feeling old.

"Don't put down your accomplishments," she replied as she took his hand in hers. "You did very well for yourself, *Schatz*. And we are not finished yet." She planted a kiss on his calloused palm, then kept his hand in her lap, drawing closer.

"It's all right," he sighed. "I suspect the end of my stint abroad is near. When I am losing my workers, it won't be long before the construction will grind to a halt. The company's bonus payments cannot stop desperate men from leaving. Let's see what will happen."

Hendrik thought that so long as America keeps up the commercial shipping with European countries, supplying the needed raw materials, and if the eastern workers could fill the vacancies left by the men now leaving for the army, the industry would chug along. "If not, I'm sure the emigration offices will soon close."

# Chapter 25

A year after the start of the war, the trench warfare in the fields of Belgium produced nothing but large numbers of fallen and wounded soldiers, their names listed in the newspapers. Like everyone else, Johanna noticed the many maimed soldiers loitering in the streets, discharged and returned home with missing legs or parts of their faces and brains gone. She thought of Willi, and of Rieke and her husband, her brother's care no doubt adding a tremendous burden on their already struggling families. The thought of her brothers and nephews triggered renewed anxiety for her children.

Many panhandlers roamed the streets. Children started to look pale and thin and joined the beggars. When Johanna left home on her errands, she made sure she carried some bread in her bag to give to the most desperate, youngest child in the street.

In early 1917, the *Reich* declared the waters surrounding the British Isles a war zone, justifying the measure so that Germany could legally defend itself in those waters. Johanna read the newspapers' enthusiastic reports. She didn't know what that declaration might lead to, so she asked Hendrik, anticipating his refusal to discuss it, but she was wrong, and he did engage with the subject.

Hendrik commented, "I bet you those Teutons won't stop at downing neutral vessels. Because Germany couldn't win the trench war, the German army desperately needs a win somewhere," he explained, and predicted that German vessels would target Allied supply ships and sink them without warning — which was allowed *only* in war zones.

"So how would that affect us, Hendrik?" Johanna asked.

"Because I'm Dutch," he spat.

"As far as I know, Holland wasn't involved in the war." She waited for a reply.

Hendrik took a breath and then painted her the picture of likely events. When Dutch merchant ships were targeted, Holland would suffer in its main business: the transportation of merchandise across the world. Hendrik's family would be affected in an economic downturn. Making it more complicated, he was also a worker in the German Empire, constructing a German railroad line, which needed those materials. "I won't be able to finish the line without the proper materials or the men."

He took his pipe out of his pocket, stuffed it with tobacco, got the box of matches out, and struck a match on the sole of his boot.

"Hendrik, you can't light that up indoors," Johanna gasped, although up to now, she had let him smoke his pipe indoors. It was a case of her patience running out with the whole damned situation, and Hendrik was the target. She wished the insecurity would end; he was hanging on to his job, and not making the decision to leave. It exhausted her. Anxiety was her constant companion these days.

He sighed, gave her a dirty look, got up, and left through the back door without a word.

***

Hendrik shared a suspicious mind with the Americans, who reacted to the German unilateral weaponization of the British territorial waters. Three days after the Germans' increase of hostile waters, the United States of America broke off all diplomatic relations.

When Hendrik, who had started to become more interested in the news, was told by one of his workers what happened, he had sent out for a newspaper. When he got home that Friday night, he told Johanna: "This is it. We will get ready to pack up and leave town. They'll be torpedoing passenger traffic next. I wonder what Herr Müller got to say for himself now."

She was shocked that her husband would walk out on the job, could hardly believe it, and held herself back from reacting, just in case he didn't mean it and reversed his decision. In a thoughtful voice, she replied. "Herr Müller hasn't showed himself since your testy question whether *Herr Nachbar* was going to sign up for army duty."

"He's shaking in his boots no doubt, now that the Americans will join the war against Germany," Hendrik scoffed.

***

And indeed, Johanna had been right about Hendrik's bold announcement. He had been just "getting ready" to pack, not actually packing.

March arrived, and nothing happened. When spring was in full bloom and lovely scents wafted all through the town, the Americans were allocating vast amounts of money to building up their military might. Then April arrived. On April 6, the American president declared war against Germany.

By this time, Johanna identified as all-German, which had become a nagging issue. She decided not to test Hendrik's loyalty to her, fearful of the way his allegiance would go. He put the Germans down, and repeatedly showed his aversion to the Teutonic nature. He loathed the German character and called its leadership's ruthless strategies for beating the enemy *the egomaniac nature of their national strive.*

She thought that her nature too was to strive but saw it as a positive trait. Without intent, or any attempts to reach a goal, life would be haphazard, random. She tried to stay calm and rational in her arguments about politics. Although Hendrik never directly blamed her, she felt compelled to defend herself and her chosen identity.

After moving into town, it had been her idea to attend the Lutheran church regularly, as decent people went to church. Today, as they walked to the church with their children in tow in their Sunday-best, the conversation about their cultural differences continued.

"Dear husband, what is wrong with having goals and being motivated to go after what you want? Isn't that called ambition?"

"Mind you, I won't knock a bit of ambition," said Hendrik. "I've plenty of it myself, you know that. But there are international standards, even in war time.

Countries agree to abide by these. Breaking those rules is egotistical and disrespect-ful of international law. It makes for unreliable negotiating partners: you can't trust their word."

He straightened his sore back, forced back to working on the line as his men disappeared. Yes, it was time he quit the heavy work. Johanna pulled his arm through hers and squeezed it. She felt he couldn't stomach much more of his wife's German nonsense. But there was no stopping her.

"Isn't the early bird getting the worm?" she continued. "Isn't that the same as surprising the enemy with a new tactic?" Johanna spoke out with her free hand gesticulating, palm up, as if there was no other way of looking at it. She felt Hen-drik was unfair about the Germans. When he attacked them, he indirectly attacked her, and her skills, her nature. "Germans have initiative," she ended her plea lamely.

With a grimace, feeling the pain in his lower back, Hendrik curtly shared his judgement.

"That's all *quatch*, baloney. The Germany Empire is a bad player with a com-plex, like what Doctor Freud talks about. Germany has a very long, revengeful memory, like an elephant: the last time, France won the war. They must dominate the world. Many think Germans are hateful."

Johanna turned red, and her pace increased. She was seething inside. How dare he, what rudeness, calling her hateful. He was hateful himself. Pulling her arm free and with clenched fists, she marched on, leaving Hendrik a few paces behind her. The conversation had ended.

# Chapter 26

On his days off in April, Hendrik brought home one of his workers, an emigrant heading for America via Hamburg. The young man named Tomasz would stay for a few days before embarking. Tomasz had managed to secure a ticket with a stop-over in Liverpool.

Johanna had been miffed by Hendrik's offer of lodging without asking her first, imposing on their space in the small house with only two bedrooms. She was still angry at him for calling Germans hateful, but since the man was already here, she planned on remaining polite but nothing more. "Listen Tomasz, you can sleep in the living room on a mattress. We have little else to offer."

"Splendid," the young man replied with a broad smile. He was a good-looking laborer of about thirty. A typically eastern type, he had a full head of dark hair and hairy arms, brown eyes, was sturdily built and could be from Belarus or Hungary with his dark complexion. She softened, acknowledging the man bore no blame for her irritation with Hendrik.

"From what town are you?"

"I'm from the Stettin region, in Pomerania. I consider myself on principle Polish or Slavic, not German. I didn't like what the forced Germanization did to us."

It shocked her that he wasn't shirking from the ethnic identity issue as she had. Eagerly, without sorrow, she had dumped hers. She almost forgot her father spoke Slavic until this man reminded her. She had closed the book and didn't want to be reminded. She quickly asked, "When will your ship leave, then?"

The man was an animated talker. "My departure is in two days. First, I'll travel to Liverpool from Hamburg, and then on a different ship for Ellis Island, the landing place for immigrants in America. The fare cost me thirty marks, but I saved for a while and have some extra money for when I get there."

He explained that the sailing with the modern steamships would only take eleven days, not weeks, as used to be. He knew that the newspapers in America said over four million Germans had already arrived.

"I don't know where I will end up. I'll be just one of many." He was positively beaming.

"Didn't you bring your wife?" Johanna asked, straightforward as ever, assuming that anyone of that age would have a wife.

"Uh, no, Frau Zondervan. She didn't want to come. My wife and I had no children. She moved in with her sister, who had many, and could use her help." He continued telling her that two mates of his had planned the same trip, who went ahead, and were already in Hamburg. They all had bought tickets from the sales agent visiting the worksites to hawk his tickets. "I will miss my wife," he added quietly.

"Yes, life can be tough," Johanna said. "You could send for her later. Or did you both decide to start over with somebody else?"

Hendrik interrupted. "Johanna, be quiet already, you're cheeky. Leave the man alone."

She smiled at the young man, ignoring Hendrik.

Tomasz confessed, "Maybe when I am settled, she'll join me."

"If not, I have no doubt you'll find someone else, even on the ship, I'm sure," she chuckled.

Johanna recalled her own yearning for adventure when she hired on with BSN — a lifetime ago — and Hendrik's courtship. Overcome by nostalgia, she said softly, "Well, good luck to you then, Tomasz." She turned around to hide her emotion and left for the kitchen. She was past her prime and Hendrik was getting older as well. If he continued the hard work, he would be old soon. She wished she was still young and remembered her brash look at the world at sixteen, such a child she was.

A few minutes later, when Johanna looked out the window, she saw that Hendrik and Tomasz had joined the boys and kicked an improvised soccer ball around with much yelling and arm waving. The ball was a bunch of rags tied with string into a sphere. Heinrich was trying to kick the ball as he pushed Johan aside, who was much bigger, but not as quick. She watched a while longer and saw that Robert had the most trouble getting a kick in.

The voices of Elfriede and Klara reached her then, playing house with their stuffed dolls and a teddy bear in the corner of the room. They were copying a couple arguing in high-pitched tones. She realized her children had heard her arguing with Hendrik. "Come girls, you two can help me get dinner on the table."

***

In May 1915, a week after having said her goodbyes to Tomasz, Johanna heard from the neighbor about the sinking of a ship. As soon as she could, she ran out to buy a newspaper. Walking home from the shop, she read the headlines and almost got run over by a speeding vehicle. Startled, barely able to avoid the horse's hoofs, she tucked the newspaper under her arm and hastened home.

The front page announced that a German U-boat had sunk the British luxury steamship. The Lusitania had been traveling home with 1200 passengers including several Americans, although it also had some steerage space for low-income travelers.

She felt for the families of the more than eleven hundred passengers who had all drowned. She didn't know that those ocean liners could carry so many people. Their bodies were not even recovered, and many would still be floating in the ocean. How terrible if you couldn't even bury your child, or your husband. Next to the article, she saw the massive advertisement offering rewards to private entrepreneurs for every corpse recovered. Imagining the scene, she shivered at the thought of it. How gruesome. She didn't care about the financial disaster it supposedly was for the shipping company.

As Johanna read, her hand covering her mouth, in distress, she mumbled, "*Ach, Du, lieber Gott,*" reading about the number of missing passengers and imagining how the families back home would feel, reading the same newspaper. Bursting with anxiety, she couldn't wait for Hendrik to come home. She needed calming down, somebody to tell her this act wouldn't lead to all-out war. She threw down the paper and turned to the children. In a daze, still thinking about all those children on board, "missing", she helped her own children off to school, then sat down again, and reread the whole front page, and every page inside, to see if there were passenger lists or any other details. She thought of Tomasz, was he saved? Did he drown?

She tried to recall a name, but that didn't help her. Tomasz hadn't named the ship he was to travel on. Then, on the third read, she realized the Lusitania had been going the other way. It was returning *from* New York to Liverpool — without Tomasz. A stone rolled off her chest.

Slowly it dawned on her that she had invested an inordinate amount of energy in the fate of a man she hardly knew. Somehow, she had associated Tomasz with her father. He was her Slavic connection and would represent his tribe in America. It wasn't till this moment that she realized she'd been looking at Tomasz as an option for her children to resettle as adults, far away from war-ridden Europe, and an alternative to emigration to Holland.

She would just have to wait for a letter from Tomasz to Hendrik, although she couldn't assume he would, after his safe arrival in America, bother at all with writing letters to his old boss. He would have other priorities. She might as well drop that angle and had better focus on moving to Holland with her family.

*\*\*\**

Johanna had already noticed that Hendrik was in a foul mood on his return. He was absentminded and forgot to kiss her, but immediately went to the boys to slap them on the shoulder, then kissed the girls. Hendrik would never read the whole paper, averse to politics as he was, but this time he grabbed the front page, lying on the table with a cartoon prominently displayed. The Osterode newspaper showed a caricature of the American Joe, portraying him as a clown with oversize, unwieldy shoes, falling over himself and tumbling into the ocean, drowning. Another cartoon on the next page suggested the British ship Lusitania was stuffed with explosives in its cargo hold.

Seeing the mockery of the funnies, he slowly and thoughtfully commented.

"After already having recalled its ambassador earlier, America now will have to declare war. It's unavoidable. A joke cannot hide the Germans' fear. With all these American soldiers adding more power to the war on the opposite side, *I* think all Germans should be afraid."

"They probably are," she replied, then added with a careless breeziness, "What else is eating you, dear husband?"

"I'll tell you after dinner," he replied without looking at her.

It shocked her that she had guessed right, and he admitted to having something on his mind. She hoped it was good news, but it probably wasn't. The estrangement between them was beginning to bother her, and she feared she was losing him. Why was he so moody?

After dinner, Johanna sent the children to play outside with the neighborhood kids. Hendrik sat down heavily in the living room, carrying the weight of something invisible. As soon as Johanna joined him with cups of coffee on a tray, he burst out in an angry voice.

"The bastards took my second-in-command. I can no longer take off every weekend. If it continues like this, we're leaving the country. I'm worn out. My body can no longer take it," he growled.

"Hendrik. The company did? How awful." Johanna said, and waited, seating herself on the two-seater, her new, dainty piece of furniture. She immediately thought of the side effect of his misfortune: Hendrik quitting, and her hope to get away from the war, so long squished to almost nothing by delays was suddenly growing. The company would decide for them, and in her favor — again.

After several minutes of silence, followed by a deep exhalations, Hendrik continued speaking in an unusually gruff voice.

"No, not the company. The army did. I stayed on the job only by the grace of my second-in-command. With him gone, I can't do it anymore. The army is recruiting every damned man that can hold a rifle. Even after I identified his position as an essential service, it still wasn't enough. They cannot touch my brother, Jan, a Dutchman, but still, that doesn't make for enough people." He looked up, rubbed his face with both his hands, took his cap off, and threw it in the corner of the room. His mustache was uneven and looked ratty, angry and as disheartened as the man himself.

"Oh, dear," she said, trying not to talk him out of anything, listening, and proud to be his sounding board, which was impossible for him with his crew as their supervisor. If the past was any indication, she feared he might not take the next step, but find some other solution. His resolve would blow over. Her faint hope this would be the moment of truth and they'd make the move, died softly with the realization. If this would continue, they'd never have a farm, and the children would grow up here, and she'd be as downtrodden as Hendrik was becoming. As hope died, sorrow began settling in.

She was right. After a weekend of rest — and some spoiling from Johanna — Hendrik went back to work early Monday morning. He didn't tell Johanna what solution he had found if any.

# Chapter 27

The children were doing well in school. They had friends in the neighborhood. Despite her expectation of a future move to Holland, Johanna settled. She liked her life in the quaint town of Zeeven. The war continued without affecting them in a direct, physical way. Hendrik's income was more than sufficient to buy what they needed. She looked away, and simply refused to notice the signs of war around her, the poverty it caused to others. She hardened against the grief of the fallen members' families and her own disappointment.

However, she couldn't ignore Hendrik's aging beyond his actual years and began to worry he wouldn't be able to farm, even if he wanted it badly. She settled into the idea they would never reach Holland. She had her sister close by, and when she made a bit of an effort, she could visit her other relatives. The necessity to adjust to her situation became obvious, and she changed her dreams.

***

Then, things dramatically changed on the international stage. When the German Empire forged an alliance with Mexico to attack America, the German navy resumed torpedoing American and other foreign ships, loaded with civilian passengers. America had by then understood that staying neutral was futile and declared war in April of that year, 1917. When Johanna read about President Wilson's declaration of war, she understood that this would mean another pivotal decision for Hendrik.

The newspaper reported that the United States Congress voted to declare war on Germany on April 6. Johanna read another article with more detail about America's decision-making process. The House of Representatives passed the resolution with an overwhelming majority of 373–50. In the Senate, the resolution had passed 82 - 6. The House members who voted against the resolution for so long until now, mostly represented the Midwestern and Western states.

Johanna mulled over the info for a while. Many were immigrants from the German Empire — millions of them — and their opposition shouldn't surprise her. These new Americans obviously still felt loyalty to their German relatives (who voluntarily enlisted, or were drafted) and would fight in the battles against the Americans. She recognized her own ambiguity about choosing sides, discovering an unexpected affinity with this contradictory behavior of some Midwestern Americans.

Hendrik would not be at home for a couple of days yet, so Johanna went to the post office to put in a call to her sister, Hannah, with whom she had the most contact. Hannah was not politically informed, so Johanna didn't get much relief from talking to her sister, although it was nice to hear her voice and tighten the family bonds. She told Hannah she feared that with America involved in the war, her move was finally coming up. Now the moment of moving away to Holland came near, she had cold feet. She'd miss everybody, her comfortable life, and the familiarity of her people.

***

On Friday, Hendrik came home earlier than usual at one o'clock in the afternoon. He barged into the house through the front door and found Johanna not there. Looking through the kitchen window, he saw a shadow moving in the backyard. He stepped closer to the windowpane and peered into the backyard, where Johanna was busy hanging laundry on the clothesline. He strode the three steps through the kitchen, opened the backdoor, and loudly called, "Johanna, will you come inside, please," and closed the door again.

Startled by his sudden appearance, Johanna threw the article of clothing in her hand down into the basket and hurried toward the door. She pulled it open, stepped inside, and slammed it shut behind her. With a quickened heartbeat, she managed to speak as she exhaled, "What's the matter? Is the world coming to an end? You came home early."

"You could say that," Hendrik grumbled. "You need to pack up everything. We're leaving Germany this weekend. I have already rented a wagon, and an extra man for loading it. We are going to Hardenberg. Only the most essential stuff we'll take; the rest can be sent later."

"But Hendrik, really?"

Johanna crossed her arms. It wasn't that she hadn't expected this, but she just wasn't ready. Fear for the unknown, for having to be Dutch, a strange extended family to disappear in — it all scared her. She wanted to resist, delay, plan with care. She glared at him as she tried on sentences to convince him it was a foolish idea. And so late into the war? It would be over soon.

She reminded him he was forty-six, and the children were all in school and settled. She admitted to him she didn't look forward to becoming a farmer's wife. The reality of endless delays had forced her to give up the idea already. She doubted Hendrik could still be an effective farmer with his back issues. She locked eyes with him as she said all this. He glared back. What was he thinking?

He stepped toward her and unexpectedly laid his arm around her shoulders.

"*Lieverd*," he said softly and kissed her on the cheek. "We talked about this. It's time. You will do fine, don't worry about that, but I cannot stay. When Holland gets involved, we will be allies on the other side, fighting the Germans. My nephews will sign up. Anyway, with the Germans sinking all those ships, it's only a matter of time before America gets involved."

"Oh, Hendrik. That happened already," she cried out. "Haven't you heard? America declared war on Germany."

He didn't know anything about the American declaration of war. Still, Hendrik always operated on his gut feelings. In the first year of the war, The Ottoman Empire joined the German alliance, as Japan sided with the British and the Allied Powers. He grabbed her by her upper-arms, and with urgency, replied, "That makes it even more urgent for us to get out. The Americans are an ally of the British, and the Dutch will undoubtedly follow. The time to move is now, while Holland still will let us in, but that door is closing. Let's do it. What do you say?"

He almost convinced her, but then she thought of something. She shook off his hands and straightened her back. "But, what about me and my relatives? I have two uncles and a few cousins and young nephews in the army."

Hendrik hesitated for a second. With an uncharacteristic grimness, staring hard into her eyes, he said: "Look, they signed up to *attack* other countries. It's a matter of principle: Germany and Austria started all this without good reason. It all could've been settled with diplomacy. On the other hand, my relatives would be defending themselves against the aggressors. What's the matter with you, pushing me to move all this time? I'm not going to discuss it anymore. Pack up to come with me, or stay behind, if you wish. Just so you know: I quit my job."

Johanna realized there was no reasoning with Hendrik, and she backed down. Facing her anxiety, her resistance seeped away, and silently she began organizing. She found and filled boxes, packed suitcases, and sorted through what to take and what to leave behind.

After a couple of hours, the children came home from school. She instructed them to get their clothes and a few toys and stuff it all in the suitcases she had collected, some of which she bought off the neighbors for a decent price.

Hendrik disappeared to contract a mover for the possessions they would leave behind, to be taken to Holland later. Jan would stay behind to help the mover with sending off the possessions, as a favor to Hendrik. They would see him in Hardenberg again.

Hendrik had found local men to load the wagon, referred to him by one of his crew members and had hired the two workers from the Zeeven area. These two weren't too bad. The rumor that her husband was a weak boss got back to Johanna via a chatty churchgoer. "You mean, kind?" she had slung at the gossipy wretch. That shut her up.

Hendrik had told Johanna he preferred the easterners, who wouldn't walk off the job so readily. Most of the laborers on his crew came from the eastern provinces of the *Reich*. But the army recruiters would pick up any unemployed man in a flash: a fate harder to stomach for the Slavic migrants, planning on returning to their eastern homes eventually. Hendrik was lenient with the easterners, to prevent them from walking off the job for good. If they feared a raid, these men just disappeared for a few days, to return when the danger was over.

Despite his insistence to stay and make more money for the farm purchase, Johanna understood now that Hendrik had been itching for years to move back to his home country. It might explain his bad moods, and his uncommunicative shell she couldn't penetrate.

She insisted that her new furniture be moved to Holland. When Hendrik had first seen her choice of furniture, he had scoffed, "Those are no *meubels*. That dainty stuff is more suited to a mayor's parlor than a farm." So be it. She, Johanna Zondervan, *would* have a parlor in her next house.

When she had seen the furniture in the carpenter's store catalog, she had to have it: an elegant sideboard with cut-glass windows in the hatch, a dining table, six chairs, two armchairs, a two-seater. All these pieces in an ultra-modern style called *Noveau*, matched. Each piece had scrolled copper designs attached to the backs, and the tapering legs were copper-shod, like elegant, dainty horses.

If she couldn't change the plan, she'd at least bring what she considered hers. Having only lived a few years with her family in an actual house, she would not leave behind any unnecessary items, let alone the stuff she loved and needed. She would make the best of the circumstances as she always had, including becoming a farmer's wife.

At the end of the packing frenzy, surveying the downstairs chaos of packed boxes and crates, the furniture stacked together in the living room, she sighed. It had finally come this far, Hendrik's dream was to own a farm, then move to Holland. Now she had to face the *unknown* challenges. Not able to imagine the hurdles, she quickly looked around for anything left to pack. Only the kitchen had some room left to stand in. It struck her that she hated leaving her country.

Tears filled her eyes as she climbed the stairs to the bedroom. As she folded her clothes for the open suitcase, waiting on the bed, she mumbled softly, *Fool, get it together.* It didn't help. Her determination couldn't halt her regrets. She would not be saying goodbye to Hannah, her husband, their children, her elder sister Rieke and her brothers August and Wilhelm, their wives, and all her surviving aunts and uncles on mother's side, her nephews, nieces, and cousins. There was no time; Hendrik wouldn't let her.

Nevertheless, with certainty she knew to follow Hendrik wherever he would lead her, even knowing she would sorely miss, her blood, *her tribe*, and possibly lose them for good. As she impatiently passed her forearm over her eyes, wiping away her tears, she hoped it would all be worth it.

# Chapter 28

The summer of 1917 passed, and the children entered school in early September. It could be said the Zondervan family had successfully made the transition to Hardenberg in Holland.

Eight-year-old Heinrich burst into the living room of their new home in his dad's village and declared: "Mutti, I don't like it here. I want to go back to Zeeven." Dressed in his school clothes, he looked like a miniature office clerk, so neat, although the children in Holland didn't wear school uniforms, so he wore his Sunday clothes. The boy pulled off his cap, threw it towards the hooks of the clothes rack in the corridor but failed to hit the target, and it fell to the linoleum floor.

From the love seat, Johanna watched Heinrich's attempted acrobatics, but didn't reply. She was almost finished reading and rereading the newspaper, from which she could only make out a fraction. However, the photographs and cartoons gave her an impression of some of the subjects.

"*Komm mahl her, Bub,*" she said. "Come here, my boy, I need your help. After two months in Holland, I bet you already know a lot of words, right?"

Heinrich forgot his quest to complain about his rude classmates and the teacher and sat down beside Johanna, flattered by his mom's words. "Let me see." He helped his mom decipher a few pieces of the Dutch language puzzle, its phonetics so much like his native tongue, and its words so very different. After five minutes, he had enough.

"Can I have a cookie and milk?" He jumped from the rug to the threshold, trying to avoid the linoleum — an imaginary deep ocean, which would swallow him whole if he fell in. He already stood by the kitchen door.

"Where are your brothers and sisters, Heinrich?" she asked in a neutral voice. "Did you lead the way again? I'd feel better if you stayed with them, so nobody will be tempted to tease you with Johan around." Her eldest son had grown into a big boy.

Heinrich kept jumping up and down. "They're lagging. I saw Klara trying to drag Robert away from a game of marbles with some boys from his class, but I don't know what Frieda and Johan were doing. I don't need them to protect me. I'm a big boy now. Can I have that milk, and a cookie too, please? I'm hungry." He was already in the kitchen, waving his arms in anticipation.

Johanna put the paper down, got up, and slowly followed Heinrich to the kitchen. Her knees were stiff and sore lately. It must be the rain. In the kitchen, she laid her hand on her smart son's shoulder and held his eyes with hers.

"I know you are a big boy. What did you want to tell me earlier?"

He looked at her for a second, then remembered. His little face showed his sadness when he remembered the incident in school.

"Oh, yes. I almost forgot to tell you. My *meester* changed my name. He said Heinrich is too difficult to say, so he'll call me Henk instead from now on. He told me that is Dutch for the same name. *Now you are in Holland, and you should do as the Dutch do,* my master said. Mutti, I'm the only one of us with a German name. Why did you call me Heinrich?"

Stunned, Johanna didn't know what to say. Her son's complaint reminded her of her own experiences with her last name, and the identity matters her Vati and Ur-Opa used to complain about, but she also knew that if you didn't lose your Slavic identity and became German, you'd have a hard time.

She recalled Hendrik's reminder to her after the boy's birth, not to forget her German heritage — if only a semi-borrowed ethnicity. It had been different for Hendrik, because his sense of identity was already something of value, and didn't need to be protected and lived up to. For her, identity was a burden, at the most a jacket, changeable as the weather gets colder, and not an inherent characteristic.

She wondered how this German heritage would turn out for Heinrich, whose sense of self seemed solid enough to question his mother's choices. Would he ever remember this moment, this shift from turning from a German boy to a Dutch person?

"I thought it was a beautiful name, *mein Schatz*," she said softly, and, knowing he loved his dad, added after a pause, "Your dad thought so too. It is his name in German and many of the men in his family had his name, and in my family, too. It means *honest heart*. It will remind you not to lie and to be fair and honest with the little ones around you. It's also the name of German kings, and of the husband of your Queen Wilhelmina, a German prince. It's a good name."

She smiled at him and nodded for emphasis.

Heinrich's face brightened. "Oh, that sounds all right, but could you not say it when my friends come to play, if I ever get friends, Mutti? Just call me Henk from now on."

"Of course, you will get friends, plenty of them. It's only a matter of time. You are a wonderful, smart boy."

Johanna asked him to bring up the smallest milk pan from the cold cellar underneath the storage room, cooling off there after the first boil. He carefully brought it up the steps without spilling.

"Good boy," she said and pushed the thick surface skin in the pan aside with a spoon and poured him a glass. She found some cookies in the blue tin jar and put it all on the kitchen table.

"Here, my boy, eat up. I will call you *Henk* when I remember, but you must always stay proud of where you came from."

Feeling a tad guilty for not living up to her own advice, she moved her hand through her precocious boy's hair, left long on top and shaved up at the sides, just the way her son had wanted it. She was amazed at his ability to articulate what he wanted and how he had instructed the barber about his wishes. That he had already developed his tastes at this young an age was unusual. He would make it far; she just knew it.

The calls of children's voices coming from the front door announced the arrival of the four twin children, bringing her back to reality.

"I better think about dinner," she said to no-one in particular. Heinrich was already gone from the kitchen.

***

Their new home was a marvelous farmhouse with attached stables for a cow and a few pigs in the back. The bedrooms were located on one side of a long corridor, the living quarters on the other side. Above the first floor stretched a large attic under the tiled roof, suitable for playing on a rainy day, or for guests to sleep in a pinch, and the laundry. The property sat on two acres at the edge of town within walking distance of everywhere. It had an orchard.

Johanna had written Hannah about another loss in her life: the privacy of a real bathroom. "*The only thing it doesn't have is a clawfoot tub, like in Zeeven. We have no real water closet or bathroom. There's only a privy in the house's back part with a cement floor, next to the stable and the hog stalls. Hendrik hired somebody to empty the can. We're all relegated again to taking weekly Saturday baths in the galvanized laundry tub in the kitchen, with water heated on the stovetop. The house is not old, but I guess the Dutch don't have bathrooms. Or maybe it's only this way for farmers. There is a pump with a sink in the kitchen to wash up there with cold water on regular days. Dear Hannah, I don't know if I'm cut out to be a farmer's wife.*"

Hendrik was building a chicken coop on the side of the house, bordering the neighboring property. He was whistling and smiling and seemed happier than Johanna had ever seen him before, not even when they just got together. Since their return to his homeland, the undefined tension he had carried in him had left him. He didn't have to work for a boss, and he had his additional land out of town for growing crops. He had made a concession to Johanna for their house's location within the town boundaries. His brothers and sisters were here, right in the town proper. These sturdy farmer types who didn't speak a lot were the kind of people Johanna had to get used to.

She was happy for Hendrik but missed her sister Hannah, and Germany, especially the language. Since she had moved so far away, she'd written many letters — her way to tell someone who knew her what she was going through. She hadn't known how good she had it, until it ended. She wrote Rieke:

*To be able to open my mouth and say what I want to say, without tongue-twisting or scraping your throat to get the proper sounds out: what luxury! I hadn't appreciated before now what language gave me, the self-confidence, the ability to communicate, reading the wealth of our literature, and our shared history. It all has fallen away. I am nothing without our culture."*

Rieke didn't reply, but Hannah promised she would come for a visit, as soon as the war was over. Shortly after America had entered the war, the borders had closed, and she was unable to leave the country for a visit. Things were tough in Germany in many ways, but Hannah wouldn't elaborate, and only told Johanna to count her blessings and stop complaining.

Johanna's heart was heavy in contrast to Hendrik's happiness in Holland. She saw the growing delight of the children, already fluent in the Dutch language, competent after four months. They adored their new place with the large yard and fruit trees, a virtual heaven for children to play in: they could bring any new friend home after school. All five of them crowded into the kitchen, Heinrich not averse to another turn of a snack as the four latecomers demanded: "Mutti, Mutti, cookies and milk, please."

Johanna obliged. As her noisy brats were eating and chatting around the kitchen table, she sat on a chair and watched them for a few minutes. They were handsome children. Each twin looked certainly like their fraternal sibling, the dizygotic sibling of a different gender. Frieda and Johan were both tall with similar hair and grey eyes, Johan on the bulky side because he loved eating a bit too much. Frieda's facial features were more delicate, and she was fine-boned, with dark, shining tresses — a girl's jewel.

Heinrich — no, she should call him Henk now — was a year younger, just a singular boy, and his nature was just like it. He had a strong jaw and lots of coarse brown hair. He likely would be the one to copy his father's bushy mustache as an adult.

The youngest two had turned nine years old, just this month. Klara and Robbie were shorter in stature than the others, still the same height now, but that might end any day now. They took after their mother: stocky and heavy-boned. Both had their mother's round face and silky hair, sleek and shiny, and resistant to any grooming attempts. Klara's braids would've just slid out of their elastic bands by the end of school. She hoped that Robbie would find a good girlfriend, someone as devoted to him as Klara, who had not let go of managing her twin brother, yet.

Johanna contemplated if and when to tell Klara to find her own friends. She saw the weakness in Robbie but hoped that would only be a temporary adjustment. After the move to Holland, it would be cruel to demand anything of them now; they were still adjusting. Children were so lucky. They learned a new language within a few months.

That reminded her of the mix of German and Dutch she heard the children speak, right at that moment.

"How was school, my darlings?" she asked. "Did you learn lots?"

"Oh, Mutti, somebody told me I look like a girl," Robbie complained.

"*Ach*, that's because his hair is too long," Klara answered for him. "He needs a haircut, just like *Henk*." She already used the new, Dutch name for him, pronouncing the hard "k" at the end, the way Henk had said it — exactly right.

Johanna shook her head in wonderment. Yes, Klara was bossy. Then she turned to the boy. "Do you want to do that, Robbie?"

"*Jawohl, Mutti,*" he nodded enthusiastically.

"We'll do it tomorrow then, alright? Is anybody teasing you with your name as well?"

"No, but I told everybody Robert is my name. It's a normal name, even Robbie is. You should say Robert now, Mutti."

Out of the blue, Johan asked, "Why are there no soldiers here in the streets?" He was a quiet boy, but something must have attracted his attention. Alert to the possibility of her German boy becoming the target of teasing, Johanna responded with tension in her voice.

"Why do you ask, my boy, did somebody say something about that?"

He looked at her with caution in his eyes. "No. I'm just wondering. There were so many soldiers everywhere in Zeeven, but none here." He didn't say anything about the words some of the boys had hurled at him: *dirty German, go home.* He had told Frieda, who was always practical and had told Johanna. Noticing the wariness on her young son's face, her heart broke. She was surprised she hadn't noticed before he was growing up. Living in Zeeven, her explanation for the military presence had been *to protect the country from the enemy*. She hadn't identified who those enemies were. How in heaven's name would she tackle this?

She put her hand on Johan's arm, and held it there as she replied, "There is no war in Holland. This country is at peace, so no soldiers are traveling to the front or to the depots for training. Nobody is fighting here. In your father's Holland you don't have to sign up for the army at majority age, if you don't want to. Isn't that wonderful? You have grown up, *mein Hertz*. You are my biggest boy, Johan." She kissed the top of his head, put her arm around him and pressed him against her hip for a brief second, and softly added: "Don't listen if anybody calls you names, dear."

# Chapter 29

After the Americans entered the fray in 1917, many Dutch volunteers signed up for the army, in case of an invasion. As the war continued in Germany, Johanna followed it all in the newspapers. It was not easy to replace the German magazines. Luckily, her sister sent her the odd German magazine, but she didn't read those openly, for fear her husband and his relatives might view her as disloyal: the Dutch were all for the Americans. But she had a defense for reading those: concern for her German relatives.

Johanna, concerned with the Czar and his family, knew the Russian Empire had its own problems with an uprising of its people. Before she had left Zeeven, the newspapers there reported about the workers' uprising. Russian troops of the Petrograd army garrison opened fire and killed demonstrators. But the protesters kept to the streets and didn't give up, and unable to stop them, the troops began to waver. Surprised, she learned that sometimes protesters did win.

In Hardenberg, Johanna read with the help from her son Henk, that the Russian cabinet had given in and formed a provisional government, and a few days later, Czar Nicholas abdicated. He was to leave the country with his family, the Romanovs. The new rulers had no appetite for continuing the war, so the eastern alliance had fallen apart. She assumed the rebellious Pomeranians had just snuck home.

A few months later when preparing for Christmas, her first winter in the Netherlands, she made lots of decorations with the children out of pinecones and cookies. That evening, she read about the Bolsheviks — the popular name for communists — who under Vladimir Lenin had seized power in Russia, and immediately negotiated peace with Germany. She was relieved that the war was coming to an end for the sake of her relatives.

The rumors that the new leaders had the Czar' and his family assassinated upset her greatly. From the beginning of the demonstrations in Russia, she'd been worried about the family of Nicholas II and his German wife, Sophie, and their four lovely daughters and one son. She'd seen dozens of lovely portraits of the royal family in her magazines, the whole family often dressed in white — virginal clothing. She tried to find out what had happened to the Romanov royals. While she had to seek a new source for her magazines and newspapers in Holland, she had a copy of a weekly edition sent to her from the nearest German city. In the town of Hardenberg, nobody cared.

"*Lieverd*, what is this obsession with royalty?" Hendrik asked her one day with barely suppressed irritation. "I don't get it. There are so many of them, a dime a dozen. I think my cousin is dating a guy of the lower nobility. Big deal. They go to the toilet same as us."

She shrugged, lost for words, now that Hendrik always spoke Dutch with her, a language she barely understood, let alone carry a full conversation in. "I don't know," she answered in her own language. Not even in German did she want to tell him about her Polish-German grandfather, his story of the princesses Eliza Fryderyka and Wanda Johanna Radziwill — her namesake — and her father's grief over his lost relationship to his culture, his identity. How could she explain the romance of it to this practical, down-to-earth husband of hers, and tell him that royalty are also people. Hendrik wouldn't understand, and he would probably laugh if she told him. Feeling fragile, she couldn't take that risk. Hendrik laughing at her would surely bring on a crying spell, as she missed her relatives terribly, this first Christmas in a foreign country.

***

As the days got longer, Johanna was increasingly able to speak better Dutch, helped by her children, enough to have a minimal social interaction in stores, which helped her recover from loneliness and homesickness. She wanted the war to end. When Germany's remaining allies, Austria-Hungary and Bulgaria backed out of the battle and signed their own armistice with the Allies, she and Hendrik celebrated. Truly a worthwhile cause for a celebration. Left on their own, the Germans would soon have to surrender.

Two of Hendrik's brothers and their wives came over for a visit, and Johanna served wine and her own salty, home-baked pretzels. When the wives complimented her on the tasty treats, Johanna smiled at Hendrik. He smiled back at her lovingly.

***

The next year in October, American troops joined the western front, and the war finally came to an end. When Hendrik brought the news home of Kaiser Wilhelm's surrender and his abdication, Johanna cried out, "Danke, Gott — thank God." The armistice agreement with the Allies was signed on November 11, 1918. That was the end of the German Empire, but she wasn't sorry, as it stopped the danger for her relatives, Kaiser or no Kaiser. Now she could see them again. When she heard that *der Kaiser* was not killed — her comrade-in-arms of a sort: both surviving expatriates — she was pleased he didn't suffer the same fate of the Czar and his family. He would be safe now.

She had adapted enough to the Dutch way of life to realize how fine and peaceful their lives were. Every day she was grateful for Hendrik's decision to return to Holland, and for her wisdom to have followed him. "I am happy again, grateful for having you and our children," she told him.

"That's *prachtig* — wonderful," he said and embraced her in a tight squeeze.

***

Some positive changes had come to the new Germany, according to Hannah. She wrote about the right to vote for all citizens, even women. Johanna read with envy how Hannah felt tremendous pride for being part of choosing the new coalition in the German Republic called Weimar. Although Hannah was not looking forward to the final peace treaty, she was sure Germany could deal with it, she wrote.

***

A year after the armistice on a sunny, fall day, Hendrik seeded the winter rye during the morning. Before he went home, he decided to pick up some provisions for Johanna — a habit from his railroad days. He dropped a newspaper on the table.

"For you, *schat*, so you will know what happened."

He smiled and winked at her.

Johanna blushed, interpreting his solicitude as his way of letting her know he wanted to get closer. She smiled and eagerly picked up the paper. She read that in the final Treaty of Versailles of 28 June 1919 Germany had to pay a vast amount of reparations and had lost several areas, essential for their economic recovery, and restricted to have no more than 100,000 men in its military.

Choked by its severity, she looked up from the paper and asked, "Did you read it, Hendrik?"

He nodded; his face serious. "That serves them right, that war-hungry lot," he said with a gruff voice. Her face must've fallen, because he quickly added, "But not you, dear. You almost never fight me, and you're not a typical German, anyway. You're half-Polish, right?" His face had turned all smiles.

She looked down and, ashamed, covered her face with both hands.

"Horrible," she whispered. "That means much hardship for my relatives. There won't be any money for school, or maybe even food for my brother's children, and two of my cousins had children who served in the war. They'll be without income. It's not fair for the Germans."

Hendrik walked over, sat down beside her on the two-seater, took the newspaper out of her hand, and dropped it to the floor beside the couch. He put an arm around her and gave her a quick squeeze, then took her hand.

"We could help them and send stuff they need. You should go for a visit to Hannah soon. Seeing with your own eyes how they are might do you good."

Johanna stayed silent, imagining how terrible the conditions were for her relatives and for all Germans. A bit of charity won't be enough. Her heart ached for Hannah and Rieke, whose life never had been easy and would even be harder now.

During the last year, she had followed the difficult negotiations as they were reported in the German and the Dutch newspapers. It took a while to negotiate the peace treaty, and it went in stages. The Austrian-Hungarian Empire had already self-destructed as nationalist groups battled for independence. It fell apart into separate nations, which each acquired status as independent negotiators.

Next step: the Allies divided up the Ottoman Empire as their punishment for committing genocide against the minorities in their territories: the Armenians, Assyrians, and Greeks. Stripped of its Middle Eastern regions, it was now simply called, Turkey — the last empire had dissolved.

The French insistence for repair payments was the major barrier to finalizing the treaty with Germany, a reason why negotiations took so long. It had been the country with most soldiers killed in battle, and they wanted revenge.

"The many dead German soldiers don't count," she muttered, reading this explanation. She had seen the tally. Eighty percent of German men between the ages of fifteen and forty-nine had gone off to the battlefields — many to never return home. The French justification that the Germans had started the war sounded brutal and reminded her of what Hendrik had said.

***

Robert and Klara sat at the dining table with their homework. Johanna saw that Klara was listening to their conversation. Henk — always finished first — was outside already, picking apples for a bit of pocket money. He had skipped a whole year of primary school and did well in his first year of secondary school at only eleven years old. He definitively would go on to higher education, maybe even university. He would fulfill her own secret promise to have at least one of her children be university-educated.

Johanna's two eldest, Johan and Frieda, were now thirteen years old. They were doing homework in the kitchen for the second year of their secondary programs, but Johanna heard a lot of talking and joking coming from them. With little interest in school, their brains were not made for studying, and they were just wasting time. Johanna had already resigned herself to those two leaving school soon. She only hoped she would see them complete their third year of the M.U.L.O. — an adequate secondary preparation for the working class. When they turned fifteen, they would be allowed to work.

Hendrik felt little mercy for the Germans, she realized, looking at Hendrik, even as he was prepared to send some charitable aid packages to her relatives. Nothing she could say would change that. If she wanted to raise their children in peace, she had better leave her German relatives to solve their own problems and not test his patience. Hendrik was still holding her hand as he sat beside her. She inhaled deeply and exhaled, then changed the subject. "Isn't it astonishing how fast our children grow up?"

"Yes, *lieverd*, I remember their births as if it was yesterday," he smiled, looking at her with as much love as ever, letting go of her hand, satisfied the danger of a difficult discussion over reparation payments had eased.

Johanna whispered in his ear: "It was a much happier time then. We were still innocent. I don't know if I ever can get back to that ."

"Doesn't matter, *schat* — darling," he whispered back. "Just being with you is enough for me." He continued in a regular voice. "It doesn't matter what punishments the Allies invented for your relatives. We'll help them the best we can. Don't feel bad. The war wasn't your fault. I don't blame you at all, or your relatives. Don't blame yourself."

Hendrik's generosity and his acceptance of her relatives soothed her bruised heart; he was better than she gave him credit for. Recalling his tired look after the job this morning, she said out loud, "Maybe you should lie down for a nap, dear, while you can. I'll stay with the kids and their homework, until they're finished." Not in the mood for romance, she knew he'd be asleep when she found an occasion to look in on him.

***

The end of the war didn't mean the end of all misery. People got sick from an unknown virus. In the summer of 1919, she read that this new illness had already reared its head at the end of 1917 without anybody paying enough attention to it.

She recalled getting a notice from the health department in the mail about protection, but she had thought it was a bit unnecessary, as nobody she knew was sick.

The infection rate had escalated unchecked, until 20,000 of the 200,000 Dutch soldiers fell ill, and 10,000 of them had been diagnosed with the Influenza immediately after the war ended in 1918. They had contracted the influenza from the returning American soldiers, coming through on their way home.

Johanna had indeed noticed the many soldiers coming through Holland on their way to the coast for the ships repatriating them across the Channel and across the Atlantic Ocean. The paper reported that, unaware of their illness and unprepared, these 4.7 million demobilizing American soldiers spread the virus unchecked, causing a second wave of the Influenza virus. A true epidemic swept Europe and America.

"Oh my God," she called out to an empty room. Hendrik was working on the land, and the children played outside. "How sad is this."

These poor soldiers survived the battles, but then were killed by illness, and contaminated others. How awful for their families. She read on, and read that *currently* — July, 1919 — more than 20,000 people had died in Holland as a direct result and many others were still dying indirectly from complications.

The paper pointed out the measures people could take to prevent contamination: washing hands, isolation, wearing a mask, and making sure the contaminated towels and wastes of the ill person were burnt or discarded in a place where it couldn't infect others.

Johanna went to work. She rummaged in her trunk with discarded clothes, destined for rags, and fished out suitable fabrics for sewing masks for her children. She chose some light-toned cloth — ripped and worn shirts of Hendrik's — and fashioned a variety of masks, for boys and for girls, and larger ones for herself and Hendrik, to wear when they would go out in the village.

When she showed her creations at dinner time, the children thought it hilarious and laughed at her, thinking it overwrought. She stood up from the table and grabbed the newspaper, then read to them what had struck her: "not aware of their illness and unprepared," and "more than 20,000 people had already died in Holland, and many more died as a result of complications." She also read the recommendations for prevention of the infection.

That silenced them all.

Then Henk said he had seen somebody from school with his parents in the street, who wore masks on their faces. He had wondered why and if the boy was sick. Now he understood.

"Okay, let's keep your mother happy and just do it, for now," said Hendrik. "We'll see what will happen. It can't hurt to be on the safe side." He smiled at Johanna and winked. She returned the smile, feeling indulged, but it was good of him to endorse her measures.

Then the children grabbed the mask they liked, tried them on, exchanged for another, until they had each one two masks of their choice, making Johanna grateful for having read and complied with the article.

*** 

The third wave of influenza continued, which would kill many more in the winter of 1919/1920, and many more indirectly from complicating matters. Many children and adults, already in poor condition from starvation in the war-torn regions, had no resistance. Johanna wrote frantically to Hannah, hoping for reassurances they'd all be well.

# Chapter 30

Before school began again, Johanna finalized her plan to travel to Hannover to visit her sister at the end of that last week of August 1920. Just as she was arm-deep in soap doing laundry in the kitchen, the doorbell rang. She wiped her hands on her apron and walked to the front of the house to answer the door. It was the mailman delivering a telegram. She accepted the small form, a typical beige packet, folded double in the middle, and the flap secured with a tag. It was from Hannah. She left the corridor and entered the adjacent living room as she undid the string.

She read: *Wilhelm passed away. Come to funeral on Monday.*

Her knees weak, hit by sudden grief, she took a few steps and fell on a chair. The form dropped on the floor as she tried to catch her breath, her hand pressed against her chest. "Willi, oh, Willi," she breathed softly, tears welling up and streaming freely over her cheeks. "The first of us to go. Already? How can that be?"

He had returned safely from the war in the colonies. He had been home for a while after the armistice — injured, but alive. What had happened? She dried her eyes and cheeks and decided to move up her trip and leave today.

She wished they had a telephone so she could call her sister. Only the post office had one, and rich people, of course. She decided to go out and send a telegram back to Hannah, instead of to Willi's wife, who didn't have a telephone either and now, with poverty grabbing hold of the country, wouldn't have a phone for a long time to come.

Johanna had seen the candlestick telephone, made of two pieces: a mouthpiece that stood upright and a receiver, which was placed on your ear. The minister had one, and the doctor's office used it, too. She would tell Hendrik later. As she threw her apron on a chair in the kitchen, she pushed her hair underneath a hairnet, put on her summer coat, and quickly walked to the post office. After sending the telegram of her future arrival, Johanna bought a train ticket at the station.

***

She told Hendrik at lunch time. He responded just as she'd hoped.

"Yes, do go, I'll look after the kids, and stay as long as you need, dear." Grateful for her easy-going husband, she immediately packed a bag.

On her arrival in Hannover, she took a cab to Hannah's home. She sat down with Hannah in the kitchen, both sad but dignified in their grief. After years of absence from each other's lives, it was strange to see each other again. They both had obviously aged, Hannah's hair completely grey. Johanna needed to get closer, but the table sat between them. Hannah's hand rested on the table beside a cup of coffee. Johanna put her hand on Hannah's for comfort.

"Tell me what happened, Hannah. I thought he was alright. What was his injury precisely?"

Hannah looked down, as if she had something to hide. She hesitated for a couple of seconds, then began speaking with a barely audible voice.

"I wanted to tell you face to face and didn't want to leave it to Dora. It's the least I could do for her. She has enough to do with arranging the funeral and all." Hannah exhaled, and with a wavering voice, added: "Wilhelm killed himself. He shot a bullet through his head with his army weapon, alone in the park at night."

Johanna's hand flew to her mouth to stifle a groan with the thought of how desperate he must have been to do this. "Oh, no, that can't be true. Are you sure it wasn't an accident? Why?"

Hannah ignored her and continued speaking with a monotonous voice, her eyes staring blindly at the table.

"He told Dora he wanted to get some fresh air and left for a walk. The police found him the following morning. Dora had already found his note on his desk in the evening, and knew he would be dead, but she didn't know where he'd be. An early walker stumbled on his body and reported it on his way back into town. Their children were staying the night with their friends, fortunately, but of course had been unable to say goodbye to their Vati."

Johanna pressed her sister's hand on the table with force, as if her heartfelt empathy could be conveyed physically.

Hannah pulled her hand back. With a faraway look, she softly said: "He couldn't live with the treaty conditions, all the sacrifices made for nothing, *a complete humiliation*, he wrote on the note. Besides, he had terrible headaches. His left leg was bothering him as well, amputated below the knee. I think he was shell-shocked. He couldn't sleep, was a terribly strict father to his children, and often screamed at Dora. I am, well, of course not exactly *satisfied*, but at peace with his decision. He had no life, and neither had his family, Johanna." She finally focused on Johanna and held steady under her sister's gaze.

Wide-eyed, her heart thumping and afraid to be overwhelmed by sadness, Johanna swallowed the rest of her coffee in one gulp. "I need something stronger. Do you have any schnapps?"

***

Later that day, Johanna went to see Dora. It was a visit without many words between them: there simply was nothing to say. Johanna promised she and Hendrik would help Dora financially if needed and asked her to just let her know what they'd need. Johanna had to get used to calling her little brother Wilhelm. He was Willi to her. He had married shortly after he enlisted, and it didn't take long for the children to arrive, who were over fifteen now. They could work, if there was any.

"It will get better when the country is rebuilt. It'll have to be better," Dora insisted with her head held high. Johanna had no reply.

***

The funeral took place a couple of days later with a simple, short service in the church followed by the burial in the family plot. It was a sunny, gorgeous fall day. During the ceremony, Johanna's thoughts perseverated on one line: *Willi personified Germany,* like a mantra for finding meaning in his death, and to keep herself from crying and losing her control. Willi *was* Germany, his inability to live with its shame so German.

She wanted to shout out how foolish the German honor is, how it got her brother killed, how war kills everybody, even if they survive, and how it devasted the people colonized, like her Ur-Opa and her grandfather, and ultimately, also her Vati. Willi's act broke her heart. Her little brother, whom she was supposed to protect. She had failed him.

Johanna returned the next day on the train depressed, off and on weeping in her carriage as it sped through the landscape. She didn't care if fellow passengers looked at her with curiosity or with sympathy.

***

In sharing with Hendrik what happened in Hanover, Johanna discovered she had one other worry left. "I wonder what will become of my brother August's sons. Those two also served in the navy, and they're young. They fudged their ages when they enlisted. I hope they'd be all right."

Hendrik shook his head.

"Dear, they're not yours to worry about. Anyway, those boys are of a different generation, and they weren't stuck in the trenches, like the infantry. Willi's job must have been horrible for Willi, dug in and not being able to move for years under all that heavy fire. You'll see: August's boys will bounce back. I hope Germany learned her lesson now."

She nodded. "I hope so too," she whispered, having little energy left, feeling exhausted by grief.

***

When the Deutsche Mark devaluated and the Weimar government kept printing more money, the meager savings people still might have had in the bank evaporated as the Mark lost its value. Johanna almost couldn't stand reading Hannah's letters describing the disasters her sisters and brothers suffered, all documented in crisp, factual terms in her beautiful, cursive handwriting, the political unrest and the violence in the streets shocking Johanna to her core. The young republic defaulted on its reparation payments, and French troops occupied the Ruhr area, cutting off the one source of German income, in fact incapacitating Germany's ability to repay the massive debt. People were demonstrating and fights broke out in the streets between opponents.

Even her eldest sister, Rieke, wrote Johanna in her cynical way about the newest trend in decorating: *Deutschen Marks* on the walls — cheaper than wallpaper. It was a bit more work pasting them down one by one, but without jobs, time was plenty.

Johanna chuckled at first, then broke down in tears. She cried and cried, not only for her siblings, but also for herself and her affiliation with disaster, her own skewed dreams, lost and alienated in a strange land. For her country, she cried, which she couldn't even claim as hers. Until the children came home.

# Chapter 31

Following the lead of the new German republic, Holland — more correctly called The Netherlands — instated voting rights for women to Johanna's delight. Encouraged by Hendrik, she formally applied for Dutch citizenship and had the children added to her Dutch passport. She could now vote but hadn't felt comfortable enough with that weird, multi-party system to cast her vote. She hoped for a long peace to educate herself on Dutch politics. Becoming a citizen was hard work, and learning about Hendrik's people and the nation kept her busy, never mind being a farmer's wife and getting her children through school and launched into the world.

She didn't mind that her children became naturalized citizens through the influence of the education system and the loving guidance in the embrace of Hendrik's relatives. This was their country, and it was a good, peaceful place. As their life continued in peace, the children grew up and finished their education.

\*\*\*

As soon as she turned sixteen, Frieda left for the urban west and found a great, liberal employer to work for as a family housekeeper. Her mistress didn't mind Frieda continuing working after her marriage. Johanna applauded both Frieda and her employer, treasuring her own past as an independent, *married* entrepreneur on the train.

Johan took a job with Shell in the Caribbean and left the country. Not long after, he wrote he had married, and helped in his spare time on his mother-in-law's dairy farm. Hendrik and Johanna were both pleased that after his less-than-ambitious efforts in childhood, Johan landed the job, and got himself an enterprising wife and a mother-in-law. Johanna dreamed about traveling overseas and meeting them one day. Hendrik didn't, happy to stay put.

As she had hoped for her son, Henk indeed went on after high school into higher education at a technical school and found himself a job as the fire chief in a village nearby. He married a local girl. Johanna liked the gentle soul, although she was quiet and hard to get to know. Henk was his usual smart-alecky self and confident. Johanna was very proud of him.

Klara entered nurses training, and her education completed, got hired by a newfangled institution for the insane. Although Hendrik was a protective dad and worried about attacks by the asylum's aggressive patients, in Johanna's eyes, it was a perfect job for her daughter, and fit her caring skills and interest in serving others. Of course, Klara stopped working when she married Jacob, a military policeman, like all respectable husbands and employers demanded of a wife. Johanna thought it was a shame to let the training go to waste. She would've been willing and able to look after her grandchildren with Klara at work.

***

All the children were married off now, except Robert, still a bachelor and living at home. After completing the same high school as his brother Henk, the H.B.S., he stayed to help on the farm. He had inherited his father's knack for mechanical work and could fix anything around the farm that needed fixing. For Johanna and Hendrik, who both completely adored their gentle son, it was a boon to have Robert still around, as Hendrik was getting old.

Klara was protective as ever, unable to cast off her old role as Robert's second mother. When he was sweet on a particular girl his mother didn't approve of, Klara made sure Johanna knew. Johanna told Robert what she wanted from him in her way that didn't leave him an option. "Her family is a godless bunch. They have no standards. You deserve better. That's all I want to say about it."

Robert didn't have the guts to stand up to his mother and continued seeing Lizzy without telling her. His father on the other hand would try to convince Johanna to stop interfering with Robert's choices, and Johanna only nodded. When she had Robert alone later, she would nag him with questions about still seeing *that girl.*

As Johanna thwarted Robert's love life, his siblings Henk, Frieda, and Klara had their first babies — all three, sons. A delighted and gentle grandmother, singing German songs, Johanna enjoyed her role very much, all-the-more because the daily burden of caring and the mundane tasks were no longer hers. In a quiet moment, she reflected on her children having all boys: Mother Nature making a start with replacing the men, lost in the previous decade.

***

Johanna saw her dear Hendrik falter in health and worried about him, accompanying him everywhere he went, for fear he'd get into physical trouble alone. He had prematurely aged, his body bent from calcium deficiencies and hard work that wore out his vertebrae, like a willow tree under steady westerly winds. He occasionally suffered severe backaches and frequently ran out of breath. All his children felt compelled to help him with the hay harvest, and they took turns among them with the other work.

Hendrik had already stopped growing other crops, as it was too labor intensive. The cow was gone, and only a few pigs and the chickens were left. The harvest was left to rot in the orchard as nobody had time to pick the fruit. And of course, the old horse. Without Bles and the buggy, Johanna and Hendrik couldn't visit the children and their families. Only the rich possessed motorcars and the Zondervans were only moderately self-sufficient. Besides, it would break both their hearts to surrender Bles to the glue factory. The faithful mare could live out her life for as long as it lasted.

In the following year, when Hendrik came home exhausted from plowing the field together with Robert on this one particularly dreary spring day, Johanna told him.

"Hendrik, why don't you quit the farm, dear. It's too much work for you," she pleaded. "Sell the land, retire, and we'll just enjoy our old age in peace and quiet in town." She put a cup of tea in front of him. It was too early for the schnapps. "Shall I put the kettle on for a bath, *Schatz*," she asked gently.

He took his cap off, sighed, and stroked his head, still with the full mop of now-silver hair.

"Ahhh, what will I do without work? I need something to do, Johanna, or I will fade away. Yes, a bath would do my old bones good. Thank you. I will stop work early for the weekend."

As she got up and walked to the door, Johanna said: "Will you join me if I pour us a sherry?"

Hendrik shook his head. "That's a woman's drink. You know, just for today, give me a shot of the brandy. I feel a bit under the weather. It'll cure me."

Johanna disappeared to the kitchen. She put two galvanized canning tubs on the stove and filled them with a small saucepan. Then she reached for the top cabinet in the pantry, got the two bottles out, walked back to the living room, grabbed two glasses out of her pride and joy — the fancy highboy cabinet — and poured them each a drink. She scrutinized Hendrik as she handed him his glass of brandy. He seemed even paler than before. She took off her apron and sat down on the two-seater across from him.

"Isn't Klara's boy a cute baby," she began, worried about him but eager to distract herself, and him.

"*Ja, ja,* he's a strappy lad for a one-year-old. Can't sit still, just like his grandpa," Hendrik smiled, but it looked more like a grimace. "I think I've overdone the plowing today. Will you call Robert for me? I need to see him."

Robert worked outside in the orchard, trimming fruit trees. When Johanna returned with him to the room, Hendrik was stretched out on the floor, breathing shallowly and his eyes closed, and his drink untouched on the table.

"Go fetch Doctor Johansen," cried Johanna as she kneeled beside Hendrik. She slid her arm underneath his head and scared to death, began kissing his face.

"Hendrik, don't leave me, please, don't leave me yet. It's too early," she sobbed, but he didn't reply. She then got hold of herself and began to rhythmically push down on his chest with clenched fists, until the doctor arrived.

"I'll take over from here," he said, and grabbed Johanna by the shoulders, helped her to her feet, and pushed her aside. The doctor didn't resume chest compressions. He put his stethoscope on Hendrik's chest and listened for ten seconds. Looking at Johanna, he asked, "How long have you been doing this resuscitation, *Mevrouw* Zondervan?"

She was exhausted from panic but working on Hendrik's chest had calmed her. Before she answered, Johanna grabbed both drinks, still on the table, and emptied each in one gulp. She looked at Robert. "How long were you gone for?"

"Fifteen, twenty minutes, tops." Robert was sweating hard, drops collected on his forehead, his face distorted with worry.

Johanna already knew what the doctor said next: a massive heart attack had killed Hendrik on this Friday afternoon. Hendrik had just turned sixty-four. Robert and the doctor carried Hendrik's body to the bedroom. After the doctor had left, Johanna went to him and sobbed, giving her grief free reign. Sitting on the edge of the bed next to Hendrik, all her grief when her Vati had died flooded over her, as Robert waited in the kitchen for the hearse to arrive.

\*\*\*

Hendrik was laid out for viewing at the funeral home. The custom of the wake at home was not in fashion anymore, said Robert. He had checked the bank and assured Johanna, to her relief, that there was enough in the bank to pay for the funeral. Robert took care of the obituary in the local paper.

The children arrived in the early afternoon with three babies. Frieda and Klara would stay with Johanna the night before the funeral. Henk owned an automobile and would return with his wife and son to their home that night, not far from Hardenberg, and return for the funeral the next day. Johan wasn't able to make it on short notice from Curaçao.

As Johanna prepared herself for the final goodbye to her kind companion, she didn't show her grief and seemed in control, although her heart was broken. She couldn't see how she could go on living without Hendrik, or if it was worth it. To distract herself, she held the babies in turns and rhythmically soothed the occasionally crying grandchild in her expert arms until she could hand the child over to his mother, sleeping and ready to be put in his basket.

In her competent and calm manner, she gave her children her directions for prepping the food according to her reception plans. Hendrik had a large family. Although most of his elder siblings had already passed on, the nephews and nieces living in town would undoubtedly attend.

Hannah wrote a telegram with the message that she, unfortunately, had no opportunity to come down, lacking the funds. Johanna understood. Hannah's husband was out of work and, getting on in years now, likely wouldn't get another job. She thanked Johanna for the gifts: a crate of fruit and the ham Johanna had sent the family. Rieke sent her condolences.

***

After everything was over, and Hendrik was laid to rest in their newly acquired family plot, Johanna had a schnapps in the kitchen with Robert.

"*Jetzt musst du die ganze Arbeit für die Bauernhof alleine machen.* Now you have to do everything by yourself," Johanna said flatly. She added after a few seconds, "I will pay you more for the harvest work."

He stayed silent.

She prodded a bit more. "What do you think?"

Robert shrugged, and said, "It's not that much, just some hay crops and the orchard. Vater already plowed the field. I just have to seed the new alfalfa field before the first frost."

Although she knew she should follow her own advice — only a few days ago expressed to Hendrik — she wasn't ready to sell the land. She hadn't had enough years together with her beloved husband to enjoy the fruits of their labor. If she kept him alive in her mind, he was still here. Hanging on was a magic trick to make it happen.

"I don't know, Mutti," Robert said. "Do you want to keep the farm, or sell it? The land may increase in value, but if you sell it now, you'll have some extra money to live off."

Johanna doubted that Robert could share his honest opinion about the best option, always with a woman telling him what to do. He was waiting for her to give him the tasks she wanted him to complete. She just could not utter the words herself: *sell the land*. She expected him to make that decision for her, feeling weak and her solidity dislodged. The years fell heavy on her, like a winter coat of inferior quality. It was going to be a horrible winter.

***

Three years later, Robert was still unmarried, the son left behind to care for his mother. Johanna had gradually learned to live without Hendrik, still missing him every day, but not quite as sorely. Having Robert at home helped to do distract her from her loneliness. They had settled into a comfortable routine. Although he would not discuss things as Hendrik had, he had so many of the qualities she had appreciated in Hendrik, his calm and even character, his gentle humor, the skills, and clear affection for her that she settled for the life she did have with Robert.

She had rented out half of the house across the shared corridor, modified with a new kitchen, for a bit of income and Robert had found casual work as a mechanic. He had claimed the attic for himself. Whenever extra money was needed, Johanna sold a small piece of land, and selling the hay, and the apples also helped in addition to leasing land to other farmers. She still had the chickens and sold two-thirds of the eggs. Bles had finally laid her head down and died. Robert had somebody take the carcass away. Johanna counted on Robert for almost everything.

# Chapter 32

The German army had surrendered in 1918, one year after Johanna had escaped to Holland with her family. After a good twenty years, the German soldiers caught up with her in the spring of 1940. The intervening two decades of raising and launching her children and of being a grandmother had blunted the earlier pain, associated with her German identity. She had a calm and peaceful life with her favorite son close by.

In the meantime, the Germany Empire had become the Weimar Republic, based on new ideals, including a good life for the common man. Johanna thought it was going to be a country somewhat like Holland, but less wealthy, as they still had a big debt to pay off. However, what she heard from Hannah and Rieke was nothing like it. They had nothing, and every penny was taken by the state for taxes, to pay off the massive debts of the country. They had nothing, but luckily, the stores didn't offer much temptation to spend their money on, as the shelves were bare.

Rieke's bitter letters and Hannah's overly optimistic ones made Johanna feel helpless. Remembering Hendrik's harsh words about the German nature did not help, although she hoped that this time, Germany would find a way to peacefully find her way out of trouble.

She had plenty of time to read again: anything and everything she could lay her hands on. Johanna feared the new calamity brewing. With one in three workers unemployed, the German people had no trust left in any government, and her sisters sounded at their wit's end. Hannah, always trying to be positive, wrote that the National-Socialist German Labor Party with Adolph Hitler promised wealth and stability for the common man, and an end to exploitation by the Allied. Hannah's husband had signed up to their party, like many others.

In Johanna's view, Hitler's promise was impossible, an oxymoron. The common man — wealthy? This leader had been in jail earlier for participating in a *putsch* in 1923: a coup to topple the government, but that was all forgiven now. She worried that the appeal of the national-socialist party — Nazi for short — was based on a fata morgana, the people believing him delusional. Especially when Adolph Hitler ascended to power in 1933, she knew the dream would have to collapse, but Hannah believed him.

Hanna wrote, *Now he's everybody's hero. He said, it's time to stop paying and work for ourselves. He gave the order to the Ruhr industry to start producing weapons. We're growing a real army now.*

Johanna wished Hendrik was around to tell her the truth. No new negotiations about paying the reparations had been announced. She was scared and hoped that her relatives were wrong. Something was not right.

When German soldiers entered the Sudetenland in March of 1939 — the borderland of the former German-Austrian areas — Johanna had been convinced that was wrong. She knew that after the Peace Treaty in what was now Slavic-speaking Czechoslovakia, the ethnic Germans in that area lived under protest. When those German-speakers welcomed the Wehrmacht troops with waving flags, and no sanctions followed the annexation, she was confused. Was that by consent? Had the Weimar government truly made a deal with those formerly German regions to join *das Deutsche Reich?*

The Dutch newspapers predicted that after Sudetenland, Hitler's armies would target Poland next for annexation. They called Sudetenland's annexation an *invasion*. In that same Peace Treaty of Versailles, in which Czechoslovakia became independent, Poland had regained its independence. Johanna knew the Polish were proud to have their own nation once again, her Vati's wish, who didn't live to see that so many years later.

Indeed, Germany invaded Poland the following year in 1939. Johanna was distressed and utterly conflicted. That was not right. Did the Polish want them to come in and unite, just like Hannah wrote? That couldn't be true.

She bought the newspaper and got more upset every day. The Polish army battled for their freedom with German troops at the border. The Polish communities in Germany demonstrated loudly against the invasion. When the German troops — significantly more robust than the Polish army — won, she had a good cry. She had nobody to talk about it. Robert was all for the German army, and Hannah too.

Since then, Johanna worried. Her nights became mostly sleepless or dreams turned into nightmares, and she became quiet, although she couldn't pinpoint exactly what was bothering her so much. She wanted to understand whether the German invasion of Poland was as bad as it sounded. She heard that civilians and soldiers had been shot in the streets indiscriminately, a brutal slaughter, it had been. What was their excuse? Her father's belief that Germans hated the Polish came back to her. Had he been right?

***

A year went by. On April 10, 1940, the radio news announced the presence of German aircraft over the Netherlands, moving west. Ever since, it was mayhem on the airwaves. Johanna couldn't listen anymore to the overexcited voices of the reporters broadcasting their screeching news. *Gott im Himmel, hilf mir.* May God help us. She buried herself in the kitchen with work.

Johanna couldn't escape Robert, who burst into the kitchen, shouting, "German troops have crossed the border, and they're bombing the western cities." His eyes sparkled and he had rosy cheeks from excitement.

Johanna stayed silent and continued peeling potatoes, eyes on her hands. She was German. What did this mean? Are the Germans invading Holland now? No please, let it not be true. It would spoil everything. Then she had to support the German soldiers, be true to her country, against Hendrik and his people.

"The Dutch border troops were unable to stop the Wehrmacht. They'll be here within the hour, Mutter!"

Indeed, not an hour later the facts overwhelmed her.

***

No fighting took place in Hardenberg. Standing in front of their homes, most of her neighbors and Johanna — on trembling legs — watched the German tanks with their white, double-lined crosses over their hulking metal bodies thundering through their street. The cavalry followed, and many, many wagons and lorries with supplies and more soldiers passed in the street.

Nobody cheered, and the silent bystanders wore their shock, anger, and hostility on their faces. Seeing the familiar uniforms, and absorbing the shouted commands' language, Johanna didn't know whether to cry or laugh. She liked the Germans, she was German, and she welcomed them, but she didn't dare ignore the neighbors and all other Dutch folk standing here with angry faces, some crying openly, and the atmosphere of fear and sadness struck her hard.

# Chapter 33

As she stood with the Dutch in her street, she felt an alien, an enemy. Her body vibrated from the heavy equipment and their engines. Her mind worked frantically trying to determine how she felt or didn't feel, and what she should do. The noise overwhelmed her.

The German winners marched in front of her through the street chests puffed. Tears blurred her vision. Memories blew in like a bad storm, battering her with the lessons learned from her childhood years in the German Empire. The message hit home: it was smarter to choose the side of the winners. In an almost forgotten lifetime, she completely and intentionally assumed her identity as German, *not* Slavic-German, or German-Polish. Identity was just a different coat you put on as the seasons change. After their move to Holland, it was convenient to be a Dutch citizen but she had never *felt* Dutch.

With the children growing up, she'd been too busy *living* to keep up emotionally with all political news about Germany. When she got more time and started reading again, her eyes were going, and reading wasn't the joy it once was. She had to wear thick lenses to be able to see anything close up, her vision virtually shot. If it wasn't for her children, who wouldn't let her stay ignorant of the news and told her religiously what went on in the world, she wouldn't know much. Mildly interested in Germany, she'd been indifferent to the foreign nature of the political developments in Hendrik's country. The recent British and French declarations of war on Germany had awakened her latent interest, only a week after the third anniversary of Hendrik's passing.

As she wept, standing in the street, the earth's tremors from the heavy equipment gradually dissipated under her feet. She recalled it all now: the bodily sensations shook something loose, deep inside her. She remembered that third anniversary of Hendrik's death as if it was yesterday, in early late July 1939. Even the children who lived out of the region had visited her, knowing the anniversary was an important day for their mother, who still missed their father very much.

She listened to the discussions between her sons and son-in-law at coffee time. "As long as they don't invade us, we will stay neutral, just like last time," Henk, her educated son had said in his self-assured way, leaving no room for doubt. Jacob, Klara's husband, the military policeman, said he wasn't sure about that. "The Germans have proven not very reliable in keeping to their peace treaties," Jacob said. Jacob sounded like Hendrik.

Johanna had listened to their arguments about power, territory, and glory, and the Prussians' fame for their battle savvy. Henk thought that the Germans were still trying to emulate the feat of the Holy Roman Empire. "They already consider our country part of their Reich, so hardly a need to invade it. Just to put a pine fine point on it, they might invade us anyway, just to make sure," he scoffed. Robert stayed quiet through those discussions. It had been a familiar sound, this political debate. Johanna couldn't resist commenting then: "Dear Heinrich, you sound just like my father." But he had ignored her all the same.

Johanna could hear *Vati's* voice now, telling her that Europe had seen two centuries of continuous tribal warfare in the century before his birth. His Pomeranian homeland changed hands many times before this got absorbed into the unified German Empire. The hunter for power was a ravenous monster, indeed.

She recalled Robert's confession at the dinner table, just one day later. "Mutter, I joined the National Socialist Party. What do you think?" Shocked that her Dutch son would join the German-style party, so hated by most Dutchmen, she didn't know what to reply. She noticed the German *Mutter* and concluded he wanted her blessing. As she formulated a reply, he kept watching her. She paused, squeezing both hands together in her lap under the table, and with a voice full of anxiety she replied with a question: "Why?"

Not waiting for an answer, she shot up, put the dirty dishes in a dishpan, and put the kettle on as she muttered, *I'm too old for all of this.* Upset and confused, she avoided him the rest of that week and wouldn't resume the conversation. Her father had been sympathetic to the socialists, but she doubted that the national socialists were true socialists. She knew they didn't want the best for *everyone,* leaving out the Jews, the Polish, the Slavs, and any other easterners. She'd better make up her mind what she thought.

***

When the tanks were gone from the streets, Johanna looked for Robert as she dried her eyes. She wanted to know what had happened to the *Kaiser.* Was he the one who had ordered this? He couldn't have. Then she remembered: when Germany established the Weimar Republic after the end of the war, the Empire ended too, and the Kaiser was kicked out. His Excellency lived in exile at the mercy of Queen Wilhelmina, somewhere in Holland.

She went to the kitchen, grabbed the sherry and poured herself a good measure in a lemonade glass. She needed the drink to revive her. Then she put the presence of the German soldiers in context. All of last year, Johanna had listened to the lively radio speeches of their new leader, Adolph Hitler. He had meant what he said.

When Johanna's ability to read began to fade when Hendrik was still alive, he bought the radio at a competitive price in the depression. Nobody had any money for radios. Luckily, the couple didn't have much money left in savings and lost very little in the crash. Hendrik's land purchases ate up most of their savings from the State Railway.

A benefit of living close to the border was receiving German radio programs. She tuned in mostly to those stations and heard the speeches of that Hitler character and she could understand why he swept people up in his dramatic rallies. As she entered the house, the radio was still on. The radio's excited voices bothered her. The Dutch voices were upset. She switched stations.

The German radio had no reports or programs and played only classical music for some reason. She needed a breather and turned it off. The smell of gasoline from the German vehicles had penetrated her house. She opened a window and the front door for a draft to clear the bad smell. Just then, Robert came home and entered the kitchen through the back door, flushed and sweaty.

"I heard about the tanks rolling in and just caught up with them at the edge of town. I came home to see how you're doing, Mutti. What a show. Did you see that display of German might? Fantastic." His voice sounded excited, and his ordinarily cautious eyes shone.

Johanna couldn't react, caught between what Hendrik would say and responding to her son's glee. Her own German blood wanted to be proud, but she knew it was not right to invade a country. She had to protect her own position in this town. Best to get more information first.

Her voice wavered when she asked, "Robert, everybody here knows I'm German. My father and grandfather left their homes because of discrimination against Polish speakers. What do Dutch people say about the Germans, son?"

"I haven't heard much. They say to wait and see what the Germans are up to, mostly."

He tried to calm her. It was hard to know what Robert really thought. Maybe it was too late to educate him about her own past. She should try anyway. The more he knew, the better he'd be able to make up his mind. She wouldn't be around forever and couldn't protect him forever. She took a big swallow from her glass.

"Stay in your seat, *Junge*. I'll tell you a tale."

Obediently, Robert sat down at the kitchen table across from Johanna.

"I never told you this, but my great-grandfather Heinrich Münzke was the royal shoemaker in Poznan for Prince Radziwill and his daughters." She told him the abbreviated story of her father's family, the strive, the poverty, the ethnic discrimination, the rebellion, and the moves to better lives.

Robert's raised brows and his tilted head inspecting her closely expressed doubt. Then he asked, "Why are you telling me this now? What does that have to do with anything?"

"Not long after my father was born, Germany joined with the eastern regions of Prussia and became one country. When he moved to Osterode, everything got easier for him in greater Germany. Life is never without difficulties. I'm just saying,

Germany taking over Holland might prove to be a good thing for everybody in the end. Unfortunately, my Vati died before he saw the improvements."

She left out details of the nasty parts of that life to make her point. It had been inconsequential to her anyway. At the time, she had utterly enjoyed the indifference of her age and only saw a bright future beckoning her. She hadn't been interested in her father's opinions back then. She was too young.

"You're preaching to the choir, *Moeder*," Robert brusquely said.

He used the Dutch word, creating distance. It hurt her feelings, but she understood this to be an exciting time for him, and he apparently wanted to enjoy it, the German tribal brothers coming in to show the Dutch how it's done.

Suddenly it struck her that she should be happy that Hendrik wasn't around to see his son siding with the Germans. He would've hated it. He called Germans *war-hungry*, and: *have no talent for peace.*

Robert waved his hand dismissing her and continued, "I don't want to hear about the past. That time is gone. We're living in a different world now and marching towards a new future. Is there anything else you want to tell me?"

Suddenly her father's tale about Marx and Wagner popped up in Johanna's mind. Her gentle and smart father had explained the quintessential class conflict in a nutshell. Just before she was born, two famous peers had died, who'd been spiritual opposites. If she'd been a boy, he'd have named her after one of them: Karl. The Jew, Karl Marx developed Marxism, meaning to liberate the working class. Richard Wagner composed the famous Nibelungen Ring — a four-opera heroic spectacle — catering to the rich German elite creating the myth of a super race.

The metaphor hadn't meant anything to her then. Now it all came back to her, a lifetime later. She realized he meant to tell her that the rich knew about the existing poverty among the common people — their servants — but knowingly exploited them. Wealthy men cannot exist without the exploitation of the working classes. Wagner's Nibelungen Ring had become Hitler's favorite entertainment.

Yes, she reminded herself to choose wisely. She sighed and feeling rattled, wished her nerves would settle, and the thoughts of her father didn't help. The

squealing sounds of metal-on-metal and the droning from the tanks still reverberated in her body. In Germany, unaware as a child, she witnessed the battle between
socialism and capitalism, which intensified *after* she left the country with her Hendrik. It had followed her here, into *die Nederlände. Verdammt!*

In safe Holland, she had been living in ignorance and didn't know it. Now her
son had chosen the German side — national socialists. Vati always had sympathy
for the Polish socialists — the rebels. Both were socialists, but the Nazis didn't
sound like Vati. Hitler despised many Germans and was hard on ethnic people.
Still, he sounded good, his promises seductive. It was too hard to distinguish the
truth in politicians' statements, and they often lie anyway. She could cry but was
also aware of her son's admiration for *her* people. Anxiety and uncertainty made
her hypersensitive, and she remembered the condition of a perpetual upset: as if
she'd never left Zeeven.

# Chapter 34

That day, Johanna prepared lunch early. It was ready on the counter on a board as she sat at the table. When Robert asked her something, she became aware he had been staring at her.

"Well, Mutter, are we going to have lunch?"

Johanna, woken up so rudely from her thoughts, got up.

"I just want to know what the Dutch think about the German army coming here. Could you find out, *lieber Sohn*, dear son? Do they hate the Germans' arrival, or are there many like you who think it's fine? I want to put my neighbors at rest. They've got nothing to fear from our family."

She put the sandwiches on plates and took them to the table. She got the milk can from the cellar, climbing the few steps with difficulty. She poured two mugs and put them next to the plates. Bone-tired, she sat down heavily across from Robert.

He had already dug in and with a mouth full of bread, asked, "What do you mean, *Mutter*? Of course, we're no danger to anyone. We're a Dutch family. Did you forget? Besides, the Germans are here to do us some good."

Johanna thought a couple of seconds about what would be acceptable in her son's eyes and then decided to share more of her shady genealogy.

"Although my parents always spoke German at home and in public, I was well aware of our Polish-sounding name. My ancestors hadn't succeeded in throwing off the Polish scent, even after they changed their name to Münzke. I always wished it had been Müller instead."

The unusual reflective tone in his mother's voice caught Robert's attention. He looked at her and scanned her face intently.

She looked back at him, holding his stare, unsure what he was thinking, and then asked, "What do you think?'

Robert replied. "Couldn't they be just German, and be happy? Who cares, anyway. In Holland nobody cares about you as a German or a Dutch woman either. You can be whatever you want to be." He shrugged again and returned to eating.

Johanna had a revelation: her son's casual attitude towards her identity was proof that her childhood resolution had worked, she belonged to the winners' circle, just like her siblings in Germany. She was right for shedding the Slavic part, which had helped all her siblings become true, respected citizens of the German Empire, when they needed to be.

Marrying a Dutchman and becoming a *Dutch* citizen after the move made her life in *Holland* respectable. Her children were German by birth and Dutch citizens by choice. She had left the country but strangely enough, the Germans had joined her in Holland. It was a crazy world.

She weighed her old, firmly held beliefs. Were these still even relevant? Her only goal was to protect her children. Should she be moving on, like her smart son? She was old. Her children were adults and could make up their own minds. There was no need to hide what would come naturally to her: to be German.

*** 

Robert finished eating, shoved his plate away and stretched his arms with folded hands behind his head, studying his mother's face.

"Dear son, will you now have to fight in the war?"

He lowered his arms, put his hands on the table, and straightened his back and chuckled.

"*Ach, Mutter,* of course not. I only joined the Dutch National Socialist Party of Mussert, not the German army, and no, I won't join *any* army. Mussert is popular. The party is not in the government yet, but with the back-up of the Germans, it just may be a matter of time before we'll join the governing coalition." He sounded patient, indulging his mom in her ignorance.

An unpleasant thought pierced Johanna's mind. Usually, she could hold off from the impulse to express her opinion until she had gathered a fact or two. Not this time. She got up, fists balled, her face flushed. In a shrill voice, she shouted: "I get it now. You joined because that girl is a member. Don't deny it. I know I'm right. Say it, say it. I dare you."

Robert shot up from his chair and faced his mom. Unable to hold her gaze, he looked away and swallowed hard before replying with a question in a soft voice.

"Mutti, does it matter?" It sounded like a complaint. He sighed deeply, then sat down, and defended his decision, his tone reasonable, suppressing any anger he might have held.

"We bumped into each other everywhere in town without even trying. And why shouldn't I join a popular organization of active people? So many have joined already. If I do what you want me to do and avoid Lizzy, I might as well leave town. Is that what you want?"

His threat hit home. She heard the words *leave town,* and the fear of losing him escalated to panic. Forcing calmness, she replied in a gentle voice of reason.

"That family, I told you about them. I only meant to warn you, dear boy. That girl has a reputation for not being selective with her favors. You can do much better. You're a handsome and smart man from a good family."

His frown and his hostile eyes told her he wasn't having any of it.

She pleaded: "I only want what's best for you, *mein Junge,* my boy."

Robert turned around, and as he stomped out of the kitchen, he said over his shoulder: "Is our family so great? You're a German. You had a reason to ask me how the Dutch feel about the Germans: you're feeling guilty. You must know that I as the son of a *mof* am no prize to any Dutch girl, believe me, Mother." He slammed the backdoor shut behind him.

Johanna got up, as contradictory thoughts tumbled through her head. She had wanted to scream *schluss jetzt,* stop now, and cut off his arguments, but it was too late to assert her authority.

Her son's words cut into the depths of her soul: her identity. Her children perceived her as German. Yet, out of Robert's mouth, it sounded like a rebuke. He

had switched on a dime to being a Dutchman, his father's son, taking on the hate
the Dutch have for the Germans, just to hurt her, no, worse: to protect this girl,
and was so much like her: conflicted.

What in God's name had come over Robert, usually so obedient and sweet? He
must really like this woman. Her demand to abandon the woman only pushed him
away and made him more tenacious in his pursuit of this tramp. Straight-up or-
dering him to forget about her hadn't worked. She must find a different tactic.

She relaxed her shoulders, breathed deeply, and sat back down at the table,
arms hanging beside her. Her head tilted back, looking at the ceiling without seeing, she let her mind wander. All her childhood, she yearned to be a member of
the ruling elite, a member of a well-functioning society of educated people invok-
ing the world's envy. Here, in Hendrik's town, when she thought she'd finally
achieved that status, she had become a nasty Dutch epithet for a German: *mof,* a
Hun.

She wondered what Hendrik would say. She missed him, his calm demeanor,
and his simple, wise views. He didn't need to gather all there was to know from
newspapers and magazines to make up his mind. He knew instinctively what was
right. *Sehnsucht* — a yearning — for him overwhelmed her, for his arm around
her, his soft voice. Johanna sat there for a long time, reminiscing, losing track of
reality as tears streamed silently over her cheeks and dripped on the waxed-cotton
table cover.

After a while, her eyes dried up. At least Hendrik wasn't here to witness his
beloved country become invaded. They had escaped the previous war's bad ending
together and landed softly in his hometown. He passed away in the satisfaction of
having provided well for her and their children. A sense of relief that he wasn't
present for her shame overtook her. She just *had* to believe that Germany would
improve life for the better, just like Robert said. She needed another dream to go
on living. She couldn't help but think of her father, who hadn't lived to see West
Pomerania established as the independent Free State of Prussia with the Weimar
Republic, and, next to it, East Prussia as the Second Polish Republic. But neither
did he have to witness yet another German invasion: Pomerania, overrun by the

Nazis, was just like Holland, *die Niederlände*: another strategic land on an important coast.

And here she was on foreign soil, her father's daughter. Like him, she had left her home to ensure a better future for her children. Much like Germany to her dad, *die Niederlände* hadn't become her home, only a host country. Just like her, Vati had left his heart behind in Pomerania, and her heart was still in Germany.

Johanna knew from Hannah's letters that Germans had a tough time, but fifteen years later, things had improved. Everybody said Hitler had set the economy back on its feet. That he also increased his troops in contravention of the Versailles treaty, enlarging the army with the newest equipment, boosting the economy, surely was forgivable. Like Hitler said: Germany had paid its dues. The factories thrived, and people weren't hungry anymore. Optimism for the future had enveloped them all. Johanna was happy for her siblings.

Hannah enthusiastically had told her that the Ruhr land was humming with activity. The new leadership had successfully beat the massive unemployment from the time of the Weimar Republic. Since he was named Chancellor, informally called the Leader, *Der Führer* had done an excellent job. It sounded like both Rieke and Hannah were behind the Nazis. Hitler had used the new constitution to get hold of the chaos by terminating all reparations to the Allies, outlawing all other political parties and instating punishment for the revolutionaries and the communists. All had been good in *im Vaterland*.

Hannah's reports gave Johanna the confidence to trust Robert and his political sense. Robert was a smart man, even if he let that woman wrap him around her little finger — forgivable. After all, like most men, he was vulnerable to a woman's wiles, especially those of a determined one; she would know. She chuckled at the memory of courting Hendrik. She would let Robert be.

Johanna straightened her back, stretched her arms and relaxed her fists. She got up and started cleaning the kitchen. If she didn't want to drive him into that tramp's arms and leave his mother, she had better support her son from now on.

# Chapter 35

Robert and Johanna decided to ramp up the sales of farm products: eggs, cream, butter, firewood, hay feed for horses, straw for matrasses and animal bedding, and whatever else the fields could produce. They even purchased a few more piglets and a cow and Robert hired some help to plant extra potatoes and carrots. He replaced the late Bles with a new, four-year-old horse. Johanna had a plan: to supply the army with her services and goods from the farm. Most was already rationed.

The government had also rationed the scarce cream and butter, to be sold only with stamps, subsequently always in short supply, so Johanna never had an issue selling these on the side. Even if you managed to get some of the butter ration stamps, it was a problem to find shops to exchange those for the real thing.

She and Robert divided the work: for Robert was the labor, and as the brains of the enterprise, she took on the management. She found a motorized washing machine for an excellent price, and a wringer, which Robert attached to a wooden frame. She took in laundry and hired a woman for the work. When they had everything in place, Johanna told Robert to take her to Klara's town and to the Wehrmacht headquarters, practically next door to her.

***

The soldiers in town behaved politely, considerate even. Johanna was proud of the *Soldaten*, and pride welled in her heart as she encountered the dapper uniformed men in the streets. The exchange — on her initiative — was always friendly. She initially asked where they came from and mentioned her birthplace Osterode to them. On discovering she was a native German speaker among the standoffish Dutch, the young men eagerly chatted with her: a substitute mother.

The meeting with *Herr Ortzkommandant* (local commander) at the Wehrmacht Headquarters in Klara's town, Overdam, went beyond expectation. The commander was interested in regular laundry services, wood deliveries, and whatever pork, eggs, and especially butter she was able to deliver. They agreed on the prices. That business out of the way, they chatted about their places of origin. He was from Bayern and seemed a kind, jolly man with a beer belly and a big moustache, much like Hendrik's. Johanna liked him right away.

*** 

Back in Hardenberg, the neighbors, her suppliers, and her Dutch customers all remained at a referential distance from Johanna when paying the bills or cashing in the outstanding accounts. She interpreted their disengagement and distance as an indication of their respect for her — a winner, like the victorious Wehrmacht. Deference was something she'd craved all her life. She didn't realize this was the way the Dutch treated all Germans now: ignore and avoid them, and when not possible, respond politely, and disappear as fast as you could. Feeling entitled to respect, Johanna dropped her attempts to speak the coarse-sounding, native tongue, expecting the *Niederländer* to understand her, because Germany was in charge, and everything was announced in German and Dutch.

After Johanna had set up the business with the Wehrmacht commander in Overdam, Robert handled the orders and deliveries.

Feeling so much better about herself, she made occasional trips to her daughter, Klara, and her family, who lived a few miles further west from Hardenberg. Klara's husband was the commander of a small unit of the royal mounted police. The family lived in one of the four homes inside the police compound — a bit too cozy for Johanna's taste, but at least her daughter and grandchildren were well-protected there and close enough for a visit.

When Robert took care of his business with the Wehrmacht or met with his Nazi party or another customer in the village, Johanna would occasionally ride with him to meet with Klara and the boys for a visit, until Robert picked her up again afterward. Klara and Jacob's boys, Martin and August, were three and five years old. Johanna had been pleased with Klara giving her second boy Johanna's middle name. He was a quiet boy and special to her.

She had begun to teach her grandsons German nursery rhymes — the only kind she knew. Although the eldest child had trouble sitting still, the boys had almost progressed drawing together with her to the finish of the song together. Although August didn't know how to say the German words, he did his best to emulate Martin; the sounds with joy on his dear face.

*Punkt, Punkt, Komma, Strich,*

*Fertig ist das Mondgesicht,*

*Heute ist ein Kind geboren,*

*Mit zwei lange Eselsohren.*

*Mit zwei Armen wie eine Hexe,*

*Und zwei Beine wie ein Sechs,*

*Mit einen goldenen Röckchen*

*Und drei bunten Knöpfchen,*

*Stöckchen in die Hand*

*Und dann ist sie weggerannt.*

*Punkt, Punkt….*

It was the perfect rhyme for learning by heart as Johanna constructed the stick woman according to the song's instructions with a pencil on a piece of paper: two periods for eyes, a comma for the nose, a dash for the mouth, a moon for the head, two donkey's ears, two witches' broomsticks for arms, two sixes for legs, and a golden dress with colorful buttons, although she didn't have color pencils. The result was just a basic stick person, very age appropriate.

The children took to the German language like nothing. It was so lovely to have grandchildren, much better than having one's own children. Only after experiencing her grandchildren had she realized how little time she had spent with her children at this age. She'd simply been too busy, her focus elsewhere on serving her customers. After all those years, she could admit that now in all honesty. Her job came first, then her husband, and well, the children had just come along.

"Klara, *meine Liebe*, did you think I was a bad mother?" she asked one day at the end of a lovely visit.

Klara had looked at her funny, her brow raised. "You were all right. Why are you asking now?"

Johanna shrugged. "No reason, I was just wondering. Sometimes I think I was too busy as a working mother those first years," she said vaguely avoiding Klara's gaze. She got her coat, and Klara helped her into it. She kissed the grandchildren goodbye.

Klara grabbed Johanna's arm and pulled it through her own in an intimate gesture of a daughter supporting her elderly mother, as they walked through the door. Standing in the driveway together, they waited for Robert, and Klara picked up the conversation.

"You know I had Robert to play with. I didn't forget that you *ordered* me to stay with him. Same with Johan and Frieda, who had each other. Maybe Henk felt lonely, but he entertained himself anyway on his own, always with his nose in the books. He's just that way. We didn't expect you to play with us, Mutti. No parents did. You fed us and got us out of Germany. And later, we spent most of our time at school, and had our friends."

Johanna nodded and added, "I thought my job was making sure we always had food ready on the table and clean clothes to dress you all in. When I grew up that wasn't always the case, and I remember days I went hungry. Most children experienced hunger, at least sometimes. The *Fröbelschule* in Germany was for rich kids, when it was a newfangled theory to teach kids before they entered grade school. The government shut them down before I was born, blaming the schools for teaching children to rebel instead of obeying their parents. As one of the eldest children, I often needed to stay home to help, and after turning fourteen I had to work the whole day.

"Oh, Mutti, those were different times," Klara exclaimed. In a more thoughtful tone, she added with a deep frown, "It wasn't always easy for us either with Vati being away on the railroad. Every time he left on Sunday nights, I cried in my bed. I was scared going to school at first, because we didn't know anybody. But like I said, I always had Robert and the others at the same school, until we moved to Holland, and then neither of us knew any Dutch. We survived anyway. Don't worry about it." She tapped her mother on the sleeve and smiled encouragingly at her.

Johanna let go of her daughter's arm and embraced her.

"Thank you for saying that." She exhaled in relief as she let Klara go. "I agree, it didn't seem to have hurt you. I see a competent woman before me. You have done well for yourself."

Klara smiled, but her eyes remained wary.

Just then they both spotted the familiar buggy nearing, further up the road.

"Here's Robert."

With Robert's *ho* to the horse, New Bles changed from a trot to a walk, and turned into the compound's drive. The animal stopped exactly before the front door where Klara and Johanna waited on the porch.

"Well, goodbye, dear Klara, till next time." Johanna kissed her.

Johanna climbed into the cart as she grasped Robert's outstretched hand. Despite causing her trouble with mounting, she wouldn't change her black widow's clothes, the long skirt that grazed her shoes. Proper attire was the least she could do to honor her dead husband. On her trip home, she reflected on her talk with Klara.

*** 

The German powers in charge of the occupation had designated Klara's village of Overdam as the seat of the *Wehrmacht* unit's regional headquarters, as luck would have, it in the same street as Klara's home. It couldn't have been better arranged had Johanna been the organizer herself.

It wasn't long before Johanna and Robert ran a brisk business with the local *Orzkommandant*, who happened to have the same first name as her father, *Fritz*, but she wouldn't call him that, of course. She called him strictly by rank only: group commander: *Gruppenführer*. She had things arranged perfectly.

To set up the business, Johanna had dialed the telephone operator with the request to put her through to the Gruppenführer in Overdam. When she got him on the line, she offered to meet him at his headquarters to discuss business, as she produced farm goods together with her son. They chitchatted at their first meeting, arranged by telephone. The Gruppenführer was very pleased to be able to talk with her in German, and they got along like old comrades.

Johanna smiled as they passed the Wehrmacht unit, stationed in the converted hotel The Black Swan, the location having been decided without the owner's say in the matter. That was a shame, as the hotel now was closed for other business, except the bar. As a fellow entrepreneur, she hoped that the Wehrmacht would compensate the owner well for the loss of customers. She was sure the Wehrmacht would pay him, or else the Dutch government would pay for extra "guests", she'd heard.

Other soldiers had been billeted in private homes, and the local estates of the nobility also had "guests." Johanna felt it as her duty to assist for a small compensation, willing to take in some soldiers as well conditional on their good behavior, but Robert had resisted.

As the animal clopped along the elevated road out of town through the Overdam forest, home to Hardenberg, a sense of fulfillment came over Johanna. Things weren't half as bad as they said. The soldiers were well-behaved, the Dutch army had surrendered and so avoided loss of lives, and the citizens were adjusting. With the new business, she felt a sense of purpose in her life again since Hendrik had passed, and she could help the locals with her German skills if anyone wished to use her services for translation.

"What are you smiling about, Mutter," Robert asked after a sideways glance. "You look like the cat who ate the mouse."

"Nothing," she replied. "It's all good."

# Chapter 36

In no time at all, Robert's political union, the *Nationaal Socialistische Bond* — the NSB — became the most hated group in the country. A few months into the occupation, Johanna heard at their evening meal of her son's hesitations about his renewing his membership. "I don't want to renew my membership. I've had second thoughts for a while about staying in the club. I hate to attend their noisy and exhibitionistic meetings. They scream a lot of nonsense."

She couldn't believe her ears.

"Why?"

He tightened his mouth and looked at her with hurt in his eyes, then looked away.

"I don't know what I believe anymore," he replied curtly.

Slowly, he continued speaking as he looked down at his plate, listlessly moving the food around his plate. "It seemed like a good idea then, a new wind blowing through the country, and all of that, but that changed for me."

"What about the things you said about the can-do attitude without all those government and union regulations always slowing things down?" Johanna had remembered it well, such good words.

"It's different now, Mother. I don't know if I should be with that bunch anymore. Our neighbors hate us, and the guys from my school days don't want to hang out with me anymore. Not that they would say that to my face, I just get the brush-off." He had stopped eating and sat back with slack shoulders in his chair, still not looking at her.

Johanna straightened her back and dropped her fork on the plate with a clatter.

"Stand up for what you believe, for once. Be a man," she exhorted him. Then, "Is that Lizzy woman still in the *Bond*, the union?" Her tone was harsher than she meant, and she followed up with a friendlier version. "I mean do you still see her? I think it's normal that a man leaves his friends behind when he's dating. No need to conclude anything from it or drop all your friends. They just become less important when you have a woman in your life. They'd understand it. So, you miss a few meetings. No harm done."

He didn't reply, so after a minute of silence, she continued her campaign.

"I think you've got it wrong. The neighbors don't hate us. They have proper respect for us, now that we do business with important people. You misjudged their seriousness. It is proper."

Johanna tried to suppress her satisfaction, but a tiny upturn of the corners of her mouth, hardly a smile, gave her mood away, and Robert noticed it.

He responded and finally, their eyes met when he spoke again.

"You smile like the Mona Lisa," he said.

"I know," she replied, now smiling full-on. "Your dad always noticed it, too. I miss him," she added quietly, her smile gone.

"Yes, *Mutti*, I miss him too," Robert said impatiently. "I'm certain he would be proud to see how we had our business pick up, but I'm pretty sure he wouldn't have liked the NSB."

He sighed and looked at her with a look of exasperation, his hands slack, resting in his lap. "I think I will chop more wood. It'll still be daylight for another hour or so. Then I can drop it off at the Wehrmacht station tomorrow morning. They asked for more wood."

"Splendid. You do that, *mein Junge*," Johanna beamed.

Robert resumed eating and quickly finished his meal, then rose from the table, pushing his chair back with his legs. "See you later."

"Till later, my boy," she said dreamily, her thoughts lingering on Hendrik.

Suddenly she shivered and a sense of dread crept up, second thoughts about her dealings with the Wehrmacht once she her thoughts lingered on Hendrik's judgement. She remained seated at the table, hands unproductively resting in her lap, wondering about her son, about their dealings with the Wehrmacht, and the possibility of accepting Lizzy as a wife for Robert.

She shook her head. If *that's* what it would take to keep him close, she'd consider it. Ultimately, it might be worth it. She could have him continue the farm work after their marriage. Robert and his woman could live next door across the corridor in the apartment, now rented out.

She didn't care about what he had said about the neighbors and the people in town not liking her, a German. What was new, anyway? Her identity had been a worry all her life, and where did it get her? Now she was finally in a winning position, and she wasn't prepared to give it up.

These first months, nothing strange had happened, just a whole bunch of regulations were announced and billets from the Reich's Office pasted all over town. The government and Queen Wilhelmina had fled to England, leaving the deputy ministers in charge, and they were behind the new laws, or at least carried them out. What could go wrong?

In the first months under German control, she signed the declaration, called the Aryan Declaration, which documented her birth history. She had filled it out in truth, proudly listing her parents, their places of birth, and that of her grandparents, all born in Prussia or the German Empire. Their religion was required: all *evangelisch*. Here, that was called Lutheran. Yes, she had a right to feel successful.

Robert was just too sensitive and had been all his life. He had a Dutch last name, and nothing to worry about. As a fellow-Germanic tribe member, he would be fine. She would be fine too, even with Lizzy if she got them to move in next door.

\*\*\*

In bed that night, she tossed and turned. Her rheumatic bones hurt. Gnawing at the back of her mind was an incident at their last family feast. Johanna had spoken with Henk in private. He refused to speak German with her any longer, and if she called him Heinrich, he wouldn't respond. As she recalled his hostility, lying in the dark, tears welled up and wet her cheeks.

While the others were in the living room and kitchen, Henk had taken her to the back of the house. His tone had been harsh, and he held her elbow so tightly that she couldn't wrestle herself away from him. In the olden days, she would've slapped his cheek, but he was a grown man now.

"Mother, listen to me," he had growled. "Do you know that the SS is operating what they call concentration camps? The first people bound for those camps after Hitler got in were political prisoners — subversives, they called them — people investigated by the Gestapo, the secret state police. You remember the name Dachau by München (Munich). They built many more camps in Poland right after the invasion, and the SS runs them now."

She didn't want to hear this. Because it didn't concern her.

But Henk went on and told her how the guards use the inmates for forced labor projects, and then kill the many thousands of German and Polish Jews on purpose. The children were killed right away on arrival. Then they separated the rest and rounded up the adults for slave labor in their war factories, until they were too weak to work anymore. They used gas to murder them. "I know this from solid sources, who brought this information back risking their lives. It's true. Mother, your Nazis are monsters. They're trying to kill all Jews. It's Hitler's final solution to the Jewish problem: the *Entlösung*."

She gasped and had raised her hands as Henk was speaking, as if to ward off an attacker. She then whispered, "I don't believe you. Why are you saying this nonsense? You're hurting my arm. Nobody else talks about this. How do you know so much anyway?"

He pulled her arm even tighter, and gave it a firm shake, so her whole body shook, and her head flew back so suddenly that her neck hurt, but he didn't let her go.

"When will you drop your misplaced loyalty, Mother? Don't be a fool. You're better than that. You and Father didn't leave Germany for no reason. Father told me what it was like in Germany. He thought they were war-hungry monsters. Don't align yourself with them and get Robert to quit that bunch of wannabee Nazis, before it's too late. Robert will do what you tell him." He added after a few beats, "I have my sources, but I cannot talk about those. Mother, you must believe me. It's the truth."

The cow had gotten up and stared at them, sensing something unusual taking place. "No, no," she had shouted. "Go away. Leave me alone. Those are lies, told by sore losers."

Henk let her elbow go, and stomped away from her, leaving her behind in the dark stable lit with only a bare bulb hanging from the low ceiling. She had refused to believe him, and stayed behind, scratching the cow's face for a while, before she recovered and joined the others. That was the last time she saw him. Since that day, she was unable to delete his words from her mind.

# Chapter 37

In the fall of 1942, the German governor of Holland, *Herr* Seyss-Inquart, had demanded more and more of the Dutch. All extra lead, galvanized iron, and other iron- and copperware had to be handed over, the materials to be dropped off at the distribution office at the same time of picking up the coupons for food and goods. Johanna had collected a bunch of items she hardly used, and Robert had dropped those off. She understood that the scarcity of everything demanded sharing from plenty where needed. She saw it as a duty, and gladly contributed to her German brothers in the army.

When Klara found out that her mother had Robert take those antiques to the distribution office for the Wehrmacht, she had been so angry with her. "Don't you understand that they will use the copper for making bullets? And those might kill my husband, or your son, or my niece. Mutter, how could you!"

Klara had turned her back and not spoken to her for the rest of that visit, and for weeks after. Mellowed after some weeks, she asked her at one visit, "What were you thinking, Mother, to give stuff to the Germans? Are you still enamored with the Nazis, just because they are Germans? Don't you know who they are and what they do?"

She had responded that she didn't think all those rumors were true, and she liked doing business with the Gruppenführer in Overdam. But Klara had shaken her head and scoffed. "You know better than that. Have you not heard what Henk and Jacob said? They are killing people without reason, especially Jews and Polish people."

Johanna refused to believe it, although the seed of doubt was sown. It just needed time to germinate, as she had too much invested in her German identity.

***

Two years went by, and the honeymoon was waning at last for Johanna. The Dutch deeply hated the Germans, and she was aware of it. She felt her neighbors' eyes piercing her back as she shopped in town, exchanging her stamps for goods, or when she sold her eggs and butter at her back door to those few, secret customers. Without competitors, she didn't have to be afraid of anybody ratting her out to the distribution controllers. The scarcity of everything despite the strict distribution laws made her customers keep their mouths shut.

Having customers for butter and eggs was normal to her, as she had sold eggs for as long as they had the farm, and people came to her without advertising. It couldn't hurt to keep it up, but her business with the Wehrmacht became a liability for her reputation. She was in a bind. To quit now would look suspicious, and make her an enemy, and her income would be much smaller.

When Jacob, Klara's policeman, got wind of it, he curtly told her, as always right to the point. "Black-market trade is punishable by law. Mother, you're not supposed to sell anything outside of the distribution system. You know that. I may have to write you up and then you *will* have to pay a fine," he admonished.

"Good heavens, that term hardly applies to me," she replied. "Just a few eggs and a bit of butter. I call that doing a neighborly favor, not trade," she defended herself. "Besides, I'm giving it away."

That was a lie, and Jacob knew it. He didn't let up on his questioning and surveillance of her. He was so insistent that it began to drive a wedge between her and Klara. One night, as she was visiting them for supper at their home in the *Marechaussee* — the military police — compound, he confronted her.

"But you're not giving your wood and hams for free to the Wehrmacht boss, are you? It's despicable what you are doing, supplying the enemy. Have you no shame?"

Johanna was furious with him. Who did he think he was? She had replied: "What you and your men are doing is the same. Both of us are collaborating with the new government. I can't see a difference. What could possibly be wrong with it?"

As Klara watched the confrontation in horror from the other side of the table, eyes wide, her hands clasped in front of her chest, Jacob escalated the conflict. He argued that the law was not allowing what Johanna did, making a buck at the cost of others who couldn't afford the prices. And catering to the Nazis, well, that was a whole other rats' nest. He and his men were doing what the law said: trying to protect the citizens, two completely different matters. Contrary to Johanna's idea of government, the legal Dutch government had left the country in fact; only administrators were left to execute the laws. Exasperated when Johanna stayed silent, he finally exclaimed, "Don't you see that the occupiers are attempting to corrupt us? The Nazis can only get compliance by coercing our citizens with the threat of their Wehrmacht and the secret police. But you, Johanna, you do it willingly."

The children were unusually quiet, and stared at their dad, when Jacob abruptly stood, leaning over the dinner table with both hands flat on its surface as he demanded his wife's input.

"Well, Klara, what do you think of Mother's actions? Is it fair for your mother to trade goods with the enemy against all the rules of decency? She is also breaking the law against black-market trade."

To Johanna's delight, Klara, red-faced and stammering, nevertheless sided with her. "Mother can do what she wants." It would've been smarter for Klara had she maintained her usual peacemaking efforts. She could've said something conciliatory, but she didn't. It warmed her heart that Klara remained loyal to her. The dinner ended in total silence.

The family, minus Jacob, waved Oma out in the driveway only five minutes later. While Robert waited with the buggy, Jacob turned to Johanna.

"Mother, it's better that you don't visit us anymore. We have different values than you and Robert. The Germans are breaking all our rights and forcing their terrible laws on us. They are not as nice as you obviously think. Open your eyes and see the truth." She saw in his face, the clenched jaws, the avoiding eyes, the fists on his hips that he was livid, and that his effort to stay polite strained him to his limit. She hadn't said anything in reply. She could be just as stubborn but was sorry for not seeing the boys after that day. She'd miss them terribly.

That was the last time she'd gone to the compound in Overdam.

***

Several months later, she heard Klara had a little girl. Robert showed her the photographs: big, dark eyes and a head full of dark curls framing her pretty face. She missed the grandchildren, and her adult children as well. Isolated, she and Robert lived their lives, ostracized.

Elfriede was far away in the west with her sons, and she hadn't seen them since the war had caught up with them. Henk had already abandoned his mother to her great regret, breaking her heart. He never popped in anymore and was even more outspoken against the German presence than Johan, away in the Caribbean. It had almost come to blows between him and Robert about the NSB. Henk's wife with their two sons didn't visit without her husband. No, she was closest to Klara and Robert, her baby twins, who were so much alike in their caring character — Klara the bossier child.

She dearly missed having her loved ones around her on special days, the harmony of before, and most of all, Hendrik. They'd escaped one war together, and now her family was falling apart in the middle of a second war, as if the first one never counted. She didn't understand it. What was she doing wrong? Why couldn't she be like Hendrik, who was liked by everyone?

She knew she had to drop the Wehrmacht deal, but she got so much out of doing business with them. It was like an addiction. She loved the easy money and the feeling of respect that it gave her. The glances of deference, the quiet demeanor of the customers. If they hadn't liked her, they shouldn't have come for eggs and waited till the ration stamp allowed for eggs.

She contemplated getting up for a relaxing drink in the kitchen. It was cold outside, but she didn't feel like getting the stove going. Her thoughts returned to Hendrik. She had him on a pedestal for a good reason. If Hendrik hadn't saved her, she might now be living in squalor somewhere in Germany, maybe with a husband who abandoned her to fight a losing battle somewhere in the world. More likely: he would be dead already, killed in action.

She didn't know if she still had relatives in the former Pomerania province. According to Henk, that was now the occupied Polish land where the Nazis built concentration camps for Jews and political prisoners. He surely meant the people who had resisted Hitler, dissenters and revolutionaries. She just couldn't think of that and forced her thoughts in another direction. It made her uncomfortable, made the seed of her doubt grow inside her, and brought on the anxiety.

After the invasion of Poland, she indeed had heard Der Führer calling the Polish and the Germanic Slavs *mongrels* in a radio speech, more than once. She had heard about the German army taking their revenge on the Polish prisoners of war *and* of the German soldiers indiscriminately killing thousands of Polish civilians in the streets. Everybody in Holland talked about it and predicted that the Nazi soldiers would do the same when they arrived here.

But they had not, and everything had been polite and calm since their arrival. She was satisfied the Germans wouldn't do this in Holland, as they were tribal brothers with the Dutch and *Germanic*. Just like her children, many Dutch had mixed German heritage. She trusted the German sensibility not to kill brothers.

When Hendrik was still alive, she was always on his side in public and kept her mouth closed tightly as a proper wife should. When she had wanted to assert her opinions with him and fight his decisions, such as leaving her country, she'd always complied in the end anyway. He had been right after all. His judgment had been spot-on.

She remembered that Lutheranism had been a mandatory religion in Germany: if you weren't *evangelisch* you were an alien, an *Auslander*. Johanna had well understood from her time in Germany that racial purity was a must. Anything less was an abomination. All the *other* genes and ancestors made one a *mongrel*. She remembered all of that.

Now that those horrible things began to happen in the streets of Holland as well, she wished she hadn't unconditionally trusted the Germans to be fair and respectful. She'd been terribly naïve, when she knew better, if only she had remembered her Vati's words, or Hendrik's. But she'd wanted to be somebody, proud to be German, and to be part of the winners' circle. It had blinded her.

Johanna suspected from her daughter's off the cuff comments on the telephone, warning her and begging her to lay off with the Germans, that Frieda seemed to have a direct line to the Resistance and its propaganda. Frieda told her with un-characteristic grimness that millions of Russian soldiers had already died at the hands of the Wehrmacht with the inference her mother was complicit in this.

"And not only that, so many *uncounted* civilians were killed everywhere in bom-bardments, or murdered like inanimate obstacles in the way on the Wehrmacht's advance through all these countries, Mother. Do you realize what they started? First at the Polish invasion, and then on to other nations? They've rounded up the Jews everywhere and put them in camps to control their fate. And for what? You tell me."

***

In the fourth year of German rule in Holland, Johanna didn't dare linger on what Henk had told her in the first year. During the daytime, she was able to divert her thoughts and avoid thinking about the atrocities. But the images of barbwire fences and people, thin as skeletons, staring at her from behind it appeared in her dreams. She knew from Klara that one of those prison camps was located in the forest of Overdam, and she had heard people in town talking about that. Jacob had to go there regularly, Klara had told her.

After waking up from such a dream early one day before daylight, she mumbled "Oh, *mein Gott*, should I believe all that?" It was all too much for her. It had to end. She got up and pulled a blanket around her before she left the bedroom. In the kitchen, she found the last bottle of sherry in the lower kitchen cabinet and reminded herself to tell Robert to replenish her stash. She leaned both hands on the table and heavily lowered herself down on a chair, a glass full of comfort already waiting for her. She began the work of soothing her tired brain.

# Chapter 38

That October, Elfriede came to visit with her sons. After two arduous trips on a bicycle, they just stayed. Twice, as the boys were too big to both sit behind her on the rear seat in one go. It was hunger that drove Frieda eastward to the farm, where there was always food.

As soon as the boys had been fed, and she finally had time for a cup of chicory coffee with Johanna in the kitchen, alone, she said in a whisper, "Mutti, Chris is in hiding. You must have heard about the *Arbeitseinsatz* plucking all unemployed and any students off the street to work in the German industry, right?"

"*Ja, Frieda, ich habe gehört.*" Johanna confirmed that she had heard, her face blank, hating the sermons Frieda gave her, and preparing for another one.

Frieda kept her voice barely above a whisper as she looked behind her to see what her boys were doing.

"His shop closed for lack of materials. Everything is gone, the *moffen* take everybody for *their* employment services. It's got nothing to do with what Holland needs for its economy."

*Ouch.* Her daughter used that hateful Dutch word for Germans. Johanna didn't reply. She was delighted that Frieda and her two lovely boys stayed with her, and she didn't want to cause discord between them. Klara had already told her in the first year of the occupation not to believe what the radio said was happening because everything was censored and under German control. Well, she'd better face it, Frieda and Chris don't like the Germans either, like Klara or Heinrich.

\*\*\*

That winter, Frieda would keep her up to date with what happened elsewhere in the country. Somehow, her daughter kept up her contact with her employer in the west, or possibly with her husband. They didn't talk about how Frieda knew the things she talked about. And Johanna didn't want to know. She suspected Frieda wouldn't tell her anyway, as Johanna clearly wasn't on the same side. It hurt her feelings that her children didn't trust her. She would never do anything to hurt them or their loved ones. How could they think that? But she stayed silent, not wanting to stir up discord among them.

\*\*\*

The general strike began in protest of the Nazis' announcement of their plans to haul off the decommissioned Dutch soldiers and young students to Germany. The SS grabbed every student off the streets and transported them to labor camps.

"People in the cities are desperate, *Mutti*," Frieda said in November. "They're eating everything they can get their hands on, and there's no coal or wood for heating."

She shared what she'd heard. Since the general railroad strike, people even dismantled the railroad ties, burning them in their stoves for heating and cooking whatever they could find. The wood-slatted walls inside homes were dismantled. All pigeons disappeared from the roofs, and the parks had no rabbits hopping around anymore. She ended by saying, "Without their fur, you can't tell the difference between cats and rabbits. There you go: no cats to be seen either."

Frieda seemed to enjoy telling her about these horrible things. She felt her daughter was angry with her and wanted to rub it into her mother's face as punishment for her loyalty to the Germans, to *Nazis*. The term sounded so hateful, but there it was; everybody used it beside the even uglier *mof*-word. She didn't even know what the word really meant, only that it was a pejorative.

"You're making this up. You're scaring me. Happy now?" Johanna replied.

It was a blessing to have Frieda close, as Klara also started coming around again with the children, just to visit Frieda. Johanna relied more than ever before on her children, which led to the improvement of her relationships. They were even closer than before, now on a basis of equality, and no longer a mother and her dependent children. They didn't spare her their criticism about her loyalty with the Germans, but although it hurt, she accepted it, as they were right, although she was unable to admit that.

Even Jacob had made peace with her, no doubt feeling guilty about accepting her food from the farm. All her children were against her, but their punishment had passed now. Nobody tried to pressure her into defying the Germans. It was just not talked about. Only Henk had not come around yet.

One night after dinner, Frieda warned Robert that the Dutch Resistance had begun to pick off *collaborators*: NSB members, and high-ranking SS members. "You had better watch your steps, Robert," she said.

He laughed exuberantly, then gave a lighthearted reply. "A good thing I'm not a very active member then. Delivering farm goods to the Wehrmacht station is just our trade. We can't be faulted for making a living, dear sister."

Frieda threw her hands up and sneered, "Well, you can't say I didn't warn you." She got up from the table and stomped out of the kitchen.

Johanna already knew from Frieda that after every assassination of the Resistance, the SS conducted retaliatory actions and picked up random citizens, to be shot. Already in the second year of their arrival, these SS men — short for Schutz Staffel (protective guards) — had put the fear of God into the Dutch. The SS organized raids in the middle of the night to search for hidden Jews and Resistance people, their address often provided by neighbors or someone with a grudge. They were ratted out by their neighbors or people trying to get a leg up with the Nazis. "Or even maybe by people like you, Mutti, faithful to moffen," she sneered.

That was so devious that Johanna gasped. "I would never do such a thing. You're being unfair," she replied.

All Frieda said was, "Oh, am I?"

It hurt her so much that Johanna cried that night in bed, as she had seen hate in Frieda's eyes.

\*\*\*

When the staff of the national railroad went on strike throughout the country, the SS arrested many citizens from random homes to await execution in jail. Many were held as hostages for when another important German would be assassinated. The Nazi governor, Seyss-Inquart thought the Dutch should hear this measure, so it was announced on the radio as a warning to cooperate and no longer resist.

Johanna's anxiety was a factor all day and all night. After her denial of the rumors, and the warnings of her children, it had come to this. Henk's warning had come true, and she had discarded his advice. Frieda said all Jews were already deported from Holland now, except those in hiding, and Johanna believed it to be true. She had to face whatever was coming, and she no longer slept a full night.

***

She could no longer deny that she was shunned. It had become evident. Nobody wanted to associate with the family after church. The neighbors turned in the other direction as soon as she walked up to somebody to chat. She was a pariah. Just yesterday, a couple overtook her on the street. As they passed her, she heard the woman loudly say to the man with a hateful glance at Johanna in passing: *Hate is too good a word for what I feel.* It had struck her deeply. It was just too awful.

She'd been so full of hope in the first year, so looking forward to her new status. Her business with the *Gruppenführer* had been a seamless collaboration, a natural connection. Now all pride in her enterprise had collapsed like a dead horse. She had to acknowledge it, if not to anybody else but herself: the Germans had failed. *She* had failed. They proved to be the brutes Henk had warned her about. Hendrik had been right. *No talent for peace.*

In only four years, she had become a quiet, elderly woman, no longer defending the Germans — her blood. The dream had turned into an ugly reality. The German goal to improve the lands they had taken guardianship of had in fact turned into the country's destruction. The effects of their plundering were visible everywhere. The people in the western parts suffered a famine, not seen in hundreds of years. Her shame made her shuffle along the shadow side of the street with her head down.

The doorbell rang, disturbing Johanna's train of thought. Thankful for the distraction, she got up and called out to the back of the house. "Frieda, could you please answer the door? Bring some food, it's probably someone from the city."

When Frieda came through the living room on her way to the front door, she carried the sandwiches destined for their own lunch and winked at her mom. Johanna didn't comment. She had seen hordes of people from the cities on the highways traveling long distances by foot to beg or barter for food with the farmers. Located in town and not an apparent farm operation, Johanna only got the odd one knocking on her door.

She always gave some bread, or cheese, and some potatoes and offered a glass of water, and still all of it for free, plus a couple of sandwiches for the road — the least she could do. God knew they would need it if they'd come walking from Zwolle, the nearest city.

She was a feeble woman now, not even a good grandma, and couldn't sit on the floor with her grandchildren anymore, her rheumatoid arthritis the deciding factor. If not for Robert, she would have to face poverty after the Wehrmacht business would end, unless she sold all the rest of her land, but this was not a time when people had any money for purchasing land. Hendrik's meager savings that hadn't been spent on land had disappeared in the depression. At least she got a few guilders each month from his devalued widow's pension.

It was March in the year 1945, and the weather was still cool. Robert had left to put seed potatoes in part of their land on the edge of town. He had to do it after dark despite the curfew, or the food seekers might start digging, hoping to find food. Thanks to hiding the potatoes in the cellar, he had some to cut up with each slice an eye from which the plant could develop in the soil after planting. If the patrols would catch him after curfew, Johanna was confident Robert's relationship with the Wehrmacht was his guarantee for avoiding his arrest.

She heard Frieda talk with the people at the door. By the sounds of it, there was a child with them. She slowly got up and shuffled her way to the kitchen to make a new lunch for themselves.

***

That evening, Johanna drank her last cup of tea, planning to go to bed early. A sudden crash made her jump up and scream. She saw her window shattered, glass sprayed all over her and the living room floor, her cup and saucer in pieces on the ground by her feet. Panicking from fear, she pressed both hands against her ribs to regulate her breathing and still her heartbeat. A red brick lay in the middle of the room on the floor.

"*Mein lieber Gott,*" she whispered. Who could do such a thing? She bent over with difficulty and picked up the red brick. It was a regular, used piece of baked clay, nothing special about it, and she put it on the table on top of an old magazine.

"They hate me," she whispered. She couldn't wait for Robert to come home. She closed the black-out curtains over the window to keep out the cold air and prying eyes. Robert would have to board it up, as a replacement pane was probably too much to hope for. What a mess.

Petrified, her hands still shook. Her breathing and her heart slowly returned to normal, and her fear retreated some, but not completely. She left the living room and locked the front door, afraid that somebody might harass her, or throw a bomb inside her door. She left the room and locked the door between the room and the kitchen. She shuffled out of the kitchen to the stable and checked the lock of the backdoor.

The Dutch thought she and Robert deserved punishment. She almost expected something else to happen and stayed vigilant. Back in the kitchen, she made herself another cup of tea, leaving the mess in the living room for Robert. She picked up her knitting, sat down by the stove, still glowing, and started manipulating the needles with shaky hands. The rhythmic movements quieted her nerves. It didn't matter that she couldn't see what she was doing in the sparse light of one bulb hanging from the ceiling: she was able to knit a sock blindly. Anyway, even with her bottle-bottom glasses, her handiwork was now guesswork with the lenses in her eyes grown opaque, like Ur-Opa Heinrich's. She knew her embroidery wasn't as delicate and faultless anymore, although her daughters were kind enough not to mention it and continued to admire her linens.

***

An hour later, Johanna heard someone rattle the back door. She froze. Robert had a key, so if it was him, he was able to get in. She waited, stiff from fear, her hands still on her lap. It took a few minutes before Robert appeared in the kitchen in his underwear and on socked feet, having left his dirty coveralls in the stable. She let out a groan of relief.

"Mutti, you are still up? Why aren't you in bed? Is the pain in your knees bothering you?"

She turned around in her chair to face him.

With somebody there to protect her, she broke down in tears. "Oh, Robert. *Etwas schreckliches ist passiert.*" Sobbing, she told him in stops and starts about the awful thing that had happened.

Robert had pulled up a chair and sat beside her, holding her hand in his. When she was finished and had stopped crying, he sighed and let her hand go. He raised his right hand and pulled his fingers through his hair and stood up.

"Is there something to eat, Mutti?" He looked in the oven. Nothing there.

"We ate a sandwich and soup, dear, I could make you some," Johanna replied. "I'll make you one with ham, or do you want cheese? There is some soup left too."

Happy for the distraction, she got up with creaking knees and got the ham from the icebox outside in the corridor next to the kitchen, which didn't have ice, but it was still cold enough anyway during the March nights. She smeared butter and mustard on the slices of dark bread, then folded them into a double sandwich and cut them in two.

Both sitting at the kitchen table in silence, Johanna observed him as Robert ate. She noticed her son was aging rapidly. His face was still dirty from the work in the field, with some clumps of mud still stuck in his hair. She saw the grey appearance in his dark-brown hair. He was turning grey early, like Hendrik.

"I would like you to board up the window tonight, if you don't mind." Her voice sounded normal; she was in control again. "We should have some boards in the back, right?"

"Yes, Mutti," he said dutifully. Then he spoke again: "Who do you think threw that brick? Did anybody threaten you? Is there anybody who didn't pay up?"

His soft voice was barely audible. He was so much like his father, every day he looked more like him. She missed Hendrik so much more in these terribly troubled times.

"Not that I know of," she said. "I was thinking maybe somebody you ran into? Somebody envious of our good fortune?"

"I think it's probably somebody working for the Resistance, which makes more sense. We are on the wrong side, Mutti. We might as well face it now the tide has turned. *We* are the enemy. I'm relieved it wasn't a bullet."

Their eyes met, but Johanna had to look away. Knowing the truth herself was one thing, but hearing Robert say the ugly words out loud shamed her. Suddenly, she said out loud what had been playing around in her head for a while. He deserved a reward for sticking it out with her. It came out almost involuntarily.

"*Mein lieber Junge*, when this is all over, you should marry your girlfriend, and move in next door. You deserve it." She covered her mouth with her hand for a couple of seconds, her eyes downcast. It had been so easy to say.

Robert looked up with a mouthful of food and stopped chewing for a second, then chomped down to empty his mouth as he forced his mother with his stare to look at him.

She smiled at him.

"Do you mean that, or are you just saying that to appease me temporarily?" He sounded suspicious, and his piercing stare tried to read her heart.

She was still smiling as she replied. "No, really, I mean it. You're getting older, my dear, and it's time to start a family. I would've liked a different wife for you, but since she is your choice, I will not fight it anymore. But you need to understand, you are my last one, my dearest child. It took me a while to get here." A deep exhalation escaped her chest. She hoped God would not strike her dead for the lies if there was a God.

Robert just looked at her, hands on the table, his eyes softened, and quietly he said, "Thank you, Mutti."

Tears welled up in her eyes, tears of shame, of regret and of fear for the future. She hastily rose from her chair and turned her back to him.

"I'm going to bed now. Maybe you could tell Frieda what happened before you start hammering those boards. She and the boys slept through that window breaking, so she must be tired, but hammering might wake them all up. Goodnight, dear Robert."

# Chapter 39

A fortnight later in April, Johanna kneaded the dough with her sore hands on the kitchen table in rhythmic movements — much like a meditation — thinking about how it would be after Robert lived on the other side of the corridor. She tried the name out loud, Lizzy.

A loud rapping on the front door disturbed her thoughts. She wiped her hands on a dishcloth, threw it back onto the table, and shuffled as quickly as she could through the adjacent corridor to the front door. She never had visitors, and fearing it was bad news about Robert, she jerked the door open.

It took a few seconds before she recognized the dirty face underneath the green helmet, the same face she grew up with, but decades older, and her eyes swept over the man's body, dressed in a crumpled uniform of the Wehrmacht. To the side stood two more soldiers — boys, really — each a meter behind the man up front. All three looked at her with hopeful expectation. Her eyes returned to the first man, then she stepped back, brow raised.

"*Ach, mein Gott, August, bist du es*? Is it really you?" she cried out. She pulled the door open wide. With a quiet voice, she said, "Quickly, step inside. I don't want anybody to see you."

The men stepped inside, one after the other past Johanna, who held the door, and glanced into the street, checking both sides. She quickly shut the door behind them.

"Follow me," she said and with a mix of anger and fear led the way to the stables at the other end of the corridor.

She quietly closed the door to the corridor. With her heart pumping and sweaty palms, the anger at him for showing up almost choked her voice. Fearful of being found out, and the accusation of harboring the enemy, she took nevertheless a good look at August, a diminished man, dark circles under his eyes and a week's stubble on his sagging cheeks. His old man's beer belly was kept in check by a wide belt. Then she threw her arms around her younger brother, a shadow of his former self, and in doing so a sense of protection resurfaced.

He hugged her back, tears in his eyes.

Dry eyed, Johanna said in a calm voice, "I didn't know you were in the army. Aren't you too old for that? What are you doing here? And why are you bringing your mates? I thought you would be on your way home. What do you want from me?"

She watched as the men took down their gear and backpacks in silence. Despite their guns and other military equipment, they looked like a trio of schoolchildren caught in a naughty act. Two of them were maybe not even sixteen years of age. "You can use that empty pigsty over there for your stuff," she directed them. "Stay there, grab some straw bedding, but don't come into the house, or into the corridor. I don't want you — or your gear — out where everybody can see."

Finally, August spoke again. "*Liebe Schwester, dürfen wir hier übernacht schlafen? Nur eine Nacht.*"

She nodded. Yes, her brother could stay there for one night.

***

When August told her of their last two days, they had indeed been on the retreat, but it wasn't that easy, as many Allied soldiers and groups of Resistance fighters were afoot, making theirs a miserable and dangerous retreat. It sounded like an excuse and made Johanna angry, again.

"*Verdammt noch mahl*, damn, what else did you expect?"

She was really talking to herself, more than to her brother. Her face was white, and her hands were shaking for fear of the unknown, although she knew it wouldn't be good if these soldiers were discovered — for them, and for her and Robert, never mind for Frieda and the boys. Then Hendrik came to mind. What he would say, and how he wouldn't have appreciated what she was doing.

"I know, and I am sorry I signed up, but had no choice. They, they, they made me," stammered August.

She cut him off. "I don't care. And I do not appreciate you showing up here. You put me in a very tenuous position. My neighbors hate me already. They see me as the enemy, a German. You can sleep in the sty for one night only, as you asked, and don't come out. You'll have to leave early, before dawn. I'll get Robert to bring you some food and water. And be quiet, there are people living across the corridor. They just might report you. My son expects the Allies to arrive anytime now."

She turned and disappeared from the stable, fuming and petrified at the same time.

***

After she had taken care of August and his mates, Johanna dropped down on a chair in the kitchen to wait for Robert's return and covered her face with her hands in despair. How did she get here? Her Dutch son was a collaborator, she a black-market trader, her German brother on the run from the Allies in her house, her Dutch husband dead, and she, well, she probably was an enemy of the people. Only *she* knew that she was only a pretend German, a mongrel. In Germany, she wouldn't pass as a full-blooded German, even when she only spoke German and never a word of any Slavic language.

She got up and went inside the living room to look at the clock. It was close to six, and Robert would come home soon. Elfriede and the children were out for a walk and a picnic on this gorgeous April day. They had better be back soon. What was keeping them? The curfew was to start in an hour, moved to an earlier time due to the danger of Resistance attacks. Only in this province, Seyss-Inquart had sent many extra Wehrmacht to ensure the army's safe retreat as it was deemed a risky place for Germans and collaborators.

She looked at the clock again. Only ten minutes went by. The clock, her beautiful clock from Osterode — a real Junghans — had survived the requisitions by the German army officials, although her antique copperware was gone by her own stupid fault and probably converted to bullets. She wondered if any Dutchman had been killed with one of those bullets. Shame filled her recalling that Frieda, her own daughter, had to remind her of that possibility.

The bread dough was ready to be formed into loaves. She proceeded mechanically with the forming and then flipped the preformed loaves in the pans. Done with that, she set the pans to rise on top of the stove. She gave her thoughts free reign. It was as if August and his mates had waited for the last minute to take off, or else they were useless soldiers who had missed the command to retreat and find their way back to home base.

In the previous week, when Robert delivered a load of firewood to the Wehrmacht, the *Gruppenführer* had told him it was the end. It seemed a decade ago when she set up the contract at their regional headquarters on Jacob and Klara's street. Had it been only five years? Commander Heusden was a nice man, and she had enjoyed their genial talk at the time. She had seen many soldiers march through town, lately all going north-east, and not nearly as well dressed and organized as when they had arrived.

But those SS fellows were a different kind altogether, the special, *protective* forces, who marched imprisoned citizens towards their destination, and now she knew to their likely deaths. The captives were often bleeding from the head, and black-eyed. Most of them had *that look* of doom in their eyes, like a frightened horse that knows it is being led to the slaughterhouse.

Whenever she was confronted with those small groups on her errands in town, or just standing in her front yard, she averted her eyes from that spectacle, deeply ashamed. Or, she went inside, afraid to look her neighbors in the eye, not wanting to hear what they said.

***

Her anxiety for Frieda and her boys and Robert — still not home thirty minutes before curfew — was high. Johanna heard the impact of bombs and mortars in the distance. She could tell the front was quickly coming closer. It had been going on like this for the last week. The sirens went off regularly, and people scurried off the street into the nearest bomb shelter or their cellar. During the last fortnight, a stray fighter plane scattered a spray of flack over the roofs occasionally, and the odd plane crashed somewhere else with an explosion that pressured the ears. Her house had not yet been hit.

Her grandsons seemed excited, thinking it was all a game. They were too young to realize the danger, and now that the schools were closed, they wanted to roam the streets and fields to hunt for artifacts, like the bigger boys. Frieda dealt with it all calmly and didn't let them out of her sight.

The Germans had perverted life beyond what even Johanna thought was decent. From Klara, she heard that the soldiers hauled off her friend's husband — the butcher in her town — and put him on a train to a camp. Some months later, the SD arrested Ruth, Margaret's friend, and their two children and took them away in a military lorry. Klara had cried as she told her about it, and Johanna had felt awful, and indeed, *complicit*. She angry and shame overwhelmed her at those moments.

She had no idea what went on in her own town but for Frieda and Klara. Robert never told her anything to protect her, but now she wanted to know who had been deported and who was shot, assume some culpability for it, and know what she had denied for so long.

Terrible guilt about having pushed Robert along on this path which led to his complete isolation filled her thoughts at night and kept her awake. Robert was not doing well, getting the cold shoulder from his siblings and his friends. The actions of the Arbeitseinsatz and the SS had forced Henk and Frieda's husband, Chris, into hiding somewhere, trying to escape capture.

Robert didn't know where they were either. His sisters kept him out of everything and considered him a potential traitor. Her family would surely fall apart, leaving her behind, alone, if any of her children got caught. Despised, she would die alone.

She wasn't afraid for herself. Her life was over anyway, her death wouldn't be a great loss, but she became fearful for her children and grandchildren. Her beloved Germans had turned into an imminent danger to her own family.

She suspected the prison camp in Jacob's district had made life difficult for Klara's husband, although Klara spoke very little about it, except that Jacob was supposed to assist the camp operators, forced to appear to collaborate. She assumed he was playing both sides, walking on the edge, his sense of justice compromised. Well, she had something in common with him, after all.

The strange part was that after Jacob banned her from their home, he had started to come around again to the odd family celebration. But she wasn't fooled. His loathing of her was a visceral force whenever he was in her home: an ordeal. He refused to kiss her cheek or even shake hands. Although he was polite when they talked, she noticed his scowl each time she said something, felt his piercing eyes on her, then turned away. At the earliest possible moment without giving hard feelings, he'd announce his leave, cutting his time to the minimum. She feared his judgment, her loathing of her, and was humiliated into silence when he was there.

She wished the Germans had never shown up. It struck her as odd that living in Germany, she never experienced the direct effects of war, even when losing distant relatives in wars fought elsewhere. She had to emigrate to Holland to experience this anxiety for her own loved ones. It wasn't the same as for siblings: this fear was more visceral. And strangest of all, it was the people of her tribe who put her in this predicament.

She wasn't blind and knew her country had become the scourge of Europe, maybe even of the world. Served her right as punishment for her choice of identity, for pretending she was full-blood German, *an imposter,* when she was only a mutt. And her brother August was in her house and constituted a danger to her whole family in more than one way. She shook her head and told herself to get to work despite her fear.

It was as if her arms were each ten pounds heavier than usual. Her knees were stiff and caused her pain as she put her legs underneath her and got her feet to standing. She went to the kitchen, made double cheese sandwiches and a pickle for each and wrapped them in a tea towel. She filled three empty Grolsch beer bottles with water, flipped the metal bracket with the porcelain top shut, and put it all in a basket by the backdoor to the stable. Robert could bring it to August, and make sure they'd leave by four in the morning. She had no desire to see her brother again or to introduce him to the neighbors.

Johanna bent down from the waist, rummaged around in the lower cabinet and came up with a sherry bottle. She sat down at the kitchen table. As she waited for Robert and Frieda to come home, she poured herself a glass. She should get them to take the empties to the dump and buy a couple of new ones. As the warmth of the alcohol spread through her icy veins, her mind calmed, and her body recognized its medicine.

# Chapter 40

The bombardments changed and grew louder with more frequent explosions. Johanna stepped out the front door and listened to it on her doorstep. She should have never let Frieda leave with the boys. This was no time for a picnic. It turned dark outside. Where could they be? She wondered if Robert was visiting his girlfriend.

A minute later, the screaming of a bomber diving down made Johanna flee indoors and slam the door shut behind her. Seconds later, an enormous explosion made the earth tremble. She flinched as some of the ceiling's plaster fell in the corridor. At that moment, Robert came flying through the front door, just about bumping into her as he threw the door open.

Full of fear, pressured breathing changed her voice into a whisper.

"Robert, listen. I have my brother hidden in the pigsty, and he has two Wehrmacht mates with him. A lunch sits by the kitchen door. You bring it to them and make sure they leave in the dark. I think they'd better leave now. And Frieda is not home yet. She went out with her usual recklessness for a picnic with the boys, at least that is what she told me. Maybe you could look for her and the boys. Judging by all that ruckus, it won't be long before the Allied soldiers will be here. You understand?"

He looked at her with eyes wide, reflecting her fear on his face.

"I *know* they'll be here soon. I'm not stupid. You're better off in the cellar, Mutter. The last bit of fighting will be heavy. Make sure you hide in the cellar now. I'll take care of everything. In case I don't see you afterward, goodbye." He gave her an awkward kiss on the cheek and rushed off.

\*\*\*

All night, the world went crazy. She wouldn't be able to sleep with all the mayhem around her. Robert had mentioned the cellar. If she had to die today, it would be in her bed. The basement was for young people with reason enough to live. She thought she heard Frieda and the boys stumbling around in the attic at one point in the night. They usually slept in Robert's bed, while he had set up a cot in the kitchen. At least they had come home safely. They should go to the cellar.

At midnight, Frieda and the boys gave up sleeping and came down into her room off the kitchen and cuddled up in the double bed with Johanna. "The attic is too close to all the shooting," Frieda explained. "The roof tiles clattered about already. We might get accidentally hit by stray bullets."

"Didn't Robert tell you to go hide in the cellar?"

"He did but the boys don't like it there." She whispered, "too many spiders."

In the glow of the flashlight, the boys' faces showed white with tension and lack of sleep. It was no game anymore to the boys, they were scared now.

"You must hide in the cellar with Robert, Frieda. It's safer. Take the blankets from the attic with you and the hand cranked flashlight."

Frieda considered it, but only for a few seconds.

"The cellar is full of spiders," the youngest boy, Hans piped up.

"Hush, boy. Oma knows. Spiders don't matter if your life is on the line. Mutti, the cellar is also right below *your* bedroom. If a bomb hits you, it'll hit us too or we'll be crushed anyway. That plank floor won't protect us. We'll lie down under the table in the kitchen and move it against the bearing wall. It's very sturdy and gives extra protection. Come on boys, grab what you can carry, and we'll go to the kitchen. Hurry up."

The three disappeared by the small light of their dynamo light. No light from the fireworks outside pierced the blacked-out windows.

\*\*\*

The hours went by as Johanna tossed and turned under a thin blanket — thin, because of heat generated by the inflammation of her arthritis. At times she dozed, to be woken with a start by another close hit. She didn't think it possible to actually sleep as the world went mad, but she did get a few winks in, her head pushed deep into the feather pillow until the bleak dawn began appearing along the edges of the bedroom window. Now she could say she had lived through a war, assuming it was all over soon.

She didn't know how long it had been, but suddenly it was quiet outside — dead quiet. No screaming Heinkels, no Spitfires, and no Messerschmitts, or whatever these hellish machines were called. Even the chickens were silent. The rooster probably died of a heart attack. Johanna lay back and breathed deeply, afraid to get up and see the damage and face the day. She must get up. She didn't have to get dressed as she had not undressed. The light of day reflected on the wall through a pinprick hole in the blackout blind.

Hoping August had left, she slowly became aware of a rumbling sound. A tremor in the earth, barely noticeable but slowly increasing, made her bed vibrate. The door of her bedroom flew open.

"Oma, Oma, wake up, the tanks are coming! We're free. The moffen are gone, Oma, Oma, get up."

Frieda's sons stood beside her bed, each boy pulling at an arm of hers without a sign of their earlier fear on their faces. Their mother stood in the doorway smiling broadly.

"It's true, *Moeder*," she said. She stepped into the room, then pushed her sons in the direction of the door. They were getting to be big boys, seven and nine years old. "You boys go and stay with *Oom* Robert. Oma and I will join you in a minute." The eager youngsters shot out of the room.

Frieda reached out to Johanna, grabbing an arm to help her get up. As she lifted her mother's sore legs from the bed lowering them onto the floor, she asked, "Well, Mother, we survived it. How do you feel?"

Johanna rubbed her face with both hands, sitting on the edge of the bed. "Tired," she said. "Did you talk to Robert yet?"

With a cold voice, Frieda said, "Yes, I did, as a matter of fact. Stupid of you to let those soldiers in, but since one of them was your brother, I get it. Your family is a damn mess, *Moeder*."

"No reason to swear, and it's your family too, dear child," she replied with a tired sigh. "What are the boys saying? Tanks in the street? Again? I am getting used to it."

Frieda led the way as Johanna followed her, leaning on her cane, through the corridor to the front door.

***

Dust hung thick in the air, like mist on a spring day, and the smells of pulverized brick, explosives, gasoline, diesel, and burning wood made the bystanders wrinkle their noses. The whole neighborhood lined the street, waving orange banners and Dutch flags, many with a bottle of something in their hands. Every house had a red, white, and blue flag stuck in its pole bracket at the gable, all of them with sharp creases from disuse, stored in a cabinet but now unfolding in the soft breeze in all its glory — forbidden until today. Other orange banners happily flapped from hooks and business fronts.

Here they came, the tanks on their caterpillar tracks, laden with dusty and dirty but healthy-looking young men in uniform, led by jeeps with some older soldiers — officers probably. Somebody said they were Canadians. The neighborhood boys ran along as they tried to climb up. The soldiers distracted them from this risky tribute by throwing chocolate bars into the crowd, which the youngsters fought over. Pretty girls reached a hand, and a few already hitched a ride on a tank.

Johanna thought the spectacle was a carbon copy of the parade of five years earlier at the same spot in the same month. The only difference with the Wehrmacht's arrival was the bystanders welcoming these soldiers, cheering, handing them beer and food, and girls throwing kisses and flowers.

Frieda, next to her, cheered loudly and even threw kisses, as her boys collected chocolate bars. "Where's Robert?" Johanna shouted in Frieda's ear, trying to be heard over the noise.

"I don't know," she answered impatiently without looking at her mother. Remembering who stood next to her, she turned to Johanna and demanded to know: "Isn't this wonderful, Mutti? Now Chris can come home. It's all over. We're free! Aren't you happy?" She then kissed Johanna on both cheeks in a gesture of forgiveness.

Johanna turned away, not happy, but relieved it had all come to an end, the whole miserable war. She didn't want to meet anybody's eye, in fear they'd hurl a slur at her, now that the Nazi danger was over: this German was defeated, like all others. She'd seen enough. "I'm going inside," she said.

In the kitchen, she found Robert sitting at the kitchen table. He had made coffee. It was only a coffee substitute, but better than nothing. She sat down with him, put a hand on his arm and vicariously anxious for him, said: "What's going to happen next? Are you in danger, *mein Junge?*"

Robert shrugged. "I don't know. I didn't do anything bad." His trembling voice belied his indifference. His face looked pale, distorted as if he was about to vomit.

Johanna wiped a hand over her face, so dead tired, then tried to fix her hair and put wayward locks under the hairnet. She had heard about the cruel things people did to collaborators in the south, liberated before the winter, but up to this moment, she had no need to speak about it.

"I'm worried for you. Henk must've told you to get out of the NSB, didn't he? We'll have to face it. Even if *you* didn't do anything, that club of yours has done many nasty things. Frieda told me the NSB had infiltrated into the highest ranks of the Dutch government. I'm almost certain something will happen now, at least with some of your members. This is going to be a difficult day for us." She didn't know half of it.

# Chapter 41

It was still early, before eight, so after a quick wash, Johanna boiled some eggs, got the ham out, put two spoons of recycled tea leaves in the teapot, and put the bread on the table. Frieda's boys, still excited from having seen the tanks with the Canadians, asked many questions which nobody could answer, as they dashed from one side of the kitchen to the other, like puppies at play. They asked about the prospect of seeing their dad again.

Johanna grabbed the youngest, Hans, by his upper arm a second before he would bump into her, as she carried the boiling water to the table to pour on the tea.

Frieda said, "*Moeder*, I'm going to pack. I want to be ready. Maybe I can get a ride with somebody going west."

"*Gut*, okay," was all she could say.

Frieda turned to the boys and addressed the eldest as she caught his upper arm and held on tightly, speaking close to his face, "Koos, you and Hans should start packing your stuff, now." Then she let go and left the room.

Johanna wondered about the threat to Robert. She went into the stable and called out his name. He didn't answer. She stepped outside through the backdoor and listened.

The street was awash in revelers, singing and yelling *Oranje Boven*, Orange On Top, and as she looked down the driveway, she saw a crowd on the road. She didn't see her son and quickly stepped back inside the doorway, not offering the group any reason for turning into her driveway.

Her heart pumped so hard she was afraid it would give out, and she plopped down on a stool in the stable, both hands pressed against her chest, breathing hard, fear overwhelming her. She detested herself for what she had done. It would all come out. Her children would not be able to stand up for her, for Robert, whom she had forced to stay in the NSB by basically calling him a less than a man.

She should have chosen the Dutch side, Hendrik's people, and not the German side, her countrymen. Her conscience scolded her: had you made your son leave that club of collaborators like Henk said, you wouldn't be so afraid now, but no, you didn't let him leave. What would happen to Robert, or to her? To be honest, she liked the extra money, the charming commander, and the way how being a German among Germans made her feel: comfortable, part of the winners' club.

She shuddered, then shook her head to get rid of the voices in her head. What would they do to her, an old woman? She spoke out loud to an empty stable: "Nothing at all, nothing at all will happen."

Suddenly, the door from the corridor to the stable opened, and Frieda's impatient voice rang out. "Mother, where are you? Are we going to eat or not?"

"Here, I'm here, Help me up, *bitte*." When her daughter stood in front of Johanna on her stool, she reached out. Frieda hauled her back to her feet.

"Why are you sitting here in the dark, are you alright, *Mutti*?" She studied her mother's face a bit closer.

Johanna felt her daughter's eyes scan her face, as she kept her gaze on the roughly cemented, uneven floor, afraid to trip as she had once before with much trouble getting up from that prone position.

"I will be fine, just didn't sleep much. Let's have breakfast."

\*\*\*

Robert showed up in the middle of breakfast, very pale, and not saying a word. Frieda didn't speak to him either. With breakfast over, Frieda and the boys left to celebrate in town and find their ride to the west. Robert sat at the table, listless, silent.

"*Was ist los mit dir, Sohn?*"

"What would be the matter with me, Mother, can't you guess?" His voice was sharp, almost hostile.

Funny how her children reverted to Dutch when they wanted to punish her. Her bones and joints hurt, and her mind didn't function properly. She didn't have an answer. Numb, she sat with him, unable to move, fear and apathy overtaking her in the face of the unknown fate for her beloved son.

A rapid banging on the front door startled them both out of their lethargy. Robert jumped up and dashed out of the room. Johanna slowly moved her legs underneath her to get up from the chair. She heard the front door open, harsh voices, commands given, and the clattering of metal.

Then Robert called out with barely suppressed terror in his voice.

"Mother, come here."

She grabbed her cane and shuffled through the kitchen to the corridor. At the far end, she could see two men, dressed in uniform coveralls with the same cloth bands around their upper arms, long guns slung over their shoulders, and one of them had a pistol in his right hand as he held her son's upper arm with his left. The other was just finishing putting shackles on Robert's wrists behind his back. They looked like they weren't planning on letting Robert go.

When she arrived at the front door a few seconds later, she demanded to know of the men: "*Was machen sie*? What are you doing?" Then she turned to Robert. "What's happening?"

His face was beet red. "Mother, can't you see — "

He was cut off by the man without a pistol, who spoke to her in a rough tone of voice, addressing her as Missus.

"*Mevrouw* Zondervan, we're the *Binnenlandse Strijdkrachten*, the Interior Army. On behalf of the Military Authority, we're arresting your son as a member of an enemy organization."

"*Aber er ist unschuldig* — he's innocent," she exclaimed, close to tears.

The man scoffed, and said, "Innocent. We've heard that before. Just so you know: we have you on the list of collaborators as well, but because you're probably not the leader, we won't bother with you for now due to your age." He looked at her with contempt, then turned around, his hand firmly on Robert's arm, and spat on the ground. Without another word, they left.

Johanna stood frozen on her doorstep, her eyes tracking the men as they walked towards a military vehicle with a canvas back, parked by the roadside. Robert didn't look back at her. The Dutch soldiers in their marine-blue overalls pushed Robert into the back, and climbed into the front, then drove away.

Robert's disappearance released her from her spot on the porch. She turned around, and went back into the house, closing the door slowly behind her. She put the lock on as well. Then she went to the back door and locked it too. She knocked on the renter's door. No answer. They would probably be celebrating in the town square. She didn't feel safe.

\*\*\*

She slowly went about tidying up the house, folded the extra blankets, and took them to the closet, remembering what Frieda had said: she and the boys might be gone by tonight as well. Then, for the first time in her sixty-five years of life, she would be home alone in a hostile world.

Her thoughts vacillated between trying to find ways to prevent herself from sinking into despair and finding strategies to fight for her son. Because she had taught him to depend on her and Klara all his life, he was her responsibility. She was the *one* person the authorities should have arrested — the *factual* leader of their business.

Johanna contemplated the idea of reporting herself to whichever authority was in charge now, then rejected it again. It wouldn't help her son. Maybe the best thing to do was wait and see. She heard the music and the drunken shouts of Dutchmen reclaiming the streets, free from tyranny, free from Germans — from most of them.

She shuffled to the kitchen, bent down with creaking knees, and felt around for the sherry bottle underneath the counter. It was only afternoon, but everybody was drinking today, and she had a good excuse: the loss of her son. There it was. Oh no, an empty one. She threw it back into the cabinet, where it dropped with a sharp, clattering sound, but without breaking. She felt around in the dark space under the counter for another bottle. She straightened her back with an unopened one in her hand and moved to the living room, where she grabbed a glass from the highboy.

She put the bottle on the table and poured a full glass, then dropped her tired body on the two-seater with the fancy ironworks on its backrest. *Art Deco*, the German salesman had assured her. Hendrik thought it too dainty, unsuitable for a farm, but he let her have it anyway. "You are my princess, and you can live like one, even on a farm," he had said.

Her thoughts landed on what she once had, and lost. Tears broke away from her eyes, but she wasn't crying. No, she was strong; nobody would see any weakness in her. She had done nothing wrong, only provided a living for herself and her family. Like her father, she liked to sit and pour herself a drink on a dreary day. Who could blame her? Who could blame her father? And yet, her mother was always harping on him, she used words like *lazy* and *failure*, and *dreamer*, and the worst word: *Polak*. Friederike had married him, so she must have liked him at one time. It was a long time ago, but Johanna remembered his hurt face now, his crushed demeanor.

As her heart melted and the fear dissipated, the alcohol released her tears. The liquid she put into herself was shed by her eyes, drop by drop, and more to get the poison out. What had come first, the failure of her father's business, or the drinking? He stayed and did his best, and he loved his children, or at least he loved *her*. Johanna was sure of it.

Was he stuck because of having a family, or because of the anti-Polish measures? Would he have left his wife if they had no children? Having had to create a life of her own, Johanna hadn't lasted long enough in Osterode to explore her parents' marriage. She finally collapsed into outright sobs with shaking shoulders, until she laid her arms on the table and rested her head on her folded forearms, the poisonous thoughts of defeat dissipating as her eyes closed.

***

That's how Frieda found her mother: with wet cheeks and three-quarters of the bottle of sherry in her.

"Come on, *Mutter*, let's get you off to bed. You need a good sleep, why don't you have an afternoon nap? I got a ride but won't leave until the morning. We'll talk then. Where is Robert? Come boys, go outside to play, but make sure you stay in the yard. There's a lot of drunks out there right now."

The boys noisily left, and Frieda asked again.

"Where's Robert? Is he off to see Lizzy?"

"*Ach, meine liebe Tochter*. My dear daughter." She started heaving again with big sobs and couldn't speak.

Frieda pulled her up from the couch and held her up around her waist with one arm. "*Mutter*, calm down and tell me. What happened?"

Slowly, they moved to the kitchen together. The walk seemed to distribute the blood in her body, and she could focus on the question. "The military has arrested him," Johanna managed to blurt out with a thick tongue between sobs.

"Oh, that," said Frieda, seemingly relieved. In a calm voice, she continued turning the knife.

"Totally expected, Mother. We warned him, but he wouldn't listen. Don't waste your tears on him. He's a big boy. He made his own bed, now he must lie in it. You always think he is so innocent. When will you open your eyes to the real Robert? He's an opportunist, not a saint." Her tone was matter-of-fact with an undertone of impatience as if explaining something to her boys.

They had reached the kitchen threshold. Johanna had enough. Anger rose in her, and she raised her arms, wrestled herself free, and pushed her daughter away. She lost her balance and almost fell into her bedroom but managed at the last moment to grab onto the doorframe as she shrieked, "*Lass mich, ich brauche deine Hilfe nicht!*"

In a soothing voice, Frieda replied: "Yes, you *do* need my help, *Mutter*. You're drunk. Do you need to go? Shall I first take you to the privy?"

Johanna shook her head and growled, "*Verdammt noch mahl. Ich bin kein Kind.* I'm not a child." She grabbed her daughter's arm. Together they shuffled to the bedroom. Johanna lowered herself to the edge of the bed, one hand on its frame, the other firmly held by her daughter.

Frieda took off her shoes, skirt, and blouse, and unhooked Johanna's corset. She pushed her mother's legs into the bed, a move that toppled Johanna over onto her side. She pulled the down cover over her mother. Before she left the room, she ensured the chamber pot was in its spot in the bedside cabinet. "Goodnight, Mother. See you tomorrow," she said.

The only answer was a stifled moan.

# Chapter 42

The day following Robert's arrest, Frieda left with her boys. Johanna's home was as quiet as a graveyard. The German army was still trapped in the west, but Frieda went to stay with a friend in Utrecht closer to her city of Haarlem to wait for the German capitulation and the Wehrmacht's departure. Johanna had packed up a crate of food to bring with her.

Two days after the Canadians' arrival, she sat in her living room with a terrible headache, reflecting on what she was to do when she heard a key unlocking the front door. The first thing flashing through her head was: *Robert is back. They released him for lack of evidence.* Joy overtook her as she tried to stand.

It was not so and only Klara came in. "Hello, Mother."

The sense of drowning in despair overtook her. Johanna sat back down, hiding how she really felt. "Oh, dear child, thanks for being here. Where are your boys, and did you bring your little girl too?"

They embraced. Klara sat down, wiping her hair back off her face. She had come on her bicycle and a few beads of sweat were visible on her brow.

"The wife of Jacob's colleague at the depot looks after them, but I wanted to see how you're doing, with Robert gone and all. I can't stay very long; I am not supposed to travel, but took a chance."

"Shall I make some coffee?"

"No, don't bother. Mother, stay put, please."

"A glass of sherry, then?" Johanna already was up and close to the highboy, where she kept the sherry with the glasses now.

"No, certainly not. This is not the time to drink. I must get back. I am worried about you. Jacob and I talked last night. He was arrested and investigated for collaboration with the enemy. That was because everybody knew about Robert and you, and your wheeling and dealing with the Wehrmacht, and Jacob's spying work, too."

"Oh, yes. Go ahead. Your German mother has a broad back, she can carry it." Her voice sounded peevish. She wanted to pout.

"*Ach*, come on now, none of that," Klara cut in. Her voice raised in exasperation, she continued. "Don't play coy with me, Mother! It wasn't that nobody warned you. But that's all water under the bridge now. Jacob was cleared the same day but reassigned to another town, so we'll have to move. He's already gone. I have other worries.

Klara's face was set, her mouth a thin line, her brow frowned, and her green eyes were cold like a cat's.

Having to face this new problem, Johanna sat down and asked, "Aren't you going with him, then?"

Klara exhaled and paused a couple of beats, then replied: "I would stay until Jacob found a place, so I can help you for a while. But I'm here to talk about *you*. Jacob thinks Robert will be away for quite some time. What will you do?"

Klara continued telling her how the country was in a mean mood and wanted to find someone to punish for all the misery of the last years. It didn't matter if Robert did something or nothing: he was simply an NSB member — that's why he was arrested. Would Johanna hire someone else for the work?

Johanna wanted to lick her wounds, but she saw that Klara wasn't having it. She had known that Klara was five months pregnant with her fourth child, remembering it now. Klara looked it, her body swelled up, and her face showed signs of fatigue with dark circles under her eyes. She should be grateful her busy daughter would even bother with her. She exhaled and pulled herself together.

"I'm sorry for the trouble I caused you all," she said in a tone that made Klara quickly scan her face, for an unusual humility had seeped into her mother's voice.

"Oh, yes. Thank you for acknowledging it."

Klara settled back into her seat and wiped an open hand across her face.

"I must tell you what Jacob said. He's thankful that you gave us food all the time and made sure the children had food all through these lean years. He appreciated it. That doesn't mean he forgives that you were in league with the enemy. That might take a while. He doesn't want to see Robert at all. Well, now that my little brother got himself arrested, Jacob won't have to see him. We both don't understand why you chose the Nazis, mother, especially after Henk told you very early on what they did." She crossed her arms and stared at her mother.

Johanna had to say something but had no clue what she could say. The whole history of her identity crisis wouldn't go over well. As the instigator, she should have said something but knew that she had not enough moral capital left in Klara's eyes for defending Robert. She felt an overwhelming shame, but to humiliate herself before one's child is another matter. That took courage.

"Do you forgive me, Klara?" Johanna asked, not daring to look up, anxiety roaring in her gut. She was about to vomit.

Klara exhaled and rolled her eyes. She put her hands flat on the table.

"How can I not? You're my mother. Yes, I forgive you. Besides, we still owe you."

The summer before the invasion, Martin had played with Jacob's matches, swiped from the table, and accidentally set the stable on fire. The back of the house was damaged and the hole in the roof had needed fixing.

"You were generous to us when we couldn't pay. We can afford to return the favor and be charitable. But I won't forget you were on the wrong side in this war, *fout.*"

There was that word Johanna heard a lot of lately, all her sins summed up in that one word, *fout:* faulty — wrong, defective. The radio commentators spoke of it. The neighbor had uttered it, passing by and staring at her with a sneering face when Johanna opened her gate to the front yard. And Robert had been *fout* too, a Nazi, and that was her fault.

It was as if Klara could read her mind as she stared into her mother's face.

"You probably put him up to it, right?" she demanded to know, as if Johanna was one of her children instead of her mother. "You thought the Germans would save you, save the country, got you some status as a German. Right?"

Johanna's shoulders slumped. Shame and guilt were things she could recognize now, and she clapped her hands in front of her face but managed to keep her tears from flowing. She had become the dependent, the weaker one, their roles reversed. Was this what she had to look forward to? She nodded in acknowledgment of Klara's accusation, as she dropped her hands and kneaded her sore hands in her lap.

Neither spoke for a long minute.

Klara broke the silence. "Well, Mother, Jacob and I know it. Just because you weren't a member of the NSB, doesn't mean you're innocent. So, Robert must carry the burden. I'm sure you'll reward him for it. That's your business. Just do *not* make us feel sorry for him. He made his own bed."

She sounded hard, not at all the soft Klara who used to faithfully look after her timid little brother.

"You have changed, Klara," Johanna said softly.

This was all too much baring of the soul — to her daughter, no less. She wanted to regain some control and forced an upbeat tone, craving some comfort. "*Basta mit der Träurigkeit. Giess mir einen sherry ein, mein Mädchen*, in the highboy." Enough with the sadness, pour me a sherry, my girl. She pointed at the cabinet with the cut-glass doors.

Klara sighed and looked at Johanna with a frown. "Is this a time for drinking, really, Mother?" But coerced, she got up and poured two glasses of sherry, a tiny bit for herself, and a full one for her mother. She put the bottle back in the cabinet, then sat down again. "You make everyone drink," she accused.

Johanna smiled. "Come on, one drink doesn't hurt. And I am a Lutheran. Your strict, reformed-Christian Jacob has you under his thumb," she added facetiously.

Klara reacted with anger, got up, and kept standing as she empathically defended Jacob.

"Stop, Mother. Not funny. The community apparently thought that betrayal runs in the family. Because Jacob appeared friendly with the camp's staff and the local captain, he was arrested. But he had to pretend to be on their side. I might as well tell you now: he was spying for his Resistance group."

Klara went on and told Johanna in an empathic voice what went on with the Dutch SS officers in the camp, and what mayhem those prison guards caused in the village. Most of them were Dutch and trained by the SS. People died, were beaten to a pulp, shot at for fun to "make them dance" and then carted to the hospital half-dead. Others were tortured to make them betray their family and their friends, or even forced to make up accusations for innocent people to free themselves, then often shot anyway.

She ended her litany of horrors with tears in her eyes. "How could those guards do that to their own people? You were like those guards, choosing the wrong side."

Then silence.

After a while, Klara said in a quiet voice: "Jacob, Henk, and Frieda's Chris were just lucky to have made it through this all unharmed. You know already about my Jewish neighbors and their kids, hauled off to Poland. Bah, don't say anything about Jacob. You should be ashamed of yourself."

Ready to leave, she grabbed her purse.

Just as quiet, Johanna replied, "I *am* ashamed." After a couple of beats with an upbeat tone, "Leaving so soon? Pour me another one, my child."

Angry with her mother, Klara barked, "Yes. I'm leaving. You can get up and get it yourself. Send somebody to the police station or call, if you need anything, but don't get fall-down drunk today, please." Klara's face was closed off, and she avoided looking at her mother.

"Goodbye, Mother."

She planted a peck on Johanna's cheek and walked through the door to the corridor, stomping on the floor on her way out. Only after Klara had pulled the front door closed with a loud bang, that Johanna got up, shuffled to the door, and locked it, tears streaming down her cheeks. Klara was right, she was detestable, a Nazi and a coward, a danger to her relatives. She was indeed lucky nothing serious had come their way, and only Robert had to pay his debt. She sat down again and finished the bottle. She didn't know when and how she got to her bed that night.

***

In the following week Johanna found out that Henk had been the regional leader of the Resistance and that's why he knew what was going on before anybody else. Klara already had shared about Jacob having been part of the group as well as a spy, an informant. Robert certainly hadn't. She only then understood the precarious situation her own presence and Robert's membership in the NSB had placed her other children, and how it had affected their lives and their family gatherings.

A profound regret for having failed to listen to her *other* children overwhelmed her, those with a moral compass. Had they felt compelled to make up for her and Robert's loyalty to the Germans? The three had done their utmost to offset the bad family reputation while risking their lives. Ashamed, she concluded she wasn't worthy of them. Telling them this was another matter.

# Chapter 43

Klara called to tell Johanna she moved out of the police compound into a civilian home in town to await allocation of a home in Jacob's new village. His assignment was to set up a brand-new police unit in this growing suburb while living in a boarding house. He'd put out the word for a vacant home.

Johanna was grateful that Klara still made it once every two weeks for a visit without children, which she left with a friendly sitter — her next-door neighbor's fourteen-year-old daughter. Martin, Klara's eldest, was already nine and could help the teen.

In early August, Klara delivered her second baby girl. Jacob wasn't there, just the midwife. She didn't visit Johanna for a stretch afterward. Then, in the fall, Klara finally moved to Jacob's village with the children. It was a much longer trip to see Johanna now, and she had to cut down visits to once a month.

\*\*\*

Johanna's children were too busy rebuilding their lives for a visit. If it weren't for the odd visit from Klara, Johanna would consider herself abandoned. If they were ashamed to have a collaborator for a mother and a brother incarcerated in a labor camp for the same reason, Johanna understood.

The neighbors stayed away from her door — naturally, she told herself. With Robert gone, production had stopped. To place a telephone call, she was forced to stumble over to the neighbor behind her to ask, or to the post office. That was too humiliating, so she arranged a telephone installation in her home, the only luxury she allowed herself.

As she hardly could walk anymore, the homecare nurse had measured and provided two new canes, specially cut for her short stature. The telephone was a boon for her to have groceries delivered, and for arranging the occasional visit from the nurse — a courtesy her son, Henk, had set up. She ordered deliveries of bottles of sherry and jenever — Dutch gin — as necessary for the visitors. Offering a drink was the least she could do.

***

Henk dropped by once, just to inform her that all NSB members had been hauled off to labor camps to pay off their debt to society by rebuilding the country. He showed enough mercy to Johanna to let her know Robert worked in Vriezeveen in the bogs, digging peat bricks for fuel. She could send parcels to the camp if she wished, he added in a cool voice.

She couldn't confess her regrets and shame to him as she'd done with Klara. Henk didn't want to stay and left immediately after relaying the news. Even if he had stayed and showed a willingness to at least listen to her, she felt no opening. She might have needed some drinks to loosen up her tongue and her heart, but Henk had no time for her.

Admitting to Henk, who had warned her early on, whom she had accused of lying and of being a sore loser, that was the most difficult. She was in awe of her middle son and wondered why she'd been so gullible to Hitler and so resistant to her own children's good advice. Indeed, as Henk said: Robert stayed away for a long time. At that time, Henk threw it in her face that even her beloved *Kaiser* Wilhelm had commented already in 1938 that for the first time he was ashamed to be a German.

The second Bles died, too. After discovering the dead animal in the stable, Johanna stood and watched it, until her feet hurt. She called the sanitary people to haul the horse's carcass away, satisfied she had allowed him to live out his life, but sad it had ended so soon, at only nine years old. She would never have another horse.

Frieda, back in the west, did not visit. Travelling by train was at the best of times already tricky with many tracks still in disarray from bombardments. With the whole country actively rebuilding essential infrastructure and growing food, it would be indecent to pay a social visit. She didn't have the money either, she wrote.

The neighbor behind Johanna — a customer for eggs during the occupation — agreed to do some errands once a week, like paying her electricity bill. Johanna paid her a small fee. That amounted generally to free eggs, as she had kept some chickens. When she asked the woman if she knew Lizzy, she heard that NSB women were also arrested. They did different jobs than the men in the rehab camps. Johanna imagined maybe sewing jobs or making radios. Suffering the common hardship would likely forge a bond between Robert and Lizzy. Damn. She'd never get rid of her.

After Robert's arrest, Johanna faithfully listened to the radio — the only source of information. Within days after the liberation, the Allied Military Authority transferred the power to the Dutch Military Authority. The responsibility for the Dutch *Volk* — the people — went back to the cabinet and Queen soon after. She had already installed the old cabinet with some modifications earlier, when the south was liberated the year before.

Johanna liked Queen Wilhelmina, who had offered Kaiser Wilhelm refuge after he fled in the night via Belgium in 1918 at the end of the Great War. She was proud of him for firing Otto von Bismarck, the one who persecuted the Polish/Slavs and caused her father's family's suffering.

From her German royalty rags, she knew that Queen Wilhelmina let Emperor Wilhelm stay in Castle Amerongen with forty lackeys for which he didn't have to pay, until buying his own estate in Doorn — his luxury prison under the Nazis until his death in the spring of 1941 at the age of 82. She wondered where he was buried. If only Hendrik had grown that old...

\*\*\*

The newspapers and the radio programs were inundated with talk about the traitors who had collaborated with the Nazis — a crime that had not existed until now. Johanna cried when she heard about the reinstatement of the death penalty for their criminal betrayal. She mourned that peaceful Holland had reverted to executions. For this purpose, the government erected a special court for the trials of the civil service's traitors. The people's hunger for revenge demanded that no-body would get off the hook. How Hendrik would have regretted this barbarism.

Once the court's judgments came in, Johanna was glued to the radio obsessing over knowing every detail. The national news station ANP meticulously reported the results. Many of the highest-ranking leaders were convicted of "extensive be-trayal and conduct unbecoming," and the verdict generally was the death penalty in quite a few cases.

Their arguments in court were heard in the broadcast excerpts — that the oc-cupational force made them, and resisting would have meant the loss of their job or even their life. This was their excuse for approving German orders and acting in tandem with German officials. Still, the highest-ranking collaborators had to pay the consequences for their choices: police commissioners, deputy ministers, and administrators.

When Johanna heard these verdicts, relief overcame her. She finally realized why she wanted to hear all this misery: she needed proof of the harm done. She no longer minimized the severity of what had happened right under her nose without her having taken it all that seriously *while* it was happening. She had waved away the rumors, calling those "fables" and "exaggerations" and had found excuses for other behaviors that had severe consequences for the victims.

As her three children proved to her, there was always an alternative — risky, yes, but, nevertheless. Those public servants could have acted with courage, like so many others. It all made her think more than ever before and it hurt her brain as she applied the new insights to herself. She unraveled the layers of her self-deceit, her delusions of grandeur, and her need to be loved, admired, and valued, all by joining the German Nazis. Here, she said it, that ugly word.

The radio reporter didn't spare its listeners the gruesome details of the charges and the way in which the victims died. The reporter described how the sentence was executed: a commander with a peloton of soldiers would take the convict out to the designated spot in the dunes close to the prison to shoot him. Johanna cringed hearing that, grateful that Robert was just a minor traitor.

Klara told her with remarkable eagerness about the execution of Jacob's regional boss, the commissioner.

"At least his death makes up for some of the hardship Jacob suffered, and for
all that man's victims. He deserved his punishment," she said with a grim face.
"He completely sold out the police department to the SS. His actions cost many
lives, people who ended up in the prison camp but had only broken the idiotic
German rules or who tried to avoid the labor camps and working in the war machine. What Jacob went through with him will cause him nightmares until his
own death, I'm sure of it."

Johanna replied, "I see." Once she had understood her own need for confirmation of the real events, she found it difficult to hear about all those men, tried and
convicted for their collaboration with the Germans.

When reports of the killings of the millions of people broke through the trials'
publications, it came as a big surprise to her that *die Entlösung* — Hitler's Final
Solution — hadn't only been a rhetorical idea. She realized politicians should
never be believed without further scrutiny of their statements. If they dare say
something publicly, they were likely also willing to follow through.

***

She learned to avoid the news, so she could drop her vigilance. She stopped listening to further details about the convictions on the radio. Convinced, she knew it
was bad, but why pick at the scab? When Klara left her house after her last visit,
Johanna looked back on the last five years.

She had been caught up in her family life, her own private goals, the dynamics
of their marriage, and Hendrik's death. Hendrik's views were simple and clear; he
had been right after all. His warning about the Germans should have sunk in at
the time. She had to admit that even a well-stated Nazi goal, such as restoring
Germany to its former glory, never justified the means.

She had chosen not to emphasize the bothersome parts of the Nazis, and lost
herself in denial. When the first Jews in Germany lost their rights and had been
ordered to gather in ghettos, she should've known things were getting out of hand,

but Hannah or Rieke had not told her about those. Until Henk had told her about it, she waved it all away as rumors. By then, she was in over her head, emotionally invested in denial.

Her new wisdom had come at a price: she had lost the respect and maybe even the love of two of her children. In a country with freedoms, one cannot take any of them for granted. Today it was peace; tomorrow the tanks could roll in. She knew the rest of her life wasn't long enough to make up for her errors, her betrayal of the country Hendrik loved — her children's country. Her shame would not end.

***

It was about a year after the war's end when Klara came for one of her visits to help clean the house and do errands.

"You are a good daughter, dear," Johanna told her, "Loyal to your elderly mother despite the damage to your reputation, and I appreciate it. Thank you."

Klara didn't answer, suspicion written all over her face. She set out to clean, starting with the bedroom. Johanna was not mobile anymore. Arthritis practically reduced her to the fate of an invalid, hobbling along, leaning heavily on her two canes when she had to use the bathroom. They didn't speak about Robert, or Frieda, who hadn't spoken with her mother yet since she'd left for the west, not even a phone call. Johanna had received one letter only.

During the lunch break, Klara made Johanna listen to the radio and the special presentation of Queen Wilhelmina. As they both sat quietly at the kitchen table, sipping their tea, the Queen announced with the cabinet's support the end of the executions. Under the motto, *we need to move on and forgive, to heal the nation*, the Queen pardoned all those sentenced to death and converted their verdicts to life in prison.

Johanna sighed in relief. The Queen had turned away already. "Now others will forgive too. It was too hard to hear, all that betrayal, that pain, those shameful behaviors — too much to bear. I know."

Klara commented with an edge to her voice: "That includes that nasty boss of prison camp Erika, the Dutchman Jacob had to face almost daily."

"Is that right," Johanna said quietly.

"Jacob told me that ogre managed to adjourn his case this long with legal tricks. Must have a smart lawyer. Even Jacob's crewmembers confirmed his crimes, but Jacob himself never actually saw him beat any prisoners. That sly fox was too smart for that. Jacob warned the guy many times to tell his Dutch guards to lay off from their games of shooting at the prisoners. When Jacob hears this, he probably would say that the Queen has no spine."

"Is that so," Johanna said. She didn't dare say anything that could be construed as defending the enemy, even to her own daughter. "Did I tell you that Robert will come home next week?" She knew this was a controversial subject, and she made sure her voice sounded casual: not a big deal.

Klara looked surprised, then relaxed. "Oh? So, what's he going to do? You sold the cow and pigs, and only have the chickens to look after, and your neighbor is even doing that. He'd better get a job. There're enough jobs around to fill." She put a sandwich for lunch in front of her mother and refilled her cup of tea.

Johanna had already decided to keep the promise she made Robert, but not to tell Klara.

She didn't share either her hopes that Robert may not want Lizzy anymore for his wife, once his mother agreed with it, or that the woman might have dumped him for another man. Realizing her own business with Robert hadn't turned out too well and had become evidence against her beloved son, she decided to just wait and see how things would turn out.

"Yes, I will speak with him soon. Everything has changed now. Luckily, I still get a bit of rent from next door. We'll be fine."

***

A week later, Johanna was having a coffee in the front room. A lorry of an un-known automaker drove up and stopped in front of her home. A man dressed in mud-colored overalls, and a woolen skullcap jumped out of the back. He briskly walked up to the front door in his rubber boots.

She immediately recognized Robert's somewhat slumped posture and was already on her way to the front door. It flew open just as she entered the corridor. As the canes fell with a clunking sound to the floor, Johanna threw up her hands and opened her arms.

"*Mein Junge.*"

With her eyes and heart flowing over, she let him envelope her in his arms. For a long time, they stood, absorbing the mutual joy of the reunion.

"*Mutter*, thank God I'm back," Robert said finally, as they let go of each other. He picked her canes off the floor and offered them to her. Keeping his hand on her shoulder he followed her to the living room and then dropped down on the two-seater.

Johanna leaned on her canes as she scanned his face. "Coffee?"

He nodded.

She turned around, hung one cane on the table rim, reached for her cup — hardly touched — and moved it to the other side of the table, in front of him.

Robert grabbed the dainty porcelain vessel off its saucer and emptied its contents in one gulp. He returned it to its dish with a vigorous move that made a loud noise but didn't crack the saucer.

Johanna smiled, then turned to move to the kitchen using both canes. "Bring the cup," she said. Obediently, Robert followed her carrying the cup.

As she refilled it, she sank to a chair at the kitchen table, not up to carrying a cup back to the living room. She hadn't even bothered pouring herself one. Suddenly, her legs were heavy like lead. Her exhaustion wrapped itself around her shoulders heavy like a horsehair blanket. Her ordeal alone in the house was over, and Robert was safe and sound in front of her.

"Well, what can I say." She wasn't going to rake up all her mistakes, that she was responsible for Robert's incarceration — at least in part — and didn't want to hear the humiliations he had gone through. It was too painful. As Robert sat across from her in the kitchen, she filled him in on her life, completed in a couple of sentences. She didn't want to ask about his past year.

"I'm so delighted you're back in one piece. I'm not going anywhere with my arthritis, so I sold the pigs and the cow, and only the chickens are left. Bles died of old age. I should be so lucky."

"You will be," he grumbled.

"Are you going to see Lizzy?" She held her breath for the answer.

Robert hesitated for a couple of beats, then replied with a firm voice, and a bit louder than usual: "We've been able to write to each other, and I've proposed to her. We will get married soon."

He fumbled in his pocket with one hand, and a pack of cigarettes with a tiny box of matches appeared. He pulled a cigarette out of the package and put it between his lips. Looking at Johanna, he struck a match and lit his smoke.

Johanna exhaled audibly. Robert had never smoked before. She didn't say anything and only stared back at her son, trying to formulate a sentence, afraid to say the wrong thing.

Robert just looked at her, eyes steady, then said: "Well, Mother, aren't you going to say what you think? Let's have it. I'm ready for it." He seemed more formidable, his skin deeply tanned from working outside, his shoulders and neck clearly developed with ropes of muscle, like a boxer, and no sign of a potbelly — a leaner and meaner Robert.

Johanna took a deep breath before she willed herself to speak.

"That's great. I'm happy for you, my boy."

"*Ach*, Mother, why are you pretending?" he scoffed.

Then he smiled at her with his sweet, lopsided grin.

"I know you hate the idea, but that's all right. I can live with your disapproval, and I'm holding you now to your promise, made when it was easy for you to make it. I want you to give notice to the renter."

He went on to lay out his plan to live next door in the duplex together with Liz and pay her the same rent, moving in on May first. "I don't want your charity. I'll be looking for a job."

"That's wonderful, Junge." She said swallowing her pride.

He took a deep drag of his cigarette. As he exhaled a cloud, he sat up. "Mother, let's talk about the real things. They put me away for almost a year. It wasn't easy and I feel I paid more than enough for the mistakes I made, no thanks to you. When I wanted to quit the NSB, you should've let me. Giving in was my mistake, but you carry part of my shame, whether you admit it or not. Now it's my turn to live as I want. To get around, I'll buy myself that motorbike I always wanted."

Robert stopped talking. With pursed lips and his shoulders pushed back, he raised his chest and chin and stared at her as he smoked.

Johanna had no words, taken aback by this new Robert: a grown man. Although it was hard to hear him stand up to her, she knew he was right. She looked down at her hands, now slack in her lap. Her youngest was no longer loving her unconditionally.

As she lost control of her last child, upset by the changes in him, her heart thundered in her chest. She needed all her brainpower to not cry and kept breathing: in and out, and in, and out, and repeat. After a few minutes, she regained control and suppressed the urge to throw the coffeepot at him. She exhaled once more and opened her mouth, but her son cut in.

"No. I don't want to hear it. Save it for someone else. This is the first day of my return. I'm going to do things differently from now on." When he pulled hard on his smoke, Johanna finally got a space.

With a cracked voice she blurted out, "Of course, my boy, of course," but Robert cut in again.

"It's time for me and *my* future family. I will not be used anymore, and Liz will help me with that, as she knows I didn't stand up for myself. Mother, I'll help you when I can, but my life for me starts now. You can pay for the motorbike. You owe me that at least."

He sat back, his shoulders and chin relaxing and added, "Now you can say what you want to say, but you are not going to change my mind."

Johanna inhaled sharply, changed her mind at the last fraction of a second, and calmly said, "*Mein Junge*, you're right. Grab me the sherry from the highboy and pour us a drink. We must celebrate."

Robert stared at her, then chuckled. "*Mutter*, you're incorrigible. No wonder I'm this way, too: everything is negotiable, right? Good, you'll have your distraction medicine, but I meant what I said." He squashed his cigarette on the saucer and got up, wandering off to the living room while shaking his head, leaving his mother behind. Relieved, she kneaded her sore hands invisibly under the kitchen table.

# Chapter 44

Soon, Liz and Robert moved in next door. They came to see Johanna on moving day around nine in the morning. As Johanna had expected, it was an awkward introduction, although she did her utmost to be non-threatening to the new woman in her home. She let them into the front room and offered coffee, but the couple declined. Liz was dressed in a pair of loose-fitting overalls, very modern, all farmer's wife. Her dark hair was done up in a ponytail, her face heart-shaped, with light gray-blue eyes. She looked young. They sat down around the table in silence, looking at each other.

Liz spoke first. Her eyes roved around the room for some moments and finally settled without expression on Johanna's face.

"What should I call you? Mother?" She had the husky, low voice of a smoker.

"That's good," Johanna said. She saw Robert smile and their eyes met. He nodded in encouragement.

"Mother Zondervan, would you want me to feed the chickens and collect the eggs? As I will be here every day anyway…" Her voice trailed off.

Johanna jumped in, unintentionally showing her disinclination to cooperate, dressed up as politeness. "Oh, no need. I thought Robert could do that. I don't want to be a bother to you."

Lizzy shook her head, her eyes challenging. "Nonsense, no bother at all. Robert will be working. He's looking for work. With his talents, he'll surely find suitable employment in no time at all." She looked at Robert with a triumphant expression on her face.

Johanna glanced at Robert, who took it all in, seemingly unaware he was expected to say something. After another uncomfortable silence, Johanna spoke.

"Well, you can just put the eggs on my kitchen table and take what you need for yourselves first. Robert will show you the food and how much to give them."

They discussed some more details about what the chickens needed." She stood up, leaning heavily on the table.

That was the sign Liz and Robert were waiting for. They got up in a shot and rushed to the door, and he held the door open so Liz could step into the shared corridor.

"*Dag, Moeder*," both said in tandem, and Robert closed the door behind them.

"See you later then," Johanna said to the closed door.

***

She sat in her chair for a long time, unable to move, as all initiative was taken away from her. Thoughts tumbled through her brain about having to rely on Liz and about Robert's withdrawal from the jobs he used to do, as she tried to make sense of how to respond to those changes. With mixed feelings, she was nevertheless overwhelmingly grateful that the worst was over. The German occupation was in the past. None of her children and grandchildren had died. It was time for a new beginning, but she couldn't shake the sense of looming disaster.

***

Robert and Liz got married at the town office. There was no announcement in the newspaper, and Robert told Johanna only after the fact when he dropped in for a few minutes.

"You didn't invite anybody?" she asked in wonderment.

"Nope, not needed. Even if Liz's parents gave their approval, I suspect they'd bail out attending anyway. We had witnesses — an office clerk and Liz's aunt. It's just about getting a piece of paper anyway." He still had the doorknob in his hand and was half out the door already.

Johanna had no comment, just one question: "Are you going to tell your brothers and sisters?"

"Maybe, we'll see. They'll find out soon enough," he grinned and left the kitchen.

*** 

Now that her son was back, Johanna started sleeping better. Of course, a nightcap also helped to relax her. She arranged for Robert to do her groceries and to include sherry and some schnapps. For future visitors, of course.

Frieda and her husband, Chris — still a handsome fellow — finally arrived for a visit with their boys on her birthday in May, two years after the end of the German occupation. Frieda had mellowed out and didn't criticize her mother. Even Henk had forgiven her and visited with his wife and three children, the last baby a little girl.

Johan, his wife, and his mother-in-law had arrived from the Caribbean on a furlough from the oil company. He drove up to her house in a huge, ivory and toffee-colored Chevrolet automobile, imported for his use on their European vacation, and it attracted the neighborhood youngsters crowding around and marveling at the soft purr of the powerful motor.

With all her children gathered at her place, it was a family reunion of sorts. When Klara and Jacob and their four children joined them too, it was almost like the olden days before the war, with grandkids crawling or running around in the orchard. Johanna couldn't contain her joy. After the terrible war and the Nazi years, and her unforgivable loyalty to the Germans, this reunion meant a new beginning. She pushed thoughts about the past down immediately. This was a celebration and no place for guilt or sorrow.

They hauled the tables and chairs into the orchard close to the back door, and sat together in the backyard drinking, munching, and chatting. Johanna claimed the attention for a toast and offered her regrets about her loyalty to the Germans. She quickly thanked her children for their forgiveness in the same breath.

A deep silence made her very uncomfortable, until Chris said, "*Proost dan maar, Moeder* — okay Mother: cheers."

Grateful, she smiled at him and mouthed the words *thank you*. At times, she noticed a spate of whispering, as some heads bent closely together but she couldn't hear what was said. However, she couldn't ignore the coolness of her children and their spouses when they spoke with Liz. Except Robert, who seemed to want to make up for the lack of enthusiasm for his new bride by demonstrating his affection for her. Liz didn't often sit on a chair and sat mostly on his lap.

Oh well, Robert was an adult and must scrub his own alley clean, as the Dutch said. Johanna didn't intend to justify her actions to her children. If they had a question, they should ask her, but nobody asked about her arrangements with Robert and Liz.

# Chapter 45

As the country rebuilt its infrastructure, times were hard with a lack of everything. In the meantime, Klara had another child four years after the end of war, her third girl. Goods slowly became more available, and the ration system was terminated eventually. With five children at home to care for, it was impossible for her to tear herself away often and she did not visit to clean Johanna's house.

After Liz and Robert had moved in next door to Johanna, Frieda didn't feel the need to visit either. She kept in touch by phone, and Johanna in turn kept her, and Klara too, informed of what went on in her world, or at least of what she wanted them to know.

The lack of extra income forced Johanna to sell off pieces of land to pay Robert and Liz for their services, and to pay the bills. The roof needed repairs. Johanna still had some hay growing for a while, but when Robert got a job as a mechanic, the costs for the help to harvest the hay surpassed the proceeds. It seemed more economical to lease it and sell pieces of land for cash, as Robert had no wish to take over the small farm. He was interested in mechanics.

***

Liz and Johanna's frigid relationship deteriorated further. The dynamics of their interactions, starting with a request followed by a rejection became predictable. Even for Klara, it proved impossible to manage, so she eventually gave up trying. Often, she ended up in screaming matches with Liz on behalf of her mother. Finishing an argument, Liz would slam the door shut like a shot, its sound reverberating in Johanna's ears long afterward.

***

It was like a war, never knowing when the landmine would explode for any unknown reason. Before Johanna went to the privy, she would first listen at the kitchen door for footsteps, then tried to decide in which direction in the corridor the footfalls disappeared, trying to avoid running into Liz. She became a stranger in her own house.

When Liz became pregnant, she was not to exert herself with the high-risk pregnancy, so she lay down most of the day on doctor's orders. When Robert told Johanna about the pregnancy, it was obvious he was delighted with becoming a dad. His joyful anticipation stopped Johanna from asking disparaging questions, and she didn't share her suspicions or question the doctor's orders. Instead, she quietly paid for a cleaning woman once a week for both homes.

To everyone's delight, Liz had a healthy boy to carry on the family name. The couple named the baby Robbie after his dad. A week of joy and peace reigned on both sides of the corridor. It didn't last. Soon after Robbie's birth, Liz added the boy to her litany in her next outburst. "You don't care about your own grand-child."

***

As Klara bailed on her, Johanna whined with despair as she squeezed the phone in her crippled hands, afraid to drop it. *"Ach, ah, ach."*

"Mother, you know it's not Robert that needs some sense. It's *she* who needs more manners, but I think that's an impossible task. You'll have to accept that he married her. It's his life. I can't tell him anything. I won't. You can ask them to move out. Goodbye, Mother."

She was sorry for Robert, and for his baby boy born in 1953, who would grow up with a volatile mother. Most of all, she was sad about facing her last years alone, living next door to her beloved son and grandchild, but condemned to watching enviously from across the corridor.

She threw her spoon down on the table and cursed in anger and frustration for her helplessness. She got up and shuffled to the living room, opened the cabinet, and took out a glass and the sherry bottle. She sat down in the living room and soothed her hurting heart.

# Chapter 46

Johanna fell into a long silence that winter as the war between the two sides of the corridor continued and Johanna had learned to give in and stay silent. On visits from Klara, she relaxed.

"You want me to shampoo your hair, Mother?" She reached up, took the hairpins out of Johanna's braided coil on top of her head, unbraided the sole tail, and spread the waves of long hair around her mother's shoulders like a silvery fairy-tale mantle. With eyes closed, Johanna anticipated the comfort of her daughter's fingers massaging her tight skull — such a rare occasion. She let out a deep sigh.

\*\*\*

During coincidental encounters with Lizzy in the demilitarized zone — the corridor — an explosion was still possible and positively dangerous after Johanna had a schnapps or two in the late afternoon. She needed her canes with everything she did and dreaded the uneven ground in the poorly lit backhouse, where the privy was.

Although she had lost weight, her body was sore all the time now, her knees in particular. With her hands cramped around the grip of the canes, she only was able to move centimeter by centimeter. The walk to the convenience store was too far and she ordered delivery of her groceries. Klara noticed her mother's pain. On her last visit, she broached the subject of moving, again.

"Mother, I think you cannot live alone anymore, and I spoke with Jacob about it. You're welcome to live with us. We'll empty out the front room downstairs for you. It's right across from the WC. I can help you with everything. I was a nurse, after all."

Johanna's facial reactions prompted another comment from Klara.

Klara abruptly got up from her chair without apparent reason, so Johanna knew she had hurt Klara's feelings. "You look as if I proposed locking you up in jail. It won't be that bad."

"No, my dear, sit down," urged Johanna. "You didn't finish your coffee. I just don't want to be a burden to my children like my mother to my sister. When my Vati died, he had nothing saved for her. Rieke's family had hardly anything to eat themselves, and she had to work at the funeral home all through her life, just like our mother."

Klara promptly sat back down. "Mother, it's not like that for us."

Johanna fumbled with a set of four needles, getting them sorted to continue with the job at hand: knitting socks. With a gentle voice, she added: "Klara, I thank you, and thank Jacob for the offer, too. Robert is looking after me."

Klara scoffed, opened her mouth, then pressed her lips together. After a few minutes of silence, heavy with unspoken criticism followed by a visible swallowing effort, Klara finally broke the silence.

"Tell you what, *Mutti*. Only our youngest is living at home. She can help Jacob with cooking a meal. I could come more often again, say once a week. Would you like that, Mother?"

"Yes, dear, it'll be nice to see you more often. Frieda can't come until my next birthday, and I haven't seen Henk or his wife." She didn't need to look at her work as her fingers were busy manipulating the thread around the needles. Her thick lenses made her eyes look huge, awash with a coating of blueish grey, like dead fish eyes.

"Yes, everybody is busy," Klara sighed. "You can't blame them, Mother. My eldest ones have their own children now, just like Frieda's and Henk's, and as you know my youngest is in secondary school. She'll soon leave home. But you have Robert's boy to visit you, don't you?"

Johanna smiled. "True, when he is allowed to come over, but he's not that little. He's such a sweet boy, much like his *Vati* at that age. Sometimes he is not allowed, and I won't see him for weeks. Maybe he was grounded for something. It's understandable; his parents are in charge, as it should be."

Her face brightened, and she stopped knitting, resting the work in her lap. "Maybe when I turn eighty we can have a party in the orchard, like we used to have. All of us together again. What do you think?"

"That's a good idea, Mother," replied Klara, mirroring her mother's upbeat tone. "Johan is back in the Antilles and won't visit again until he retires. We'll see what happens."

They agreed on weekly visits. Johanna didn't see Klara crossing her fingers under the table. She picked up her knitting and let her mind meander.

"That Johan of ours inherited my father's *wanderlust*. He had to leave his family in search of a better life. Come to think of it, I did that too, getting on the railroad with your Vati, and Hendrik did that, too. I guess it's in our blood." Just like the taste for schnapps, but she kept that thought to herself.

As Klara stood, she declared, "All right Mother, I'll vacuum first and then wash your hair again, since you liked it so much last time."

*\*\*\**

From then on, Klara arrived weekly on Johanna's doorstep.

Johanna had given up wearing corsets as they became too difficult to get into. She knew this hornet's nest of her poor relationship with Liz had to come down somehow, expecting to be stung, although she couldn't quite predict how it would happen. She closed her eyes and recalled Hendrik's face and mannerisms, creating his image from memories to soothe her, assisted by an alcoholic haze.

# Chapter 47

The sixties restored the economy and made *Niederlände* into a progressive nation. The war was forgotten. Conservatism was on its way out and a new vibe was hitting the world. Nobody talked about the past.

Johanna dried dishes standing by the sink when the kitchen door flew open. She dropped the plate. It clattered to the floor and broke. She turned around and saw both Lizzy and Robert standing in the corridor.

"*Was gibts*? What's the matter? Is there a fire?"

Robert spoke first in his soft and respectful voice: "May we come in? We must tell you something." His face was closed, his eyes not meeting hers but looking at a spot over her shoulder.

Drying her hands on her apron, she mumbled, "come in, have a seat," then touched her hair to tuck any wayward locks underneath the hairnet, grabbed her canes hanging from the rim of the counter, and shuffled to the table.

Robert sat down on the long side of the rectangle and Lizzy, on the short side. Johanna sat down across from Robert and hooked the canes with their handles onto the table rim. She didn't want to face Lizzy, who thankfully stayed quiet. Her mind frantically looked for a possible reason for the visit in preparation for what was coming. It couldn't have been a quarrel with Klara, as she hadn't been for a visit yet that week.

"Mother," began Robert and waited a beat. "I'm not sure if you need to prepare anything, but we're giving you notice. We have an option to buy a home, and we decided it's better for all of us to start out on our own. In two months, we'll be out of here. If you want me to do anything for you, it'll have to be now." He offered to butcher the chickens and sell them. He could put an advertisement in the paper for a renter, or anything she needed him to do for a smooth transition.

Johanna didn't know what to say, whether to laugh or cry. She sat still and stared at Robert. This was not what she had expected. Panic started eating at her nerves and her hands began to shake. She quickly put them on her lap underneath the table. She didn't dare look at Lizzy, afraid of an outburst. She could not protest, as that would surely bring on an explosion. She wanted to scream but forced her emotions down.

As if she read her mind, Lizzy spoke with her usual, agitated voice: "It's not my doing, believe you me. I'd rather not spend the money, but you made it hard for us to stay. It's your own fault your son wants to leave you, and I want to take *my* son out of this unhealthy and hostile home." She turned on her chair and looked at Robert, then turned back to Johanna.

As Liz spoke, Johanna's breath accelerated — unwelcome anger overtaking her panic — and she made herself breathe slower while still staring at Robert: in and out, to control her heartbeat and not retaliate in anger.

"You can't even look at me," Lizzy spat at her. "What have I ever done to you that you hate me so much?"

As she ignored Lizzy, Johanna finally managed to say to Robert in a quiet voice, "It's fine, do what you want." As soon as she glanced at Lizzy, she couldn't hold herself back anymore. With a breaking voice, half crying, she blurted out: "I cannot begin to tell you what you did to me and my family, how you have wrecked our lives."

"Yes, please, let's hear it," Liz taunted her.

"No." Johanna grabbed her canes and got up. "*Hau ab, jetzt! Raus!*" she said with clenched jaws and dry eyes and pointed with her cane at the door: get lost, now!

Standing already, Robert growled, "Come on, Liz, we're out of here." He pulled Liz off her chair with her arm, and out the door while Lizzy with burning eyes loudly exhorted Johanna to share her thoughts. "Yes, tell me more of your fables, come on now, don't hold back!"

The door slammed shut behind them.

*\*\*\**

Johanna sank back onto the chair, dropping her canes beside her on the floor. She covered her face with her hands, wishing she'd kept her mouth shut. As tears of sorrow streamed from underneath her fingers and gathered on her chin, she whispered "*Ach, lieber Gott in Himmel, lieber Gott*, what did I do to deserve this?" Dear God in heaven didn't answer.

*\*\*\**

Once recovered, she wiped her face with the lace-trimmed hankie always hidden in her sleeve. She bent down, and fished the canes off the floor, got up from the table and shuffled to the door, turned the key, and pushed the extra latch shut to make sure nobody could surprise her again.

She made her way through the kitchen to the front room and locked the door to the corridor as well. Since she was in that room anyway, she opened the tallboy and got her glass and bottle out. She had relocated her medicine from the kitchen to a better spot. She figured she deserved a bit of medicine to calm the rattled nerves and sat down in the living room to contemplate what had just happened.

Klara would be glad Liz was leaving, but Johanna was not. Besides losing her dearest son Robert, it also meant the witch Lizzy would take sweet little Robbie away from her. She remembered what it was like to be all alone after Robert was arrested. Without Robert's help, she was an isolated, handicapped old woman, one of those pathetic leftovers. With Liz and Robert her only contacts, she was even more isolated from her neighbors than at the end of the war.

She didn't want to move into one of these modern homes for old folks, like Hendrik's sister, Dientje. The poor woman had turned completely demented as soon as she was interned there. She would have to pay a high fee in such a home, too, unless she went into a home for the destitute, which she wasn't yet.

Another problem would be finding a renter who would put up with the primitive sanitary amenities in her home. Henk had told her long ago she should have a proper bathroom installed and offered to help her find a contractor for the work.

"Sell a piece of your land then, Mother," he had advised, but he would have to be the man to arrange it for her. He wasn't around, however.

She couldn't possibly live with Klara and Jacob: the war would always stand between them. Besides, Jacob was a dominant and impatient man, retired early, so would always be around and he had no respect for her. She was the enemy. To live under his reign would be an ordeal. No, she couldn't possibly move in with Klara, but how to tell her daughter without losing her too? Had it come to this? Was the only way left to die alone in her own house?

The tears welled up again, and she didn't bother wiping her cheeks. She poured herself another measure of sherry, whispering what Hendrik would say: *pull yourself together, you silly girl.* After a half-hour, she shuffled to the radio cabinet, turned it on, and grabbed the magazines from the shelf underneath it. Returning to her chair, she turned the pages, thankful for Klara, who had bought the royalty rags but wasn't aware her eyes had gotten so bad. She dried her eyes with the soaked-through hankie. Since her sight had become so bad, she could not read the stories and didn't gain the same satisfaction from the magazines, so she threw them down on the side table.

She sat back and let her mind wander. As life retreated more every day, her memories had become more detailed and added their own coloring, making up for what she missed. She remembered her classmates in Osterode, even their names. *Vati* and his stories were clear, the sadness in his eyes, the dead babies in their framed photographs on the sideboard: it all came alive in her mind. She heard the voice of *Mutti* reciting her old saws, her no-nonsense ways — almost cold. Now that she was older herself, she understood her mother's need to protect herself with a barrier of practicality. Sentimentality made one weak and vulnerable.

Lately, her memories had become everything to her, meaning almost more than the disappointing reality. The birth of her babies, the midwife Frau Mattias, and of course always Hendrik — she now lived every day with those dear memories, savoring them, even dreaming about her old life. She had a good laugh with Hendrik in a dream about the prim and proper railroad inspector, who kicked them out of the railcar after seeing all those toddlers and getting a whiff of little Frieda's stinky diaper.

The piercing beeps of the one o'clock time signal on the radio of the ANP news woke her out of her reveries. She should eat something. Klara always nagged her about eating sufficiently. As she heaved herself up from the armchair and took a step, she almost lost her balance. She grabbed the canes and made her way to the kitchen as the newsreader's voice blared through the house.

She wasn't hungry, but remembered some cold chicken in the fridge, the new appliance she liked. It saved her from having to get into the cellar. Maybe she'd try the new television after lunch and see if there was a children's program playing: the adults had their evening program.

Robert had bought this new-fangled thing she didn't need, never having known anybody who had one. He bought two, one for his family and one for her. Got a deal on them, he said. He asked her to sell a piece of land to fix the roof and threw these in too, said the television was the new window to the world, and important for their growing son, as well as great entertainment at home for their only child, who now already was ten years old. They had been protective of Robbie, as long as their bad reputation had lasted, having been *fout* in the war.

She had signed the agreement for the land sale and never questioned him, just paid for her share of the costs. She trusted him. The reality of going to miss him hit her again, and the tears flowed. *Oh, no. I messed everything up.*

# Chapter 48

A stumble, a fall, and a sharp sword pierced her lower body, making her cry out in pain, then she disappeared into the black nothing. When she became conscious of her world again, she found herself lying on the floor in the kitchen. Pain hovered at the edge of awareness. She heard a moan, then realized it was her own voice. The radio was still on and crackled without any program playing. It must've gotten late. She opened her eyes.

It was dark around her. She saw the kitchen table and chairs in the faint light coming from the full moon through the window. She was lying prone on the floor between the kitchen and the front room, unable to get up or move. The pain was unbearable. She tried to shift her body, and agony followed, like somebody stabbed a knife into her hip, and she faded out within two seconds.

She didn't know how long she had been out when she came to. She let her head rest where it was: on the prickly coconut-fiber mat, and she moaned. Her mind was cloudy, and she couldn't grasp what had happened, although she knew she was at home on the floor. She gathered all her strength and called out *Robert, Robert,* but only a pitiful sound left her mouth, more like a cat's meow than a human voice. Searing pain ran through her, and she plunged into the blackness.

When she came to for the third time, full consciousness took a minute or two to reappear. She knew this time to remain completely still and not move anything except her eyelids. She cleared her throat and tried her voice, *ah, ah,* then louder, then full strength, *Robert, hilf mir,* help me, and sank into silence. Not a single sound permeated from the other side of the corridor. The two walls were solid brick: good insulation for sound. She'd never heard her son and his wife arguing.

She wondered what time it was, how long she had been out. Robert went to bed early on most days. Liz may turn in later, but she wouldn't accept any help from her, and would rather die, right here on the floor. Her foot was going numb and started to prickle, so she tried to move to shift the weight. The same sharp pain shot through her, and she froze in time to prevent passing out.

She needed to urinate, but how could she? Despite her efforts to gather herself, she sobbed about the humiliation, the pain — what a conundrum she'd gotten herself into. There was no other way than just to let go. Leaking from her eyes and her bladder, she kept her body immoveable, nevertheless. The warmth underneath her was comforting at first, but as the liquid cooled off, she started to shiver. This caused another flash of pain, so she breathed in and out in a controlled manner, keeping this up as she focused on keeping her muscles relaxed. *Ach, Du, lieber Gott, hilfe mir,* she prayed silently, hoping her godlessness of the past was forgiven.

Nobody came, and why should they? Obviously, it was late, maybe even past midnight. Even if Robert was to check on her, it wouldn't be until morning. She recalled her outburst; had that only been this morning? Now she remembered: she locked both doors to her home out of fear. Exhausted, she faded out. She closed her eyes, just for a minute, and entered another nightmare.

***

Crouched underneath her bedroom in the cold cellar, which smelled of urine, she heard the bombs falling, and her body cramped up, stiff with fear. No, it was something else. Slowly, she returned to reality and became aware of the hard floor of the kitchen underneath her, and as she tried to raise her chest to sit up, the same sharp pain from earlier startled her fully awake. She froze and listened. The radio program had resumed and announced rain for the day.

A loud banging on the door coming from the corridor reverberated through the house.

"Mother, are you there? Mother, open the door. Mother, answer me." Klara's voice. And Robert's: "Mother, open up."

"*Danke Gott, danke, lieber Gott im Himmel,*" Johanna sighed, then she called out as loud as she could: "*Ich bin gefallen und kann nicht aufstehen, hilf mir, Klara.*"

She heard her talk to Robert in the corridor: "She fell and can't get up." A few seconds later, a crash sounded, and she heard the door slam against the wall. Klara kneeled beside her, face wrought from worry, staring into her eyes.

Johanna closed her eyes, relieved.

"How long have you been on the floor like this?"

She felt Klara's hands scan her body, and when touching the hip, Johanna bit her lip and then screamed.

"It's the left hip, she might have broken it," she heard Klara say. "Turn that darned radio off, will you?"

Johanna opened her eyes and spotted Robert on her other side, bent over and peering into his mother's face.

"Call the ambulance, Robert. Mother, you're going to the Emergency. All right? I'll stay with you. Are you in much pain? I can ask the attendant to give you a shot."

The room became silent. Johanna growled, keeping her eyes closed, didn't want to face the wetness on the floor or her daughter's sympathy. "Yes, my hip hurts," she whispered. Robert's footsteps disappeared into the kitchen; he used the phone.

"I don't need a hospital, I'll be all right, just help me up," she murmured. Her right hand was in Klara's warm hands. It felt good. She remembered Klara was a nurse. Her practical no-nonsense nurse's bedside manner did a world of good. She opened her eyes and forced a smile.

"You'll be all right, Mother, just keep still." Klara smiled back at her. "Did you forget I was planning on cleaning today? You just made sure I was needed, didn't you?" She chuckled and gave Johanna's hand a little squeeze. "Better not move. The attendants will know how to get you safely onto the gurney."

Johanna closed her eyes, keeping her body completely still. She heard Robert coming back and say: "They're on their way." It was not long before she felt a prick in her upper arm, and many arms and hands hauling her up and away. With her eyes closed, she let it all happen. She noticed movement. It wasn't easy formulating answers to the doctor's questions. She let go and sank into soothing darkness when she felt something softer than the floor or gurney beneath her.

# Chapter 49

A voice in the distance, a touch on her arm, then somebody near her asked, "Can you hear me? Are you in pain?" The queasiness became more urgent. She fluttered her eyes tentatively, then was able to keep them open, and she recognized the blurry face before her by its voice as her daughter. "Well, hello, Mother, how do you feel?"

Johanna focused and tried her voice. "Hello, Klara. What happened? Where am I?"

"You're in the hospital." Klara patted her hand.

She tried moving that arm, but Klara held on.

Johanna pulled her other hand from underneath the cotton blanket and wiped her face to awaken her senses. The memory of searing pain in her hip appeared and she carefully moved her right foot, and low and behold, lifted it carefully a few centimeters. Relieved, she felt nothing now, and let it rest, then tried the right leg. Even tightening her muscles caused significant pain, so better not. This wasn't half-bad.

"Oh, yes. I remember I fell. How bad is it?" She sighed. "You can be honest with me. Can you hand me my glasses, *bitte*?"

Klara got up and walked away, returned, and put the glasses on her mother's nose. "Better?"

"Much better. So, tell me," Johanna croaked. She was parched and nauseated, and her throat was scratchy. "Can you get me some water, please?"

Klara got some water from the sink, then sat down on the chair beside the bed and helped her mother drink from the glass. Klara's sharp intake of breath before she spoke scared Johanna, afraid it was bad news, but her daughter put on her professional demeanor and gave her the diagnosis.

"The fall dislocated your left hip. The emergency doctor took care of it and it's back in its socket. You'll have some afterpain, but that's normal. You are fortunate your hip didn't break in the fall, Mother. An angel must be watching over you. How come you fell, anyway? Were you drunk?"

Klara's voice was neutral, without blame, but the question was uncharacteristically blunt. Its blandness fooled Johanna into thinking her daughter held no judgment on her mother's taste for a drink. "Not really, just had a few."

Klara shot up from her chair, her face distorted in an angry frown.

"That's exactly what I was afraid of. This is *it*. You cannot stay in your house anymore. Jacob agreed. You're living with us."

Klara glared at her mother, and sat down on her chair, prim and proper, very upright, probably expecting protests.

Johanna wouldn't oblige and remained silent. In her heart, she agreed. Her first impulse had been to seek the relief of the sherry. The reality had dawned on her: without Robert next door, she wouldn't be able to live alone. She should let her daughter make the decisions. And Jacob, well, she would hope to keep her wits about her to formulate some defense, if he harassed her with her love of Hitler. *She* knew that to think the Germans were the good ones had been a mistake.

She might be forced to say it out loud and apologize to him: *I was wrong.* You were right, Hitler was a monster. He would gloat. She'd have to denounce the Germans, her own blood — at least partly. Her chosen identity was an aberration, her belief a delusion. All her life she'd wanted to be a full-blood German, and now see what a pathetic fallacy that turned out to be. There are no good Germans: they all elected the monster to power and nobody had stopped him from carrying out the hatefulness. Jacob would judge her and find her a fool, humiliate her.

"Mother," Klara said in a soft voice, taking Johanna's hand in hers, "it won't be as bad as you think. Don't exaggerate. Jacob is all right. He has mellowed too. We don't talk about the war. Anyway, you took care of us then, so we'll take care of you now. That's just life."

Suddenly it was as if a dam broke loose inside Johanna, and tears flowed down her cheeks. She cried without sound, letting herself experience the relief of her daughter caring for her. Powerless to defend herself, she no longer had to face the fights, the humiliation of her failures. The heartache of losing her home and her beloved son, and the grief of being old and helpless overwhelmed her.

Klara, next to her, still holding her hand, let her be. When she calmed down, Klara spoke again.

"I am going to speak to the hospital staff. I'll be right back. Don't you worry about a thing, *Mutti*."

\*\*\*

The next day, a ride in the ambulance took her to the town where Klara and Jacob lived. Johanna was to sleep in a proper hospital bed on loan, and the Green Cross staff installed it in Klara's front room.

"You need a good sleep, Mother," Nurse Nightingale told her.

"You're kidding me. I had a good sleep last night, so why have two in a row?" She joked, but Klara wasn't having any of it. She had to go down for a nap, clothed but without her orthopedic shoes. Klara gently draped a thin cover over her, then left the room.

She heard Klara's and Jacob's voices murmuring in the next room behind the closed sliding doors between her room and the living room. The curtains were drawn to give her privacy. Soon she drifted off.

\*\*\*

On waking up from a snooze, she waited. It wasn't long before Klara was there to help her up. As they chatted, Klara took the bull by the horns.

"Mother, you will not be able drink here as you like. You can't afford to fall again. The doctor prescribed some pills for you."

Johanna decided to keep quiet and see how things would turn out. She could always go home again.

\*\*\*

The afternoon went by without much talk. Jacob read his newspapers, then went out for a walk. Klara rummaged around in the kitchen. Johanna sat in a special chair, higher than the others, to reduce trouble with getting up. She'd asked for her knitting, and Klara had brought it. She didn't feel well and dozed away the rest of the afternoon in her chair.

After a decent early evening meal of meatballs, mashed potatoes, spinach, and some chitchat, Klara helped her to bed. The powder room with a real, flushing toilet was conveniently located right across from her room, only a few steps from her bed. Exhausted from the day's events, she handed her canes to Klara, who hung them on the headrail of her iron-framed bed. Johanna sat on the bed's edge as Klara lifted her legs, and she slipped between the fresh sheets. Assisted by the sleeping pill her daughter had made her swallow, she fell into a deep sleep.

# Chapter 50

The soldiers were severely wounded; one man's face had shreds of flesh hanging down, exposing his facial muscles, another had no eyes, and holes where his eyes should've been, and the third man without legs was moving forward on his ass on the pavement. The screaming projectiles in the air hurt her ears. Three of her five children were with her — the youngest ones only — then they disappeared from her view. Heinrich stood before her with a big grin, with Klara and Robert watching from a distance. She called his name. Then he disappeared too.

Now she stood by some sort of chicken-wire fence. On the other side of the wire, she saw a muddy field of hard-packed dirt full of scarecrows standing in unusual positions. Oh no, they were moving — these were actual people, dressed in rags, with hollow eyes, white faces, their emaciated skulls only covered with a shadow of stubble for hair. *Lieber Gott,* take me away; these are the Jewish prisoners. Why am I here?

Then Klara's face appeared behind the fence, singing a song to her sons, but the boys weren't even there. Klara's thin voice wavered, and she had trouble keeping the song's tune: *Maikäfer flieg, Dein Vater ist im Krieg, Deine Mutter ist in Pommerland, Pommerland is abgebrannt, Maikäfer flieg.* June bug fly, your dad is in the war, your mom stayed in Pomerania, Pomerania burnt to a crisp, June bug fly.

A voice screamed, kept shouting and wailing and wouldn't stop, causing her a terrible headache. She needed to vomit.

"Mother, what's the matter? Your screams are waking the whole neighborhood."

She opened her eyes. Klara stood beside her bed, shaking her shoulders.

"Wake up, Mother, were you dreaming?

"Why am I in bed, Klara?" She tried to get up and raised herself on her elbows, but Klara pushed her back.

"I need to vomit," she breathed, barely audible, so tired.

Klara disappeared, then returned with a pail, just in time.

Johanna threw up until only bile came out. Exhausted, she lay back on the pillows. "I was at one of those camps you and Henk always talked about," she explained. "Hendrik was there too. You were singing that *Maikäfer* song. Why am I in bed? Why are you pushing me down? I have a terrible headache. Who screamed?"

Klara looked at her funny. "What are you talking about, Mother? You've never been to a camp. You were dreaming."

Johanna didn't understand anything. What was she doing here? Where was Robert? Her leg hurt, but she'll have to get up because the chickens need feeding. If Robert won't do it, she must. Oh, her head hurt so much.

"Turn off that light," she grumbled in a strangely hoarse voice. "My head hurts. I need to get up to feed the chickens." Anxiety about not being understood flashed through her as she tried to move her hips and legs to the rim of the bed, but pain shot through her hip, and Klara held her shoulders down. She sank back into the pillows, exhausted.

Klara's voice came from far away.

"Mother, you're confused. It's four in the morning, you fell, and now you are with us. Go back to sleep. Shall I give you another pill?"

What was she doing here? "I want Robert, not you." The pain in her stomach and head wouldn't stop. Somebody moaned and moaned. "Stop the moaning already," her voice croaked. It dawned on her that the moaning came from her own body.

She reached a hand to Klara's face, checking if her daughter was a dream. Her hand shook and couldn't find its way to the tired woman's face, hovering over her. The stranger by her bed grabbed her hand and held it.

She heard a man's voice and perked up.

"Is Hendrik here? I want Hendrik. Get Hendrik for me. Or Robert."

"No, Mother, that's Jacob," the woman beside her bed said.

"I don't want him, I want *Vati*," she growled. "Not *Mutti, Vati*."

The people in the room talked, but she couldn't understand what they said. She kept her eyes closed tightly to keep the hurting light out. Her body was very cold, and she shivered. Her extremities trembled from fear. She was lost. Where were her babies? Was she in a camp? She opened her eyes and saw the people standing there. Staring ahead of her, she drowned in the blackness, frozen, catatonic.

***

Somebody shook her shoulders, a prick in her arm. Voices. Cold, cold, she was so cold.

***

She shuddered and had to throw up. Becoming aware she was flat on her back in a bed, she opened her eyes. Klara's face hovered above her. "I have to vomit," her voice barely audible.

"Here's the pail, sit up, Mother." Karla helped her up with an arm behind her back.

She vomited into the pail.

"What happened? I have a terrible headache," she said, looking around the room. Luckily, Jacob wasn't there. Klara gave her a washcloth, then left the room and took the smelly contents in the pail with her, leaving the door ajar.

Johanna heard an unfamiliar sound and realized the toilet flushed. When Klara returned to the room, she pulled up a chair.

"Mother," she said in a grave voice. "We must talk. Do you remember you fell and came here in an ambulance from the hospital?"

"Yeah, I remember something," she lied. She'd better let Klara talk. Her splitting headache made focusing hard. "Can I have an Aspirin for my headache?"

Klara got up, grabbed a vial from the side table against the wall, shook out a pill, and handed her a glass of water with it. "Here, take this, it'll help you."

Johanna sank back into the pillows, her eyes closed. She listened as Klara explained her ordeal.

"Well, where to start, Mother? After having been without alcohol for some time, I suppose since your fall, which was on the day before yesterday, it appears you have symptoms of alcohol withdrawal." She went on how at first, she had thought her mother had a bad dream, but then realized Johanna was hallucinating. Jacob called the doctor in the middle of the night. Dr. Sweet attended right away." He gave you a shot of Librium," she said and stopped talking.

Johanna stayed quiet.

Before continuing, Klara inhaled deeply, apparently finding it difficult to realize her mother was an alcoholic.

"Jacob asked that I tell you we will not let you suffer."

Good. Klara Nightingale went on to tell her that Dr. Sweet found withdrawal worse than the illness of addiction, especially dangerous in old age. She wouldn't have to go through the whole process of physical detoxification. They had concluded, she was drinking much more than she had let on. They had agreed to let her have some drinks every day if she chooses not to detox. Klara's voice during the last sentence sounded positively accusatory.

Johanna didn't feel the need to speak. Who wouldn't seek relief in her circumstances? With her eyes closed, she just listened. As she suspected her daughter would have more to say, she waited. What she most feared was judgement, derision, and humiliation. Indeed, after a few moments, Klara continued speaking, to Johanna's relief now in her calm nurse's voice again.

"Of course, if you would rather go through the withdrawal process, Doctor Sweet recommends Librium and other medications to keep you comfortable at the hospital for it to be more suitable. Last night it worked, and he also gave you a shot for pain. It's your call, Mother."

Klara was finished.

Now she had to say something, but she had no inspiration. *Lieber Gott*, it had come to that: she was an alcoholic, just like her father and grandfather. She pressed her eyelids tightly shut to hold back the tears of sorrow, grief, and shame trying to overwhelm her. No, she had more pride than that. She was better than that. She was not going to burden her daughter with the job of having to soothe her drunk Nazi mother. That should never have to fall to a daughter.

Klara sighed, and patted Johanna's hand.

"Oh well, you don't have to decide now," she said in a friendly, motherly tone of voice. "We'll talk later. You have a good rest now. Let the Aspirin and the Valium pills do their work, and then I will bring you a light breakfast. After that, we'll get you out of bed. The doctor said you need to keep moving to prevent your hip from freezing up."

# Chapter 51

On the second day of her treatment, the doctor withdrew the option of detox for lack of a decision from Johanna. Klara told her about the doctor's recommendations. In Doctor Sweet's opinion, withdrawal from alcohol was not a real option, so he gave Jacob the job of pouring her medicine: a couple of drinks of her choice each day. With that prescription, her body would be okay. She listened to Klara with her eyes closed, grateful she didn't have to decide anything.

*** 

Johanna's new life as a patient resumed. It was just she, Klara, and Jacob, as their youngest daughter had left home. The year was 1968. In the evenings after supper, the TV went on for the news, and Jacob got out the bottle of schnapps from the *dressoir* cabinet: Dutch gin, hidden in the back of the sideboard. She liked it, and it was better for her than the sweeter sherry. She had heard the phrase Dutch courage and understood it well. With two glasses of it in her, she had no problem speaking up.

"You pour a meager glass, Jacob," she scolded him every day.

"Doctor's orders, Mother," was his usual reply.

Every day she tried to trick him. "*Jacob, schenk noch mahl rein.*"

He played along, but she couldn't make him budge on pouring another drink.

"Can't do it. You had your ration filled, Mother. I'll give you an extra one on your birthday, and at Christmas and New Year, and the other Christian holidays. Did you lose track? Sorry." He winked at her, so she knew he wasn't mad.

To Johanna's relief, Klara had been right: Jacob had not brought up the war or made references to his mother-in-law's business with the Wehrmacht, or her son. It was as if Robert didn't exist. She was grateful for this and her anxiety about her past in Jacob's presence lost its bite.

***

Doctor Sweet visited her twice a day in the first week and gave her shots with a mix of medicine and vitamins to get her back on her feet. Then he only came once a day for a week. The doctor was a broadly educated man and spoke several languages. He complimented her in German about her progress: getting out of bed, sitting up for hours, and using the bathroom independently already.

"I'm from the previous century," she bragged. "We were born tough or died."

He smiled at her. "Isn't that the truth, *Mevrouw* Zondervan. Luckily, we invented all kinds of medical improvements in this century. You could get to be a hundred years old, yet."

She understood his prognosis but had an opinion and expressed it.

"Oh, doctor, I don't know if I would want to be that old," she chuckled. "What's left to live for at my age?"

Her hips and knees were like before — sore and stiff — but she managed with an Aspirin prescribed for the pain when it got too much.

Klara stayed completely out of decision-making and let the men in her house decide: the doctor and her husband. When Johanna didn't agree, she grumbled for a day or so, but didn't pull Klara in, and in doing so kept some independence from Klara, on whom she relied so much already for her daily care.

One day at breakfast, which she and Klara always had together, she told Klara what was on her mind, without Jacob present. He would have his meal an hour later, alone.

"You should stand up to your husband."

Klara smiled indulgently. In her nurse's voice, she chided, "If you're talking about the drinks, you must see that Jacob just has your interest at heart. I always thought that Father spoiled you. He had you on a pedestal. Not Jacob. You're probably right that I don't speak up for myself enough, but I like it this way. I like to keep things pleasant, just like you did when we were with Vati."

"But I would like things to be better for you, now that women have the right to vote and all these modern things. Wouldn't you like to have more say?"

"No, Mother, don't you worry about Jacob and me. We're fine. I had enough decisions to make during and after the war, when I was alone with four children."

Johanna let it go. Klara was not Frieda, and her instinct and personality were to care for people. She should be happy about it. There was only one thing that worried her. Since she'd opened her eyes in this house, Johanna had thought about Robert without saying it out loud. It popped out now.

"Where's Robert? Is he planning on visiting me here?"

Klara's face said it all: she glanced at her mother and then looked away when she answered. "He hasn't called or asked to visit. Give it time, Mother."

"He and Jacob don't get along," Johanna grumbled.

"*Ach*, Mother, you don't know," said Klara dismissively. Then she added: "He was busy moving out and preparing his new home. He has his job and his family. Don't be mean. He was there for you during your fall. Who knows, he might take you for a time in his new home."

That got her right in the gut, and she blurted out: "Never. I'd die before I live again under one roof with that *woman* he married — she had wanted to say *that devil*." She pursed her lips and folded her arms across her chest.

Klara shrugged and poured herself more tea.

"Suit yourself. The doctor said you should stay calm, as your heart is weak from poor circulation. How about staying with Frieda then? She offered to take turns caring for you. Maybe next year?"

Johanna sighed and unfolded her arms. She picked up her knife from the table.

"Pass me a slice of bread and the butter."

She wasn't going to be moved again. What did they think she was: a wardrobe? It was hard enough to get used to a new place, especially now that she was nearly blind. Imagine that: her own children wanted to treat her like an untrainable dog, *schlepping* her from one unwilling owner to another. She wasn't having any of it. Oh, Hendrik, if only you hadn't died so early, we could've grown old together in our own home.

\*\*\*

A year later, a taxi moved Johanna to Frieda's home in the western part of the country in the city of Haarlem. Klara came along in the car and would travel home by train. On their arrival, Johanna heard Klara and Frieda talking in the kitchen about what the doctor had prescribed for her, and she caught the words *no salt, only two drinks*.

"*Bah*, nonsense. I'm better now," she called out.

"Never mind," called Frieda back, and a second later stepped into the living room. "We're going to have fun, Mother. Klara's man is a stiff shirt, but mine is a lot of fun. You're going to like it with us. Say goodbye to Klara, she's leaving now."

Klara hugged Johanna and told her, "I'll call you, and you can call me too, of course, Mother, anytime."

"*Ja, ja, gut.*" Johanna didn't look at Klara, as the latter waved goodbye.

Once Klara had left, Johanna asked Frieda the same important question: "Will Robert visit me here?"

***

Caring for a willful and hard-headed mother proved to be a lot of work, and handling Johanna required great diplomatic skill, not in the least because collaboration between the two competitive daughters proved nearly impossible. As they had developed their approaches with their husbands in their own lives, each dealt with problems differently and had a different view of the world with different expectations.

It wasn't even a year before Johanna's legs swelled to an elephantine size, her salt intake uncontrolled. Her kidneys couldn't cope. Too much water in her system hampered the heart's functioning as well.

Johanna's fear of becoming an unwanted dog proved justified and she did indeed get moved. Following an unsolvable disagreement between Klara and Frieda, her daughters moved her back to Klara's home — against her will. After the move, she sat in her chair, brooding and steaming, feeling powerless, an awkward pres-

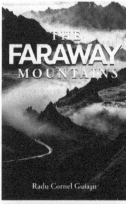

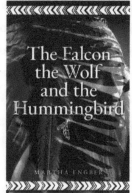
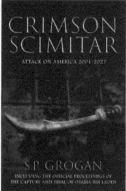